Reckless Deal

Reckless Billionaires Series

Maxine Henri

 Created with Vellum

"Wounds heal. Love lasts. We remain."
Kristin Hannah, The Nightingale

Chapter 1

Mila

"The two largest arrangements go on each side of the door from the outside to frame the entrance. Two on each side of the podium, and I'll decide on the others once you bring them all in," I instruct the flower delivery guy.

"The place looks wonderful," London Lowe, my client, exclaims as she enters.

"I'm glad you like it." I smile and she steps back. The woman seems scared of any human interaction, particularly the pleasant ones. I've been a bit mean and have enjoyed her reactions to my smiles.

"You should get ready now." She drags her eyes up and down me with a look that suggests either concern or disgust.

My hair is messy, my makeup is non-existent, and my dress is still on its way because my sister got lost.

I beam at London to hide my lack of preparedness. "I'll take care of the flower arrangements, and then I take care of myself." Or so I hope.

Almost an hour later I bounce down the steps in front of the venue, praying Annie gets here soon. Across the street, an elderly man attempts to step into the traffic with a shaky gait.

He is not your problem, Mila. Damn it. I cross the road. "Let me help you."

His eyes shine with gratitude as I clasp my hands around his elbow and help him shuffle to the other side. We still have several feet to reach the curb when the endless snake of cars moves, honking as if that could speed us up.

It speeds up my heart rate for sure, but it's not like I can rush him. When we finally step onto the sidewalk, I gently disconnect my hold of him and give it another few seconds that I don't have to make sure he's okay.

Finally, Annie trudges into sight, holding a clothes carrier, pushing a stroller and heralding seven-year old Aidan alongside the relentless traffic. Sweat covers her skin and the frown on her face screams of pain.

A pang of guilt zaps through me. I worked at a coffee shop on the other side of town yesterday and lost track of time. It shouldn't have happened. I should be on top of things more. I shouldn't have missed my rental dress pickup. For many reasons, but mostly because I can't afford these mistakes. I can't afford a contingency plan.

"It's so heavy," Annie sighs. "I could have done without the extra half hour detour."

"I told you to take a cab. Thank you." I take the bag from her and she winces, trying to disguise it with a weak smile. The dress isn't heavy, but in her case it might as well be an iron dumbbell.

Fuck. I shouldn't have asked her to do this.

"I'm so glad I could help, and get out of the house," she says, as if she can read my mind.

"You saved me." I give her a hug. "Let me get you a cab. I can bill it to this job, don't worry."

She eyes me, probably trying to confirm if I'm lying, but then she nods, the pain ruling over her intentions as always. I kiss all three of them and head back to work.

When I make it inside, my head is spinning. I didn't have time to eat or drink. Luckily London ordered sandwiches and snacks for all the staff and volunteers, so I'll eat before I get ready, and then this evening can start.

I unzip the bag and all thoughts of food disappear. I step back and shake my head, my mind racing in many directions, none of them useful. I shake the bag from the hanger and assess the black gown.

It's beautiful. It's appropriate for the occasion.

There is no way I can wear it. It's not my size. It's not the one I reserved.

I grab my phone to call Annie but stop myself. What good would it do to make her feel guilty about the screw-up she didn't cause?

I look at the sandwiches on the table in the corner, then back at the dress. For the first time in a year, the exhaustion and the finality of my dire existence bring tears to my eyes.

My breakup with Brian and his threats. My sister's illness. My nephew's needs. My duty to them and my love for them. And all the jobs I've taken to help them out.

It all crashes down and materializes in one stupid gown, and I allow myself a brief breakdown and cry.

Could I look any more ridiculous? The dress turned out stretchy enough and was only about a size too small. It would fit decently. For someone with a less generous chest region. Not my case.

A square neckline, tight bodice and a long slit up the thigh in a shimmering black would be beautiful. Just not on me.

The swanky venue is filled with laughter, conversation, and the undertones of a soft piano coming from the corner where the orchestra is getting ready for another round of dancing.

Shimmying voile curtains hang from the ceiling, forming tender pillars to soften the interior of the warehouse. Just one of the touches to transform this room into a ballroom. Most of it under my supervision.

I should feel proud. I would if it wasn't for the dress. Or all the other disasters in my life.

I tug my neckline up yet again to ensure the girls stay in. Argh. Tonight I should look glamorous. Instead, I look vulgar.

This gala hosts the crème de la crème of New York and if I ever wanted to fit in, this dress ensures I don't.

Not that I want to fit in. I'm working, after all. The evening is going really well, the guests seem happy, drunk enough to bet more in the silent auction, but not enough to cause trouble.

I should be proud of an event well prepared. Instead, after two weeks of frantic organizing, I'm teetering near a breakdown stronger than my three-minute crying session earlier.

When London Lowe called me about her event planner falling sick so close to her most important event of the year, I knew it would be near-impossible to take over. In fact, I'm pretty sure I was her last option.

Taking over at that stage and finalizing every detail I hadn't planned, then ensuring everything ran smoothly without understanding what it is I'm managing was a challenge.

And for a client with as many connections as London has, failure or even a hiccup isn't an option.

No wonder she couldn't find anyone so close to the event date. Nobody is that stupid. I'm not that stupid. But I am that desperate.

In the end, I pulled it off. Minus the dress. The result is... I'm dressed. My hair is in a high ponytail, my makeup consists of red lipstick, and my gown either exposes my breasts or raises up around my hips. My body is trying to escape it.

I can't even imagine having eaten anything today. Or drinking, for that matter. I focus on breathing, organizing and surviving without bursting stitches.

"Can you help me bid on a cruise, my dear?"

The voice startles me, and it takes a moment to find its owner. The lady is hunched over, supporting herself with a fancy cane. She looks like a fragile fairy godmother with a wicked stare. I smile.

Her dress dangles on her birdlike frame, and while she looks a hundred years old and struggles to move around, I'm envious. Why couldn't my dress come three sizes bigger?

"Of course. It's just over here." I help her navigate around the silent auction table.

"I don't have my glasses. What's the last bid there,

honey?" She points at an item. Her crooked finger reminds me of Annie.

"Twenty thousand dollars."

Shit, I know these people have money, but this is ridiculous. I remind myself it's for a good cause, but it's hard when I imagine what a quarter of it would do for my family.

"Double it, my dear."

I blink a few times. "Are you sure?"

She cackles. "Of course. I know London will use the money well. And I want to win."

"You really want that cruise." I laugh after I put her information down, wondering if there is a way I could subtly suggest another good cause.

This one would take even a thousand dollars, but while I'm desperate, my family situation hasn't robbed me of my dignity. Not yet.

"Oh, please, I couldn't care less about it, but my sister hates cruises and I want to give it to her as a present. The stick up her ass wouldn't allow her to refuse, especially after I make sure all our friends know about my generous gift. I will kill two birds, so to speak, give to a charity, piss off my sister, and get two weeks of freedom from her gossip and meddling in my affairs." She cackles again and shuffles away.

The little vengeful lady brings a smile to my lips, despite the way she throws around money to spite her sister. It's too close to home. I wish I could do the same. Not to spite. To help.

My smile dies as my eyes connect with a dark gaze I wish I didn't know. A dark brown abyss.

My head swirls with apprehension and possibly the lack of sustenance.

My poor heart thumps against my ribcage, and with my generous cleavage I'm worried everyone might see it.

Clearly, this dress has squeezed out all rational thinking.

There are three things I find sexy in a man: dimples, defined biceps, and vests. There are many things I hate about Giovanni Cassinetti.

Among them his burn-your-underwear smile with dimples, which I've only seen once or twice because the man's typical facial expression is utter annoyance.

I wish I didn't care about his hot AF chiseled biceps that fill his tailor-made suits perfectly, unlike my dress today. His frame is lean, but solidly defined in all the right places.

And, of course, the man is wearing a three-piece tux tonight. Jacket open, his black vest is hiding everything I ache to discover.

Scratch that. I don't ache for him. I don't have time for his personality. He's cold and arrogant. And let's not forget his herd of long-legged, collagen-lipped bimbos he parades around.

The first time I met him a few months back, when he came to an event in his brother's restaurant, Casa Cassi, my entire body reacted to him.

It was so unexpected, I lost a train of thought and made a complete idiot out of myself. I never lose my wits, but I guess there is always a first time for everything.

Every time he comes to Casa Cassi, dining with one of his countless models, I focus on the women in his life, hoping I can tame the unreasonable attraction.

And every time I succeed, mostly because his rude behavior knocks down his appeal. Until I see him the next time and I shake with that unreasonable need again.

It's ridiculous how the want and the dislike can cohabit happily, while the man and my unresolved attraction are driving me crazy.

We stare at each other over the heads of the guests. His entire being emanates something spellbinding and I can't look away. Something is off tonight. He isn't looking at me with contempt or his usual disregard. Maybe it's the fact he's looking at me—at anything—instead of his phone.

With narrowed eyes his gaze pierces me, and I swear the man can see my deepest hidden secrets.

I feel strangely exposed, melting in the hottest sun and freezing in the iciest storm. All at the same time. Consumed by his gaze.

He hasn't even moved to scan the whole of me. He's simply focused on my face as if it's the most fascinating thing in the world. Heat crawls up my neck.

Music and conversations fade away as the sound of my heartbeat takes up most of the space in my head. I need to look away. I have to break free from this prison of his stare. I want to. I think.

I narrow my eyes. That's all I manage, but it's something. Hopefully, I achieve two things with my mean look—to hide how frazzled I am by his scrutiny, and to allow him to see what I think of him.

Well, not about the hotness and dimples and muscles and the stupid vest, but the real, more important things. Like how shallow and arrogant he is.

Yet his stare unnerves me. What does he want? Why is he doing it? And why is there a part of me that hopes he won't stop?

The man spends most of his days and dates—as I've observed—staring at his phone. I need him to go back to that.

He shakes his head slightly like he can't believe he's spending his time looking at me. Or he doesn't like what he's seeing but can't look away either. His eyes burn me. Like the flickering flame of a candle, I want to get closer to bask in its light, but I know it would scorch me.

My head swirls a bit and my vision blurs, so I blink a few times to find my equilibrium. When I refocus, Gio is talking to someone, but he glances my way one more time. What I read on his face looks too close to concern. I'm being ridiculous.

"Mila, here is the current total." A volunteer who is minding the silent auction snaps me back to reality and my work.

I thank her and find London. "Excuse me." I smile at her companion and she steers us to the side.

"You've done an amazing job, Mila. People are having a great time, and all your additional touches to this venue and the program made this gala one of the most memorable ones. I will recommend you to everyone. You deserve to conquer New York with your attitude and skills."

I blink a few times. Her words slide down, lining my chest and my stomach with honey as pride swells inside me. "Thank you."

I know she hired me out of desperation, and probably because my best friend, Gina, her sister-in-law, sang my praises. She could have said "job well done'," but she said more, like she really means it.

I dial up the smile I've been casting around during

the evening, and this time there is a whisper of truth in it.

"Would you like to announce the donation's tally now?" I recover and give her the paper with the number.

"Are you okay?" She studies me for a moment.

"Yes, yes."

No, I'm not. I was just stripped bare by your step-brother's gaze. I haven't eaten or drunk anything all day. I've ridden an adrenaline wave that comes with jobs like this, and you've just validated me in the most wonderful way. So, no, I'm not okay, but I don't have the privilege to admit that.

"Okay." She looks down and purses her lips. "Let's make the announcement, and please make sure all the volunteers mind the silent auction."

I cross the room to the sound manager and get the mic ready for London. Walking is a bitch in this stupid dress, and I have to stop a few times to breathe and recover a semblance of grace.

After London's words, I hate the dress even more. I'm not vain, but who would have thought a dress could ruin a night like this?

London gives her speech and immediately the silent auction gets busier. I shuffle over to one of the volunteers and tell her I need to take a minute.

My head swims, blurring my surroundings as

another bout of dizziness claims me. I stumble out of the room into the deserted hallway.

Leaning against the cold wall, I consider how far away our green room is. I need to drink some water at least. Regretting I didn't walk to the bar instead of out here, I look at the double door and consider returning to the ballroom.

But I made it this far already and there are bottles of water and fruit backstage. That should be okay to stabilize my blood sugar and keep this fucking dress together.

Keeping one hand on the wall, I fight the swirling floor and trudge along. Before I practically fall into the room, the noise of the ballroom gets louder for an instant. Hopefully whoever stepped outside hasn't seen me.

I stagger around and take off my heels, wishing I could sit down, but I don't think this dress would survive that. I lean on my hands against the table and lower my head, closing my eyes.

A click of the door alerts me, but I can't move fast enough to look at who came in. Only volunteers and London know about this room. I pry my eyes open but the kaleidoscope of stars flickering in front of me prompts me to close them again.

The world continues to swirl. I fight to focus on

something, anything to pull myself out of this funk. Jesus. Am I going to faint?

And then a smoky and spicy scent wafts my way, and suddenly I have something to focus on, but it's as far from helping me recover as possible. Without thinking, I whirl around. Wrong move.

The world spins around with me but in the opposite direction, and I lose my footing. Two firm arms grab me, and luckily I remain upright. Wrapped in that enticing scent, trapped by firm muscles.

I close my eyes to breathe and enjoy the safety that surrounds me. Safety I haven't felt in the longest time. It brings me peace I didn't know I could feel again.

We stand there for I don't know how long, and for a moment my head doesn't fight the closeness. Damn the consequences. Damn the hussies he dates. Damn his rudeness. Damn his contempt. I need this peace.

"Are you hungry?" As soon as the gruff words reach my ears, the peace is gone. Wiped out by a simple question, and a tone that spikes all the hair on my nape.

"What are you doing here?" I push off Gio's chest, blocking the feel of his chiseled muscles under my fingertips.

"I saw you stumbling around like a newborn lamb. Jesus, woman, here, eat something." He hands me a protein bar.

My eyes dart between him and the bar. Jesus, he really has a flawless face. And he carries around protein bars.

"Eat," he growls.

Fuck him. I'm about to refuse when my stomach grumbles loudly. As I step back the stupid floor moves again, and I waver. I grasp the table beside me, but Gio scoops me up at the same time, supporting me with both arms again.

It's like he is squeezing me with two scorching pokers, leaving burn marks all over my skin. He snatches the bar from me and rips off the wrapper on one side before giving it back.

Right now, it looks as good as an upscale four-course meal. My mouth waters. I bring the bar to my lips, aiming my eyes at the boxes on the side. Anywhere but him.

It doesn't matter, I still feel his gaze on me. Studying me. Scrutinizing me. Zapping through me like a current.

I don't know how to reconcile the comforting hug with the rest of his behavior. I don't know how to recover from his silent judgment.

What I do know is, unfortunately, his stupid protein bar has saved me. I feel better just from the first taste of the gooey substance on my tongue. Delicious. Like the man in front of me. Wait. What?

I snap my eyes back to him. "Thank you, but I can take care of myself."

All the evidence screams that my statement is bullshit, but I straighten up and return his stare with all the confidence I can muster. Not much under his glare.

He steps closer, robbing me of any protection I thought I still had. My chest rises, brushing against his vest. His breath feathers across my face from above.

I look up, not because I think I can withstand his gaze, but because I need to try. To stand my ground, however shaky.

I meet those dark eyes, my mouth going as dry as a desert. The lingering taste of chocolate from his bar turns sour, or possibly more sweet. I'm not sure anymore.

"Can you, Mila?" The timbre of his voice has a new quality. No longer his usual disinterest and contempt. It's deep and sensual, and it reverberates deep in my core. He looks at me like he owns me, and for a split second I want to belong to him.

As if we both think the same, we jerk away from each other. Me mortified, and him... I don't know. Disgusted? I can't read his face.

"Eat the bar and drink some water," he orders.

"Yes, sir." I smile at him, because that's how I deal with life.

Something passes over his face. It's brief, but I

swear it looks like adoration. He likes my smile? The lack of sugar is making me stupid. I take another bite with gusto, because apparently passive aggressive is my new norm.

He shakes his head and then looks me up and down. Now I'm sure it's disgust on his face.

"Why would you dress like a hooker?"

Chapter 2

Mila

"Excuse me," I yell, but the print shop clerk turns and gets into a waiting car. I don't slow down. My rational mind already knows it's too late, but desperation propels me.

I reach the entrance and wiggle the door. It's closed. I needed to print and bind my presentation. Hopefully in the morning.

I allow myself a moment of panic, wiping a tear. It's been a year since I returned to New York to help my family, and to escape Brian. A year later and his words ring in my ears as strong as ever. *You screw up everything, darling. You're lucky to have me.*

I know he's not right. Deep down I know, but that confidence weakens with every day of this exhausting existence I've been living.

Deflated, I trudge back to the subway, my mind

trying to come up with a plan B. Almost an hour later, I arrive home without a solution, but the screaming that welcomes me snaps me out of the self-pity party immediately.

Ellery is crying in the playpen, her little face stained with tears and mucus.

"Annie," I call out, picking up my niece, whose skin burns. I dash to the kitchen and find my nephew in the corner, his knees pulled under his chin, rocking.

The floor is wet, spaghetti swimming around, steam mingling with desperation as my eyes connect with my sister's.

"Ellery, baby, mommy is okay," Annie croons. Ellery hiccups and reaches for her mom and my heart breaks a little. Annie holds her hands to her chest, her crooked, swollen fingers rigid.

"Sit down," I order.

She slumps into the chair and I place Ellery in her lap. She wraps her arms around her daughter, her hands and fingers stiff.

"Sh-sh-sh," she consoles her daughter.

I sit down on the floor by Aidan. "Hey, buddy, Mommy dropped the pot, but everything is okay. Do you think you can help me prepare peanut butter sandwiches and clean up the mess while Mommy reads for Ellery? We both really need your help."

His eyes dart around for a moment before they

connect with mine. The maturity in his gaze, the understanding of his family's situation, of his own vulnerability, hits me in the chest.

I'm overwhelmed with everything, so I smile. Fake it until you make it. And it's my smile that pushes him off the floor.

"I'm sorry," Annie whispers.

"Shut up," I scowl, but grin at her. "You wanted to cook for your family. Besides, who loves a peanut butter sandwich here?" I raise my hand and the children follow. I shrug. "See, much better dinner is coming up."

She mouths, "Thank you," and buries her face in Ellery's wild curls, hiding her tears.

By the time I hit the sofa, ready to die of exhaustion, it's almost midnight. The kitchen is clean, the kids are fed, and Annie has fallen asleep with them. My alarm is set for me to hit the print shop right as they open.

Everything is just slightly under control.

"I'm so sorry I'm late." I plop down across from Gina. Casa Cassi isn't yet busy with the lunch crowd, but the place buzzes with preparations.

"No worries, I had things to discuss with Massi and

Phillip." She stands up and saunters behind the bar. "Do you want a coffee?"

"Yes, please." I shed my coat and lift my hair to cool my sweaty nape. I need to get my schedule under control.

The coffee grinder roars to life and the lifesaving aroma fills the room. I close my eyes for a moment, to find my equilibrium after running like a headless chicken all morning.

Late seems to be the theme of the month. At least Aidan got to school almost on time. His morning meltdown put a serious dent in my schedule, but I did get my presentation printed.

The swinging door to the kitchen bangs open and I immediately know the beat of calm is over.

"I thought we agreed you won't drink coffee anymore," Massi roars at his wife. Well, technically, she's his ex-wife.

"It's for Mila," Gina drawls, and Massi's features soften immediately.

He walks around the counter to reach her and kisses her hair, gently caressing her growing belly. The scene tugs at the corners of my lips.

"Hey, Mila." Massi waves. "Nice to see you finally shop for clothes in the adult department." He chuckles.

I glare at Gina. It seems like my wardrobe disaster from last week is a joke in the Cassinetti household.

"No worries, you'd look amazing even in a sack of potatoes." Massi winks and returns to his kingdom in the kitchen.

"He's not wrong." Gina returns with two cups of espresso and sits down. She glows, and not only because she is pregnant. She's been glowing ever since they got back together.

A pang of jealousy licks at my insides. While I'm happy for my best friend, her newly-found second chance at love solved all her financial problems, and she is expecting. She deserves all the good fortune coming her way, but Jesus, I could use a break.

She raises the small cup to her lips, and I raise my eyebrow.

"What? Don't judge me. If the man thinks I can function without caffeine because it's better for the baby, he's wrong. Besides, this is my first." She shrugs and inhales the aroma.

"Your first?" I chuckle.

She glares at me, but a smile lingers on her face. "Let's get to business."

"Of course, boss." I bite my lip.

We spend half an hour going through all the social media plans for several restaurants Gina works with. Or I should say, "we" work with, but we wouldn't have those clients without her, so I don't pretend. I've always been her sidekick.

"Okay, I think we're set for the week. When is your meeting? Should I get Massi to make us something to eat?" Gina stands up. "I've been ravenous all waking hours."

"Maybe just soup. I'm a bit nervous."

The pitch has kept me up since I received the call. I don't know how such a big company found out about me, but just being invited to present my capabilities is an opportunity. I need to break the streak of bad luck I've been having.

"Don't be silly, Mils. You'll dazzle them. You know your shit, and they wouldn't have invited you if they didn't think you have something to offer." She raises her finger and disappears into the kitchen.

I don't feel as amazing as she seems to believe. Since I returned from California almost a year ago, nothing I try is enough. If it wasn't for my therapist, I would fall into believing Brian was right all along.

Gina returns. "Mils, London has been raving about all you've done, not only to save her gala but improve it. I'm sure this job will get you on the right track to have a pool of stable clients. Also, I'll need you to step in and take on more once the baby comes." She sits down and reaches over to squeeze my hand.

"I hope you're right, because lately I feel I've lost my dazzling powers." I smile at her.

"You've been taking on too much."

I snort. "And yet it's not enough."

"You took the responsibility for a whole family, and you juggle so many things. Let me help you." Her eyes plead.

This is not the first time she's offered. "Gina, I'm not taking a loan from you. I can manage."

Massi comes in with two plates. "Ladies, enjoy. I have to go back to the kitchen, but I'm happy to whip up something else for you."

"Thank you, this smells like heaven." I inhale the steam rising from my bowl, thyme and garlic tickling my nose.

"You know only the best for you, always." The two of them have been pampering me ever since Massi's business rival tried to sever my fingers.

"And the offer to help is on the table," Gina says. "I don't mind. You left your life behind to help your sister. No one would think less of you for accepting some help yourself."

I swirl the spoon in the rich cream and taste some. "In some twisted fate, I'm glad Annie's situation forced me to leave Cali, though."

Gina narrows her eyebrows. "What do you mean? Brian would have understood why you needed to be closer to your family. You were planning a future together—"

"Gina, it doesn't matter anymore." She's my best

friend, and she went through so much in her previous manipulative relationship. She of all people would understand, but still I can't bring myself to share. To admit my failure. My shame.

"I'm here," I continue, "and I'm stuck with all the problems—health and financial—of my family, but I wouldn't want to be anywhere else."

Everyone adored Brian. I used to love him. Until I realized that in his shadow I was loving myself less and less every day. And yet I couldn't leave. If it wasn't for one desperate call from Annie, I might have never found a reason to leave him. A reason to stand up for myself.

Gina gives me a serious look.

"The woman I used to know who brought sunshine to my life when it was at its darkest is gone. I look at your smile nowadays and most people don't see it, but you've lost your spark."

"Why thank you, you make a girl feel great." Yes, sarcasm is the newest tool in my arsenal.

She's right, and if I wasn't so fucking exhausted working fifteen plus hours a day, and still only barely paying for Annie's medication, I would find the way to bring that smile back.

"Who else should tell you the truth if not your best friend?" She slathers a generous dollop of butter on a warm bun.

"Well, if this job pans out, I'll get my spark back. I promise. How are you feeling?"

"I've never been better. Is it weird I feel guilty about it?" She chuckles and shakes her head, but the truth gleams in her eyes.

I could tell her she's being silly, but I know it wouldn't eliminate the useless feeling. The moment between us stretches in a vulnerable companionship.

"You deserve the happiness, Gina."

She smiles and rubs her belly again. "You're a good friend, Mils. And you deserve the happiness too."

"Jesus, this meeting got heavy." I laugh. "I'm happy, just a bit unsure about the future right now, but that will pass."

Will it? Isn't this exactly what Brian predicted? *You're nothing without me.*

"I know you said you were too dependent on Brian. I'm pretty sure I don't know the complete story there, and I respect your need for independence. But being independent doesn't mean you can't accept help."

We stare at each other for a few beats, and a part of me wants to ask her for help. For a check that she wouldn't miss, and that I could use to cover Annie's medication and rent. To breathe, and grow my freelance business into something more sustainable that won't kill me with the endless hours of work, and would also provide for the family.

But I can't. I can't prove to Brian—not that he cares—I really am nothing without him.

Gina gives me a sad, but understanding, smile. "Eat." She beckons to my soup.

She says it with love and care, and a hint of concern. Nothing like the growl only a week ago at the gala, but the memory flashes over me anyway.

The intense glare. The dark brown abyss. The solid muscles. The tick in his jaw. The way my body is drawn to him. The warmth spreading through my limbs against my will. The humiliation.

"Do you think I'm a slut?"

Chapter 3

Mila

I don't know why I asked. Why do I need validation from my friend? Why can't I rise above his insult? I mean, my dress at the gala... Why do I fucking care?

I know he didn't comment on my lifestyle... or maybe he did. What does he know about me anyway?

And yet, I couldn't sleep because of his comment for several nights, which in my current situation isn't good. Not at all. I shouldn't care about Gio Cassinetti's opinion, and yet...

"Where is this coming from?" Gina laughs, but her laughter dies as she meets my eyes. "You're serious? I haven't even seen you with anyone for a few months. And even when you were enjoying all the possible kinky fun after you broke up for Brian, even then I didn't for a second think that. What are you talking about?"

I shrug. "I don't know. Gio said I look like a hooker."

She gasps and covers her mouth. "Oh my God, I'm so sorry, Mils. I don't... he acts like an arrogant asshole, but I always assumed it's a mask, but... I-I-I don't know what to say. Do you want Massi to beat the shit out of him?"

Her attempt at lightening the mood falls short, but her concern is sweet. "No, of course not. I don't care what Gio thinks, anyway."

But something in her reaction doesn't sit well with me. As if she is hiding something.

* * *

Perhaps my reaction to Gio's harsh words bloomed out of proportion because of the seeds Brian planted. But that sliver of rationalization is as thin as a spider's thread.

As much as I try, I stumble, falter, trip. I don't glide smoothly like Brian or Gio. Or Gina, London, or any other person I know.

I cross the street, craning my neck. The building is an intimidating skyscraper of glass, cement, and corporate culture. Never did I imagine I might work for a large company like The Wings. At least I'd work with influencers and at the events, so hopefully not cooped up in one of the cubicles.

Though the idea brings a smile to my lips. I've been freelancing since I was in college and never considered working for a machine like this, but as I step into the large stone-clad lobby, I'm excited.

Perhaps this could be my clean slate. A chain of small boutiques across the country, The Wings is a perfect mix of small—a type of service I'm used to supporting because they cater to a specific niche of people who want to be unique—and large, because some important holding has bought them recently.

I smile at the receptionist who stops me with an erect finger while she finishes a phone call. As soon as she hangs up, another line rings. I keep smiling, but I hope she won't make me late.

A pathetic part of me wishes Brian could see me here. The thought lingers in my stomach, spreading acid. I don't want to do things to prove shit to Brian. It's been a year, for fuck's sake.

The receptionist finally gives me a visitor badge and sends me on my way. The elevator is full of people with purpose. They're all dressed smartly. I look down at my dress, pleased with my choice. A simple purple dress. Dressy, but not too much.

. . .

"This is what you're wearing?" Brian shook his head.

I ran my hands over the black pencil skirt I wore with a white off-shoulder T-shirt. "Yes." My voice is just a whisper.

"You can't be serious. This is a dinner with my partners, and you're dressed for a party. Don't you have anything more appropriate to wear?"

"Brian, I'm dressed for a party. I'm opening a restaurant tonight. I told you—"

"And I told you how important tonight is for my career. Baby, I can't believe you would rather go to some party. This is my future. Our future." He looked at me with hurt in his eyes, and for some reason I felt the betrayal deep in my bones.

"I'm sorry." Perhaps I could call Gina to tell her something came up. If I was careful, nobody at Brian's dinner would notice I was posting on social media. But without being there and taking pictures? "I have to go, Brian. I told you we can't move an opening night." I didn't want to do this to him. I knew how important his job was to him.

"You're always sorry. For once, it would be nice if you supported me."

"Let me call Gina."

. . .

I shake off the memory as the elevator dings on the fifteenth floor. I step onto thick beige carpet and into another reception area. This one is much smaller. Two men in blue overalls are attaching The Wings logo to the soft brown wall across from me.

"Mila Ward?" A woman in her late forties, dressed in black, high-waisted pants flaring at her ankles and a white button-down shirt draws my attention.

"That's me." I smile.

She rushes to me and hits the elevator button. "We'll go down to procurement, so you can get started on the paperwork. I'm Portia Krane, and you'll be reporting to me."

I'm pretty sure my jaw falls to the floor. Reporting to her? I'm glued to the spot as I try to make sense of her words, and I don't realize she has stepped into the elevator. She makes an impatient noise, holding the door open for me.

"It's going to be a six-week contract, till mid-January, and afterward we can talk about either a permanent position or an extension." She checks her watch. "You must have impressed someone because I haven't seen corporate moving this fast on approving a contract since I've been here. Mind you, the new owners might have different processes. We're all just trying to go with the flow and figuring things out on the go."

"There are no other candidates? I thought I would present my capabilities?" I'm trying to figure out if there is a chance another Mila Ward has been hired.

She frowns, checking her phone. "There's no bid for this position. I was told you're working on the social media plan execution. And while I don't like when someone makes hiring decisions for me, I checked you out, and six weeks won't kill me. Especially if you prove yourself. Don't screw me over."

I blink a few times, unsure how to respond to her unwelcoming welcome, but beggars can't be choosers, and the fact that someone recommended me here and I got hired is too good to be true for me to fuck it up. Perhaps one of London's guests from the gala?

"I hope you can spend a few days in California next week," Portia continues as we get out of the elevator. "We've redesigned the stores there, and if the rebranding is successful we'll be rolling it out to the rest of the country. Our VP, Marnie Kowalski, will go as well." She speaks as fast as she walks, and I type while I try to follow. "Are you on your phone?" She stops abruptly and I stumble.

"Taking notes." No wonder she has this fit figure if she speed-walks the endless corridors. My heart hammers in my chest, but if I'm honest, it's not just from her speed.

"Oh, great. I like efficient people. Where was I?"

She turns to march again. "Oh, yeah, it's not ideal you'll be out there by yourself with Marnie, but we have a few issues here and I'll be staying. Marnie is okay, though. You can learn a lot from her. Good, here we are."

She knocks on a glass office and opens the door, not waiting for the answer. "Rob, I have Mila Ward here. Could you set her up with paperwork and then help her find the HR department?"

An older, bald gentleman with glasses and checked shirt looks up from his computer. "Give me a moment."

Portia turns and makes eye contact for the first time since we met. "Good. Today is going to be a long boring day of trainings, instructions, manuals, etc. I blocked tomorrow morning in my calendar to brief you on everything. HR will show you your desk later. Welcome to the team, Mila."

I watch her leave, still unsure what has just happened, but before I can contemplate it further, Rob clears his throat.

I sit across from him, and he puts paperwork in front of me. I glimpse the hourly rate and my breath hitches. Even if this gig lasts only six weeks, I'll be able to get at least three-months' worth of meds for Annie and pay the rent. Maybe even take care of some credit card debt.

"For a contract like yours, I need to file three

competitive quotes, but I guess when you know the boss of the bosses, things get expedited."

I have a feeling he's more concerned about the shortcut in the procedure than my capabilities, or my connection to said boss, but my joy over the contract is suddenly tainted.

I don't even know who my benefactor is, and I already feel like I'll have to prove myself doubly hard because of his help.

I quickly fill out all the forms and sign the documents, but before I leave to find HR, I can't help but ask, "Who is the boss of the bosses, Rob?"

It's a fine balance between sounding sweet enough to get him on my side and not sounding completely stupid that I don't know who he's referring to.

I did my research on The Wings, but I didn't dig any deeper than that. I should have, since of course I missed something.

Rob doesn't even look at me, already typing away on his computer.

"What do you mean? Giovanni Cassinetti, of course."

Chapter 4

Gio

"**C**areful you don't collapse. You're pounding that belt like you haven't gotten laid in a while." Conrad whips his towel in the general direction of the treadmill I've been abusing for almost an hour now.

"Real mature, asshole." I pant, punching in a few more digits to incline.

Sweat drips from my forehead, but the release is not coming. Lately, no matter how much I try to reset my brain, I can't seem to shake off the agitation. "When did you come back?"

"Last night. I can't say I missed the fucking cold. Why does anyone live in New York during winter?" He sits on a bench and starts lifting weights.

I finish my uphill sprint and slow down the

machine, wiping my head with the towel. "You should have stayed in San Diego."

"Nora missed Christmas in New York." He pushes through gritted teeth as he raises the bar above his head. "I have two board meetings scheduled, so we decided to come here for a month. My balls froze the minute we stepped off the plane and I almost turned around." He chuckles.

"Yeah, careful, you look like a surfer playboy." His tanned skin is glowing dark compared to mine. "It might be deadly for you to go out without your wife. The socialites of New York would be drawn to your pretty, sun-kissed face." I get off the treadmill, wrapping my towel around my neck.

"I thought all the socialites were busy fighting over you," he quips, and struggles to lift the bar again.

"You need help, pretty boy? It looks like Cali doesn't have the right equipment to keep you in shape."

He drops the bar with a clank and sits up. "At least I can lift. You run like a girl."

Fucking Conrad. "Load it up, asshole."

We chest press and dead lift like idiots for about fifteen minutes, pushing each other beyond reason. Just like any other time we're together.

"Fuck, I'm going to regret this tomorrow." He stretches his triceps over his head. "At least I won."

"Hardly." I poke him in the ribs with my elbow.

"It's good to see you. Let's have dinner soon. Massi's restaurant has been the talk of the town."

"Sure, Nora would love to see you, and I can survive the mediocre company for one night. Let's hit the sauna. I have a business I'd like you to look into."

I check my watch and think of the zillion emails waiting for me, and then shrug. "Let me rearrange my schedule and we'll go for breakfast in an hour. I hate saunas."

We meet at my club. The hostess brings Conrad over to my table, blushing and staring at him as if he's a god. He flirts with her, but we both know it's for her benefit. Conrad is as pussy-whipped as they come, happily monogamous for years now.

"Don't give her ideas." I shake my head.

"She could see my wedding band. It's a fair game." He shrugs and places the linen napkin on his lap.

"Is that what Nora thinks?"

"She knows she's the one for me."

We order breakfast and Conrad asks, "What about you? Still the most eligible bachelor in the city?"

"Yeah. If I find a woman of Nora's loyalty I might consider settling down. In the meantime, I'm happy with my arrangements."

He studies me for a moment, and I get the strange feeling there is pity in his eyes. Fuck me. The last thing I need is my best friend feeling sorry for me. Why is it that once you're past thirty, everyone seems overly concerned with your relationship status? I'm perfectly fine.

"Your arrangements are stopping you from finding the one. You can't assume there is betrayal behind every relationship."

There has been, in my experience. "I thought you wanted to talk about business?"

He shakes his head, smirking. "How is the retail business?" Of course he can't help himself, and pushes the sore point.

"It's a fucking nightmare. I wish I'd never taken the bet."

He laughs. Like throwing his head back, enjoying the front-row seat at my humiliation show. "How bored you must have been to actually take me up on that challenge."

I'm not bored. "What did you want to talk about?"

"There is a vineyard for sale in Napa. Inheritance. One sibling is willing to stay and manage the operation, but she can't afford to pay off her brothers who are not interested. Nora knows the family and wants to help them." He goes on, describing a potential for expansion and the quality of the wine.

"Why would you need me? This is a pet project you can afford without a call to your bank." I take a sip of my tea.

Conrad Hermann has been my best friend since Wharton. We made our first hundred million together, and we still co-chair some companies together. And though we have diversified in different directions since then, Conrad is one of the few people I trust.

"I want the vineyard. It's good and honest, and I enjoy putting some of my money into real things, but I'd appreciate your assessment first."

"I don't have time to fly to California. I'm swamped as it is with my latest acquisitions."

"Yeah, asshole, who knew you fucking have to work for your riches?" He rolls his eyes. "Nora wants to move to Europe."

I adjust my cufflinks. "You're there every summer."

"Permanently."

Pussy-whipped. "And you're going to grant her this wish and fucking commute overseas?" I laugh.

"The first year I will. While I figure out which of my assets need to be offloaded because they require too much work."

"Too much work? Do you hear yourself? Are your retiring?" I keep shaking my head, but Conrad sits there with his smug grin, as if there is something I'm not getting.

"Yeah, I'm pretty much retiring." He shrugs. "I want to spend less time stressed and more time with

Nora. We want a family, and this fast-paced gig is just not doing it for me anymore."

I stare at him, wondering who kidnapped my friend's brain. "Fast-paced gig? It's your fucking career, your legacy. You're just going to throw it away?"

"Don't be so dramatic. Work doesn't bring me as much joy as before, so I'll consolidate, sell, buy something new to keep me occupied. But I'm done playing the big game, man."

I have no words. I imagine who I would be if I retired, but immediately I know that without my work I would be nobody.

"Okay, I see you don't understand, and perhaps when you share your life with someone else you will, but I'm actually pretty excited." He shrugs and attacks his breakfast oatmeal.

Work doesn't bring me joy anymore. What a ridiculous statement. We're thirty-three, not eighty.

"So Nora wants to move, and Nora wants to help the family with the vineyard. Are you making any decisions for yourself anymore?"

"Asshole. Just because I'm dropping the workaholic tendencies, it doesn't mean I don't think for myself anymore. Look, go and check the place out. I'll send you all the numbers. You know I value your opinion."

"You want me to spend time on your wife's pet

project like it's an actual business?" I canceled two meetings to have this breakfast, for fuck's sake.

"Don't be a dick. Look at it for me."

"Okay, send me the prospectus." I sigh. "I guess I'll see you in Italy this summer." I shake my head again and stand up.

"Don't be so sour about it. You'll understand one day." He pats my shoulder.

"No, I won't. Let me know when we can have that dinner. I'll talk some sense into Nora."

* * *

"I rescheduled your nine o'clock and your ten o'clock, but before your next meeting, Mrs. Kowalski is working from home today and needs to talk to you urgently. Can I get her on the line?"

Lydia waits for me at the elevator, simultaneously picking up my coat and pushing a hot tea into my hand. By the time we reach my corner office, she's recited my schedule for the rest of the day and I've answered two emails on my phone. We're a good team.

"Thank you, Lydia. Yeah, get Marnie on the line first."

She closes the door behind me, and I find my desk neatly organized based on priorities. When the woman retires, I'll be lost. Maybe I'll move to fucking Europe then. I chuckle to myself.

The phone buzzes and I hit the speaker button. "Marnie, is everything ready for next week?" I turn on the large monitor on my wall to check the markets then start replying to another email.

"About that, Gio." Her voice falters. She's worked for me for four years, and the strength the woman exudes scares many, regardless of their gender or seniority. I move my attention to the phone as if I could see what's wrong.

"What's going on?" I snap. Ever since we bought the stupid retail chain for hippies, something has gone awry. I can't wait to hear what it is now. At least Marnie brings solutions to the table.

"We'll have to postpone the launch. By at least one week." The way her voice trembles would suggest she is crying, but that can't be true.

"Continue."

I lost a bet to Conrad—I don't even remember what it was—and the asshole challenged me to buy a retail chain and make money on it. I wish I didn't want to wipe his smile away with the millions I make. This particular venture is headache-inducing.

"I can't fly for the retail relaunch in the foreseeable future, and the soonest I can get one of my senior staff to replace me is two weeks."

That's ridiculous. "Why can't you fly to the West Coast?"

She clears her throat and I swear she sniffles. Jesus, I hate emotional responses. What the fuck?

"Gio, I'm pregnant." She says it as an apology. Do people really think that little of me?

"Congratulations, Marnie. But unless I missed something, I don't see why you can't fly to California next week."

This conversation is dragging beyond the limits of my patience. It irritates me, because if something is wrong I'd like to move to the solution, but also because Marnie is never this sensitive.

"Thank you. We're happy, but the pregnancy has been deemed high-risk, and I was ordered to be on bedrest. Look, Gio, I'm going to work from home... from my bed... for a few more days, but then I'll go on leave. I can't risk this baby to..." And now I'm sure she's been sniffling.

"Of course, of course. And you're sure nobody can step in?"

The numbers on the large screen flicker in red and green, and the words on my laptop blur while I seek for some clarity in this fucked-up situation.

"I looked at all the contingencies, at all the projects, but we don't have anyone senior enough to leave as early as next week."

She gives me a list of candidates who can oversee the launch on the ground in California, but she also gives me compelling reasons why they can't drop their assignments quickly enough. She did assess it from all the angles.

"We can't postpone. It will cost us money and reputation. I'll go."

"You?" She almost chokes. "Gio, this is a hands-on kind of trip. Schmoozing with people."

"I can schmooze with people." *I can't.* I should have never gone into retail, and now I'm stuck with field work and a requirement to actually meet with employees and customers. I can handle suits in the boardroom, but this? Pure torture.

"Gio—"

"Marnie, I appreciate your concern, but I got this covered. Try to wrap up all the loose ends, and then let's start the process to fill your position for a year."

"Thank you, Gio. I'll send you a brief for the events in California and all the necessary details. I appreciate your understanding."

"No worries. Take care of yourself. And congratulations again."

I hang up and lean back in my chair. *Hands-on trip.* I hope the employees involved are capable enough.

As I leave for my first of many meetings of the day, I shoot a message to Conrad.

Me: I'll be in California next week. I'll check out the property.

Conrad: I haven't even sent you the details yet.

Me: It's your lucky day, asshole.

The meetings are long, tedious and dull. Okay, maybe one is kind of interesting, but by the end of the day I'm somewhat pleased with the prospect of an out-of-office engagement.

"I reviewed your schedule for the California trip, and I made the hotel reservations." Lydia once again proves she's on top of things as I return to my office late in the afternoon. "There is a team of people on the ground, and there are only four key locations planned for the first week."

"Great. Thank you. I need to make a detour to Napa Valley while I'm there. Can you coordinate with Conrad Hermann and have it arranged?"

"I will. If you don't mind, it's my grandson's birthday today and I'd like to leave."

"Of course. Thank you, Lydia." I glance at my watch, surprised it's five o'clock already. I sit behind my computer and attack my inbox with determination.

Two hundred messages later, I squint at the screen and it blurs in front of my eyes. I text my driver and make my way out.

The elevator stops on the fifteenth floor and the

blond princess floats in. Jesus, I forgot she works here now. I wonder what job Marnie offered her.

She's typing on her phone and murmurs a greeting without raising her eyes. Is she pretending not to see me? Fine by me.

Mila holds her coat over her arm, balancing her large laptop bag and her phone in the other hand. Unlike at the gala, she's wearing a decent dress.

My eyes wander down her curves, stopping at the perfectly round ass. The woman has the body of a goddess. I force myself to lift my gaze before I cause problems HR would kill me for.

I inhale to snap out of my unreasonable fixation, but that doesn't help much because lavender wafts my way. Something about her essence is so intoxicating, but then I remember her bubbly personality and her unwarranted glaring every time we cross paths, and I return my attention to my emails.

"You?" she yelps as we get off the elevator. What the hell? Was she really unaware of my presence?

"Me." I nod.

"Is this some sort of a sick joke? You want me to be indebted to you for some weird reason? You have to control everything and everyone?"

"You make no sense." Scratch the bubbly personality. This woman is crazy. Fuming for some reason.

"This job." She drops her laptop between her feet and yanks her coat over her shoulders.

"This job?" Is she seriously upset I got her a job? It's not even a full-time position. "You don't like the opportunity?"

Mila jerks her head back, staring at me. "I like the opportunity just fine. I don't like you meddling. Pitying me. I can get a job on my own without your sympathy gestures."

Is she for real? "Look, if you think I'd have given you a job without knowing you're capable of doing the said job, you're delusional. You're not here because I wanted to help you. The favor was for Gina. And even that wouldn't have happened if London didn't sing your praises. The only thing I approved of was giving you a six-week contract. I won't hire you before confirming you're the right fit."

She steps back and blinks a few times. Without thinking about it I step forward, my gait long enough to invade her personal space. This woman draws the worst out of me. Fuck, the HR team will have a field day with my behavior. I step back immediately.

She opens her mouth and closes it again. And as if cornering her right now or my ogling earlier wasn't concerning enough, despite my annoyance with her, I fixate on those lips.

Perfectly shaped, dark pink, glistening with something, but not lipstick. Fuck, I want to sink my teeth into that bottom lip, full and sensuous.

Her breath hitches and my cock stirs, just like in that dingy storage room at the gala. I need to get laid soon, because this attraction makes no sense. She hates me, as she has suggested many times with her cold shoulder behavior, and frankly, she seems more trouble than she is probably worth.

I better call Lydia to organize a date for me before California to release this stupid sexual tension.

"The last time I checked, talking with respect with your coworkers is one of the prerequisites for the *right fit*."

To her credit, she raises her chin and smiles. "I didn't know Gina interfered. I'm sorry." Okay, another point for the ability to apologize when she is wrong. Why am I even rating her? She's Marnie's responsibility now.

"Look, based on what I've heard, you need the job, but I'm not forcing it on you. If you don't want it, you're free to go."

It would be for the best, anyway, because I don't need her here, tempting me and irritating me at the same time.

I should just leave, but instead—no restraints, Cassinetti—I step closer. Not too close, I'm still aware of our current professional relationship.

She counters my move, steps back and hits the wall. There is enough space between us for another person to pass, and yet her heat spreads over my body.

"What is it going to be, Mila? Are you walking out?" *You're on a roll, Cassinetti.*

The blue of her eyes pierces me with hatred, and something else I can't place. She bites the inside of her bottom lip, but doesn't waver from my glare, and something about it draws me in more. Like a moth lured to a flame, I lose myself momentarily in the deep blue of her eyes.

The elevator door beside us dings and I jerk away, shocked back into reality. I adjust my cufflinks, annoyed by the whole situation.

"Thank you, Mr. Cassinetti, I appreciate the opportunity. I *will* prove myself." She turns on her heel and walks away, head held high, tossing her silky hair over her shoulder.

Now I understand why so many CEOs have a private fucking elevator.

Chapter 5

Mila

My efforts to avoid Gio Cassinetti lasted for two whole days. The car his company—or my client/employer—sent pulls to a stop in front of a house the size of which I didn't even know existed in Manhattan.

I take a fortifying breath, in the hope that I can survive this meeting without the lingering feelings of frustration and humiliation crawling up my spine every time I interact with my new boss. Or the boss of my boss.

Just my luck that a last-minute health concern would put Gio in charge of the project I've been assigned to work on. I can be professional. I am a professional. I can put my unreasonable attraction to the side easily, because the man is as warm as an igloo.

I just need to wrap my head—or rather my attitude

—around the fact he's no longer an arrogant brother of Gina's husband, but my boss. I can do that.

Jesus, this house is a mansion. My heels sound obnoxious on the stone pavement leading to the main entrance. Flanked by two white pillars, the door is adorned by a wreath.

It seems so domestic, I wonder for a second if I'm at the right house. And why is he working from home, and taking in-person meetings here?

I'm tired and cranky. I don't like being cranky. That's not who I am. I put on a smile and take three more breaths, but as I raise my hand to ring the bell, I can't do it.

Yes, you can.

Can I? I've felt and acted like an idiot around the man since our encounter at the gala. Stupid protein bar. Gio is insufferable and rude, and yet he noticed I was lightheaded and dizzy. He sought me out to help me. In his very weird, obnoxious way, but he did. And then he gave me this gig.

I wish I could ask Gina about it, but I'm avoiding her because I've been unreasonably upset about her meddling and getting me this job. I'm a horrible person. Her family has been so good to me, but my pride is suffering. While well-intentioned, this kind of help is only a bitter reminder of the failure I am. Perfect. I'm also ungrateful now.

Mila Jessica Ward, snap out of this. Be yourself. I close my eyes for a moment.

The thing is, I don't know how to reconcile the man I thought he was with the man who did those small deeds of kindness. Well, kindness wrapped in an insult, but still.

Let's start with a clean slate.

"Or let's start with why are you standing here, wasting time?"

I snap my eyes open and meet Gio's glare. Dark brown, bottomless pools. My heart jumpstarts.

Apparently I speak to myself out loud. And, of course, he has cameras, or heard the car. How long have I been standing here?

I give him a million-watt smile. "Sorry, my sister called."

His gaze drops to my hand where I hold my phone, and back to my eyes. He licks his lips. It's all happening in slow motion, while in my mind I'm watching the freight train hurtling forward to kill me. For lying. Or just out of mortification.

He shakes his head slightly like he's annoyed, disappointed and done with me. Then he lifts his own phone, starts typing and turns. "You're late."

I watch his back receding into the long hallway and the door closes slowly. I put my foot in to prevent it from slamming in my face, but then I freeze. Is he expecting me to follow?

"Are you coming or what?" he growls, without turning or stopping. He *is* expecting me to follow.

I don't make it too far, because as I unfasten the sash of my coat, I don't quite know what to do next. There is no coat rack. Should I take my shoes off? Are there guest slippers?

"The door to your left." Gio's voice carries down the long hallway as I glimpse him turning into a room.

I stare at the wooden paneling to my left. Door? I groan and start patting the wall, and jump back when a click sound reveals there is a door after all. I shed my coat and hang it in the disguised closet, and not wanting to waste more time, I take off my boots quickly and pad my way to where I think Gio disappeared.

Leaning against a large table in the middle of what seems like a dining room, Gio types on his phone, a deep crease splitting his forehead.

He lifts his gaze. With narrowed eyes, he takes in my bare feet and shakes his head. "I shouldn't have worked from home today."

I chuckle. Why, I don't know. "Why did you?"

"Friday to Sunday I always do. I rarely do internal meetings on those days, but this is important." He walks round the table and sits. "This project has been the bane of my existence."

"Why did you even acquire a retail chain? It doesn't seem your typical portfolio?"

He snaps his eyes to me, and I flinch. "What do you know about my *typical* portfolio?"

"Just what's readily available. I want to know who I work for." I smile at him, but it's like trying to break a diamond. He repels any kind gestures.

He observes me, frowning. "Have you read the briefs from Marnie?"

Let's work, I guess. I let out a long breath and take a seat across from him.

"Yes, I have reviewed all the plans and I emailed the team on the ground with questions. I think for the most part, the events are well covered. I have a few suggestions to improve the flow of people, and I think we should set up a VIP area at the two larger events..." I continue rattling off my suggestions without looking at him.

In my element, the nerves slowly melt away and I relax into the chair. When I finish, with some level of satisfaction, I look at Gio and jump to my feet.

Without realizing, as I spoke, consulting the notes on my phone, I leaned into the chair and brought my knee to my chin. I'm wearing a dress with a flowy skirt, and I'm pretty sure I just flashed my boss.

Seriously, can I ever recover my dignity around this man?

If it wasn't Gio Cassinetti, I would have sworn there was mild amusement tugging at his lips.

"You seem to have things under control." He leans back in his chair. "So, you think the team on the ground is reliable?"

I fidget with my phone, my eyes darting around, the train of thoughts derailed. I'm grateful he's not addressing my comfy posture, but that doesn't mean I forgot about it.

"Sit down and talk." He growls, impatience lacing his tone. "And keep your legs under the table this time."

I collapse into the chair and move it as deep under the table as possible. I find the notes on my phone.

"I can't answer your question. I don't know anyone on the ground. Based on their responses to my inquires, they seem prepared. Whether they're competent or if they're sold on the re-branding is something I can't assess from my position, or in the two days I've been here."

"Yet you seem to have grasped way more than expected in two short days." He leans forward on his elbows.

Sometime during my speech, he rolled up his sleeves. Jesus, now I understand arm porn might not be a myth.

Wait a minute... did he just praise me? I blink a

few times because the combination of his sinewy fore-arms—how do you even exercise those muscles?—and his cold but definite comment bring on yet another wave of fluster.

"Thank you." I smile and he nods. "I spoke with the manager of the San Francisco location, and I got a feeling—just a feeling—the employees might feel this is too much money spent for no apparent reason. I feel the re-branding should start internally, so people understand and buy into the new direction. Culture is a part of branding, and I think the change has happened on the corporate level but hasn't reached the ground."

Jesus, did I just criticize the project and potentially rat out the employees?

"Okay, let's leave on Sunday instead of Monday and schedule internal meetings prior to each event, so we can get them on board, at least somewhat. Let's talk to the team here to prepare a presentation for me, and to brainstorm the benefits of this change for the employees."

He's delivering the task list with the collected precision of a surgeon. His coldness feathers across my skin despite the distance between us. Each word is like an icy shower, so I smile more broadly, seeking any semblance of warmth.

Is he just being efficient? Is he mad at me?

Annoyed by my judgment? He prompted the question. Why do I feel so freaking insecure around him?

"I'm sorry if I overstepped. I've been on this for too short a time to make such an assessment." *You keep saying sorry.* Brian's words echo in my head. A screw-up.

Gio looks up from his tablet and studies me for what feels like a year. I'll drown in that whirlpool of his gaze. I have no chance against this man. He looks like he is sick, or disgusted. I straighten up, internally berating myself for my cowardice.

He shakes his head like a wet dog, discarding something annoying. "Well, you made the assessment anyway." He shrugs and stands up. "Let's take a ten-minute break. I'll call my assistant to coordinate things in the office, and then you can present the media plan." He stands up and leaves.

I'm lingering between elation from a productive meeting and a bitter aftertaste from his attitude. He's efficient, and not shy about giving credit when it's due, but he still is the coldest, most aloof person I've ever met.

I stand up to stretch my legs and walk around the room. I peek through the double door he left open, but I don't hear him. The long hallway stretches in both directions. I guess it's not that long, but being used to shoe box-sized apartments, it looks like a highway.

There are two console tables on each side of the wall, with beautiful, large flower arrangements. Who takes care of them?

This home is warm, unlike its owner. I walk around the room where we've spent the morning. The open space—larger than my apartment—doubles as a dining, living and sitting room, with an impressive library lining the three walls and floor-to-ceiling windows.

I tiptoe—not sure why—to the shelf with photo frames. One is a family picture with many teenagers. Four girls and four boys, one of them Gio, are frowning at the camera.

Annie and I used to hate having our pictures taken at that age. I guess it doesn't matter how much money you have growing up, some life phases are universal.

There is a photo of a couple getting married. The man is incredibly handsome, and based on his features he must be Gio's father. It's his parents' wedding picture.

Two other wedding photos stand beside each other. One is of a beautiful couple. The woman is a famous model, Nora Flemming. It's the next pic that surprises me. It's Massi and Gina's first wedding. They look so young.

I take in the room, needing to confirm where I really am. He keeps these mementoes of happy moments of his family and friends, and it's so at odds with the man that I step back, suddenly feeling like an intruder.

I hurry to the window, because I want to see my first private garden in New York—I didn't believe they existed. Also, staring out of the window feels less intimate.

The landscaping is simple, with an English lawn and trees. They look lonely and bare this time of the year, but I can imagine this yard is an oasis when in full flourish.

Gio walks in, but I don't turn, surprised by the colorful discovery in the far corner of the garden. "You have beehives?"

"You discovered my secret."

I jump, his voice much closer than I realized. He stands behind me to the side, not necessarily in my space, but still too close for comfort. His smoky and spicy masculine scent reaches me, raw and enticing.

I force myself not to move, because I don't want him to know what effect he has on me. I can't even define the effect, but it's a mixture of pleasure and disdain.

"Do you have a beekeeper, a housekeeper, a groundskeeper and other keepers?" I resort to mockery.

"Are you judging my lifestyle?" He steps closer to stand beside me, and this time I step aside. Only slightly, but still. The man draws the worst out of me. And he is my boss currently, so there is that. Screw the goosebumps liberally covering my skin.

"Judge away. You're right, I have all those keepers, a driver, a cook, a trainer, a pilot, a personal stripper."

My eyes widen and I chance a look at him. He's staring at me with hooded eyes. Dark brown and bottomless. Oh, God help me, the dimples make their appearance. It's like his appeal grows with my desperate effort to deny it.

The sight of humor pulling at the corners of his mouth is addictive. I just got a taste, and I really want to experience more of it.

I grin at him. "I can't imagine the reference check for a personal stripper position. What a hardship."

He chuckles and then shakes his head again, as if disturbed by such a display of normalcy. We stare out the window in silence, and an unexpected feeling of companionship descends on me.

We're sharing a moment—I don't even know what the moment is—but there is no tension, no need to deliver, no goals and results, none of his arrogance or my self-doubt. It's just us, taking a break.

"I don't have a beekeeper." The words ring like a secret admission.

I don't turn to look at him or acknowledge I even heard him. *You discovered my secret.* His voice, so sharp usually, softened at its edges, and I wish he would continue.

"It's my hobby." He fidgets, putting his hands into his pockets. It might be a casual stance, but it feels like a fortifying position to hide his unease. Though I don't understand why he would offer the information if it makes him feel vulnerable.

"You're a beekeeper?" I don't want to sound incredulous or mocking, but I fail. Jesus.

He chuckles. It's a low rumble and it hits me like a beautiful melody. Maybe it's because he never does, but every time he chuckles feels like a special reward.

"It's the only way I can dress like an astronaut."

I whip my head around and there they are again. The dimples. The smile reaches his eyes, and the dark abyss shines with mischief. I'm so taken aback by this layer of him that I blink a few times, but my smile stretches farther.

"I'm pretty sure you can get a real astronaut uniform to wear in your spare time." I bite my lip, but this unexpected showcase of personality amuses me too much, and I can't help but grin at him.

"It's called a spacesuit, Mila." He sounds more like the Gio I know, but the spark is still in his eyes.

"I'm sorry. Though I'm pretty sure it's not only about the suit. Is this some sort of stand in eco-activism?"

"God no." He runs his hand through his hair. "I'm too selfish to take a stand on things I can't influence." I want him to smile like this more, but he turns to face the garden again. "The buzz and the gentleness are soothing. The hive is a box of calm in the middle of a busy life. Holding a frame of bees, I have to move slowly, holding something precious in my hands. I have to breathe."

Every word is like a caress, slowly peeling off a layer to uncover a man I've just met. I like the man. Oh, I really do. Jesus, the last thing I need is to develop a real crush. But then he continues, and I have to keep reminding myself this is the man who's usually rude, dates socialites, and disrespects me. A man who called me a hooker.

"I always have to rely on myself." His voice is a pleasant rumble. "So I guess the hierarchy, the hive mentality speaks to me. I can be at peace with nature in the middle of the city. I learn from them. A queen is the leader, but she knows her role without interfering. I try to lead the same way."

He operates under immense pressure. A fast-paced, results-driven environment is where he thrives, but it must be so lonely. Most people fear him, or judge him, or expect something from him. No wonder he shows the world a mask of coldness.

It's a necessity for him. Distance. Yes, he's short

with people, rude even, but I wonder how much of it is a personality and how much is a survival mechanism that has grown over time into his second nature.

I turn my head to watch him. The perfect profile, with his square jaw and chiseled cheekbones, and just the beginning of a five o'clock shadow on his flawless, tanned skin. I see it all in a slightly different light. A ghost of inner beauty I would never guess he possessed.

"And I'm severely allergic to beestings."

Wait. What? "A dangerous hobby then."

"The other option would be to give in to fear and miss out on something great. Let's talk media."

He snaps me out of my reverence so quickly, I almost trip rushing to the table again.

Gio sits to the side of me this time, leaning back in the chair, looking almost relaxed. I don't really have a reason to look at him differently, but I do. The rolled-up sleeves, one ankle over his knee, casual gaze.

A glimpse of the considered man I got at the gala, with this job, today watching the currently empty hives, forces me to reevaluate my attitude. Perhaps I can give him a chance.

So he seems superficial in his personal life with all the models and the phone practically attached to his hand. Who am I to judge on the latter, after all? But I have to acknowledge that he built a great company and doesn't impose his ideas on people, judging by today's meeting.

We talk about the media plan. He asks only a few questions, mostly about his role, and I get the feeling this is his least favorite part of the job. He likes to be behind the scenes. If he spoke to people with the passion he just showed me when talking about bees, the media would love him.

We conclude the meeting and I stand up, for some reason expecting there to be more casual chat, but Gio immediately focuses on his tablet.

"I'll have Lydia text you the flight details. You can see yourself out."

Dismissed. I guess the rare glimpse of humanity was just a fluke.

"Sorry, if you don't mind, I need to use the bathroom." I shove my notebook into my bag.

He looks up from his screen with an expression of annoyance. "It's to the left at the end of the hall. Good job today." He dips his head back to continue his work.

Truly dismissed. The interesting man from earlier is gone. Really a fluke.

I take my things and hurry to use the bathroom. I have to spend a week with him, and then hopefully someone else takes over and I can go back to avoiding him.

Though a week together, working, might be a very

difficult endeavor. With the arms that distract me. The scent that robs me of rational thought. The deep brown eyes that fluster me.

All of it was easy to ignore—okay, feasible, not easy—before that glimpse of an interesting man flashed in front of me. Before he remembered to shut it away.

Hopefully, he'll be rude enough to keep this relationship professional. Well, that's an oxymoron if I heard one.

As I walk from the bathroom, taking a peek at an impressive kitchen, I wish I had asked him for a tour. The idea of his probable response, with that tensed jaw and expression of a suffering animal, brings giggles to my lips.

"Thank you, Lydia, and please have someone pick up Ms. Ward on Sunday." Gio speaks on his phone with his assistant. He's looking at the garden, his back to me.

The broad expanse of his shoulders, stretching out his shirt, begs to be touched. Okay, in my mind. I wonder if he makes love with the same intensity as he works. With that frown on his face.

Jesus, Mila. I roll my eyes at myself, and then I regret stopping to listen. Well, technically I stopped to admire, but I do hear his next words, and any idea of a man I painted in my mind is wiped away.

"Oh, Lydia, please set up a date for me upon my

return, or even this Saturday." A casual request, as if he was reserving a table at a restaurant. He has his assistant schedule his dates?

"Oh, not with her." I don't know who Lydia suggested, but Gio shudders at the mention. What the hell?

He nods a few times, listening. "Sure, let's see if she is available."

He turns and I scurry away, grabbing my things in the weird closet and running out the door.

He saw me. He caught me eavesdropping. But what I overheard is way more... pathetic? Weird? Sad?

Chapter 6

Mila

"Are you sure you'll be okay?" I wrap my arms around Annie for the tenth time.

"Stop it. Of course we'll be fine. You spent all Saturday cooking for us. We'll have meals for weeks, not a few days." She rolls her eyes. "Besides, thanks to you I've had uninterrupted treatment, so I'll be fine."

I don't tell her I put the medicine on my maxed-out credit card. She doesn't need to worry about that. I'll get my paycheck for the gala and the Wings project soon. If she gets the drugs regularly, her symptoms might improve enough for her to even pick up few more shifts at work.

I kiss Ellery and squat in front of Aidan. "I'll be back on Saturday morning. You're the man of the house now. Help your mom, okay?" I ruffle his hair, and he snakes his arms around me.

Leaving them for a week is harder than I thought, but we need the money, so I have to hope Annie won't have a flare-up and Aidan won't have an episode.

As the car pulls onto the vast empty tarmac, nerves and excitement dance around my stomach. I haven't been to California since I broke up with Brian. I've certainly never been in California on a private jet.

I'm excited about the events, and I have some cool media opportunities lined up. I wish the trip didn't involve Gio Cassinetti, who seems to occupy too many of my thoughts and fantasies lately.

Thoughts about his dates, his emotionless detachment, his rudeness. All in such sharp contrast to the family wedding photos, protein bar rescue missions, beekeeping, or his ease in commanding the conversation when it comes to work, but completely failing to maintain it outside of the business scope.

Oh, and then the fantasies keep popping up. His long, calloused fingers playing with his cufflinks. The timbre of his voice when he's relaxed. The muscles bulging under his shirt. His dimples, and the small lines around his eyes when an occasional smile reaches them.

Everything about this slight obsession is inappropriate, and useless. It's not like he sees me in any other way than a charity case. Yes, I might help him at work, but I wasn't his first choice.

I wouldn't be his choice for anything. I'm not his type. His assistant would never call me to arrange a date. Jesus. He thinks of me as a hooker, anyway.

Not that his cast of dates looks like nuns. I'm not a prude. I've been enjoying casual hookups since Brian, mostly to soak up the freedom I didn't have for so long. But I'm not a slut.

The driver opens the door and I step outside. An airport attendant appears from somewhere and helps me with my suitcase.

I'm wearing high stilettos and they echo on the pavement as I approach the plane. The frosty wind bites deep through my light jacket, since I'm dressed for the mild weather on the other side of the country.

Despite the chill, the sky is blue, and the mid-morning sun reflects off the plane's sleek silver exterior.

I want to savor every moment of this luxury, but the lack of a coat forces me to rush up the stairs. By the time I reach the smiling flight attendant—blond, tall, fake lips and boobs, just like Gio likes them—my cheeks are burning from frost.

"Welcome on board, Ms. Ward," the blonde greets me, and gestures to the cabin.

My heeled feet wobble on the soft carpet and I

stop, unsure what to do or where to go. Gio is working, frowning at his laptop. Am I late?

He lifts his eyes and stares for a moment before his gaze travels down, slowly taking me in from head to toe. I swallow, uncomfortable under his scrutiny, but when his eyes meet mine, heat spreads like wildfire hitting my core.

The hunger in his eyes is undeniable. Raw. Terrifying. Wonderful.

I packed my best wardrobe for this trip. As Gina always says, dress for success. My deep green dress perfectly combines casual and dressy, hugging my curves in all the right places, while covering my cleavage and falling below my knees.

The flight attendant speaks to someone behind me, a coffee machine hums, and my heartbeat echoes in my temples. The moment stretches, but I'm unable to look away.

This is inappropriate on so many levels, but Jesus, is there a bedroom here?

As if my thought traveled through the space between us, Gio breaks the eye contact and glances to his right, toward a door at the rear of the plane.

Something dark flickers in his eyes and then he adjusts his cufflinks, looks at the computer and growls, "You're here, finally. We can leave now."

The last few weeks have just culminated in a

discovery—whiplash is Gio's superpower. Well, mine is a smile.

"Good morning, Gio." I add a note of enthusiasm that makes me sound comical, but I'm done with his growling and glaring.

He sighs. "Sit, for fuck's sake, the pilot is waiting."

I open my mouth to tell him off, but said pilot's voice floats through the speakers to emphasize his point. In a much nicer manner.

"Of course," I chirp, and plop down across from my grumpy boss.

"Buckle up." Well, the velvet of his voice is definitely only a part of my fantasies. He doesn't even look at me. Asshole.

I fasten the seatbelt, the attendant offers me a beverage, and we take off. Gio continues working, as if I don't exist, so I indulge in my surroundings.

This plane is amazing. I could get used to comfort like this. Aidan would love it onboard, probably begging me to get into the cockpit.

Though if I had a plane with polished brown paneling and soft leather seats at my disposal, I'd probably sell it to get Annie's meds. It might last her whole lifetime. Clearly, I'm not a very good businessperson. That's why I don't have a plane like this. I chuckle inwardly.

I feel his glare immediately. I guess the chuckle wasn't completely inward.

"Do you always work on Sundays?" I scoop my feet up under my butt, carefully covering my knees with the dress.

"Do you always sit like a child?" He runs his eyes down my chest to my legs, but catches himself and returns to the screen.

"Do you always answer with a question?" Two can play this game, though comparing me to a child rings truer after my retort.

He sighs again, and I swear it sounds like he was just delivered a death sentence, but he closes his tablet and leans back. His expression would fool anyone into believing I'm subjecting him to waterboarding levels of torture.

"What else would I do?" He adjusts his cuffs.

"What?" I cross my arms over my chest.

"If you force me into a conversation, keep up, Mila. What else should I do on a plane?"

Oh, he's decided to answer my original question. With a question, of course. "I don't know. We can talk." I don't particularly want to suffer through a conversation with him, but I'm having fun taunting him.

"I thought you prefer to eavesdrop." He licks his bottom lip, amusement and challenge on his face.

Damn it, of course he saw me in his doorway on Friday. "I happened to pass by. If you don't want your personal conversations overheard, wait for your guests to leave." I smirk. "How was your date?"

He drags his tongue over his upper teeth, and I still. I can pretend all I want, but I'd like to taste those lips. *Jesus, Mila, stop it.*

"That's none of your business," he deadpans. "But it didn't happen after all." He glances at his tablet. Missing work?

"Sorry to hear that, perhaps it was short notice. Or maybe she would have preferred you called her yourself." I shrug innocently.

"She knows how the arrangement works." He straightens up and opens his tablet, frowning. He said too much, and now he is escaping the conversation.

Maybe I overstepped by asking, so there is that. Arrangement? I wish his comment wouldn't spark my curiosity.

"I don't know what the arrangement is, but I'm sure a woman would appreciate a man calling her instead of his assistant. Like normal people do." Why am I pushing this?

"Well, not everyone has the freedom to do things like *normal* people, Mila."

He starts typing, and I'm left with the regret for pursuing this, for challenging. Freedom? Is his status and his money really in the way of having a normal life? Is that how he perceives it? What a sad, lonely existence.

I'm bored so I continue asking him questions, but after all the one syllable answers or grunts, I just freestyle and talk to him about anything and everything.

"Do you always talk so much?" He sighs.

I snort. Is he seriously offended by a friendly chat? That's what people do on a plane. "No, sometimes I sleep."

He types for a moment. "Feel free to use the bedroom in the back."

"So there is a bedroom." My excitement is inappropriate for a business trip, but come on. I'm on a private plane.

He glares at me, probably thinking about throwing me out, and then he returns his attention to his screen.

I scroll on my phone for a moment. "Would you give me a parachute?"

He jerks his head up. "What?"

"If you were to throw me off this plane, would you give me a parachute or just chuck me out?"

He shakes his head slightly and returns to his work. I do the same. Okay, I get to googling images of bedrooms on a private jet.

"When," Gio says, without raising his head.

I look up, frowning. Is he talking to me?

He lifts his gaze. "When I throw you off this plane, not if," he deadpans.

Did he just make a joke? Jesus. With this man, who knows? I smile, and I might imagine it, but I think the corner of his mouth quirks up.

Everything goes wrong at the employee meeting. Gio is as dry and distant as the Wings employees believed. They challenge him on everything, but mostly on corporate greed when in the name of reinventing the brand, his company spent money on new logos instead of on employees who deliver the customer experience.

He answers with sound rationale, without emotions. Like he doesn't care, though I know he does.

Tully, the manager of the store, is challenging him all the way, but in the end they remain at an impasse. The employees crave attention, some concession, but are unable to win the argument because Gio's claims are bulletproof.

I watch him in action and feel a mixture of pride and sympathy for him. He's winning on the issue, but losing the people. He was right to assign this to Marnie, and I can't help but admire him for stepping in, despite the obvious discomfort he feels.

"You really don't get it in your ivory tower," Tully accuses.

Gio adjusts his cuffs, and his jaw could probably cut through diamonds. I can't stand it anymore.

"You're right, Tully, we should have involved you earlier, taken your input into consideration." I step closer and put my hand on her shoulder. "You and your colleagues have been working for this wonderful company way longer than most of the people who spearheaded the change under the new management. Wings take care of their customers in a very personal way, unlike any other chain, and that's all on your shoulders. You're on the ground, and your input would have been invaluable."

Tully's eyes dart between me and Gio, frowning and assessing my motivation. I glance at Gio and he steps closer, looking into the manager's eyes.

"Mila is right, mistakes were made. I will take all your concerns over to Marnie and her team, and I'll oversee the next steps in the company's transition to ensure we involve you."

I step to the side, beaming. He got it. His shoulders are still stiff, and his facial muscles are arranged in that typical half-annoyed, half-uninterested expression, but he took my lead and rolled with it.

Tully looks at her coworkers, and then, with a sigh,

she extends her hand to Gio. "Okay. Let's roll it out tomorrow with a bang."

Gio nods, and an awkward silence descends on the room. He should conclude the meeting with something inspiring, but as if in slow motion, I see him turning away and reaching for the phone in his pocket. Jesus. Fucking. Christ.

"Let's move on to the informal part of the meeting," I practically squeal. All eyes turn to me, most with expectation, some with wariness, and one pair with exasperation. The deep brown abyss.

"The company is inviting everyone for drinks across the street." I noticed a bar when we came in, and now I'm begging the universe they have a table available.

A wave of excitement sweeps the room, and Gio shakes his head. "Yes, drinks are on me."

"You did well there." The relaxed velvet of his voice has returned. He leans closer, so I can hear him.

The bar teems with people, but we snatched a table in the corner and I'm getting the third round of drinks for the group. They've been more amiable since the first round of beers. And even Gio loosened up a bit.

I didn't know he followed me to the counter, but suddenly there is too much of him in the room. Crowding out my rational thinking, stealing my breath, robbing me of my composure, negating my dislike of him. His strong masculine scent infiltrates every fiber of my body. Smoky and spicy.

His arm brushes against my skin, and in that moment I wish we were alone. I have no shame.

I can't blame the reaction on his closeness, his all-consuming presence. *You did well.* His words shine a beacon of joy through my chest.

I'm so starved for recognition that the simple comment breaks me apart and fixes me again like a magic wand. I can roll my eyes at my neediness, but praise from Giovanni Cassinetti comes only when deserved.

"Thank you," I croak, and chance a glimpse at him.

The dimples. My core sighs, and luckily the waiter pushes the tray to me and returns me to reality.

"Let me help you, Princess." Gio picks up the tray and saunters away.

Princess? And why am I only now noticing how sexy his ass is? The man looks too good for his own good. What was in that beer?

"A good call on those drinks last night. I think we placated them enough so today should go smoothly." He swipes on his screen with one finger, a spoon in the other.

"Good morning, boss." I plop on the chair across from him, last night's mood forgotten.

He lifts his gaze. "Good morning. Could we have informal meetings like that at every location? I've already sent Marnie a list of their suggestions. The reasonable ones."

He returns to his typing and eating.

"Do you ever stop working?" I ask and pour myself a cup of coffee.

"No."

Not a morning person, I guess. Hell, Gio is not a person person, period.

"We'll be in Santa Barbara late tonight," I say, "but we can host a breakfast for them. The same in Sacramento. In San Francisco we can have drinks after the event."

"Isn't that too late, post the event?" No eye contact.

"Not if we invite them now. Besides, I'm pretty sure the other managers talked to Tully, so you need to do something. We can have breakfast there too, but I think it would be nice to wrap up the tour with a post-event party."

"Right. Can you take care of it?" He continues typing.

I sip my coffee and pull out my phone, searching for the best locations for these events and drafting the invitation.

Ten minutes later, Gio looks up, frowning. "You've done it all?" He looks at his screen and back at me, apparently reading the list of venues for our informal get-together and a draft invitation from him for the employees.

"Apparently working through breakfast is a company culture." I shrug, smiling over the rim of my coffee.

"Good. Eat something. I don't need you to faint on me today." He goes back to his emails, but I'd swear a smile ghosts his lips.

For whatever reason, I feel like I won a round. Though I'm not sure what the game is, and if we're even playing one.

If Gio's conversation with the staff last night was painful at first, it has nothing on his condescending brush-offs with the media. I've been operating in full-blown crisis mode by the time the third blogger attempts to take a selfie with him.

I'm half-sure these women who feature fashion and lifestyle on their accounts are hoping for a personal collection to drool over, and I'm a hundred percent sure that's what he believes, but he has to pretend and play the game or we won't get the exposure we're hoping for.

"You can't do this," I hiss, pulling him to the side.

"I can do whatever I want." He frowns, jerking his arm from my grasp.

"Okay, let me explain this to you in terms you can understand. The objective today is to successfully unveil new branding. These people came here to evaluate the change and hopefully transmit the success of it to the universe. It's your job to guarantee the results."

"No such results can be guaranteed." He rolls his lips, unimpressed, and adjusts his cuffs.

"Really? You're going to argue terminology? You know very well what I mean. Would it kill you to smile or take a selfie, or talk about the brand with a bit of enthusiasm? Fake it, but get it done." I beam at him, because we're in a public space among our guests, but my eyes are shooting daggers.

He drags his tongue over his teeth again. God, I wish he wasn't doing that. It's worse than his dimples. It's languid and predatory. Like I'm his dinner, but he's not sure how to eat me. Jesus.

"Okay." He nods.

I open my mouth to argue my next point when his acquiescence registers. "Oh, okay then." I turn to storm away, but he grabs my arm.

Hot coal. Scorching electricity. Direct line to my core.

I face him, moving slowly, afraid to get closer. I stare at his hand on my arm, and he follows my gaze.

"No more than three minutes with each of them." He drops my arm, and while the connection was light, I stumble at the loss of it.

"Good." I toss my hair and march away from him. I'm pretty sure the sweat down my spine is a direct result of his burning glare.

I approach a makeup station where some influencers have gathered.

"Don't you love these intense, brooding types? God, I wish I lived in New York. I'd be the one to finally claim him," Audrey @audrey_the_lifestyle_goddess tells her friend, eyeing Gio in the mirror.

"You wish. Claudia has been trying for a year now and can't lock him in. She's so tight-lipped about the whole thing. If it wasn't for her public profile, I wouldn't believe they've been dating."

"She's too desperate. I know how to handle men like Giovanni. Imagine the lifestyle that comes with that package." She purses her lips to apply a coat of lipstick and saunters toward him, adjusting her top to show more cleavage.

Gio is typing on his phone, leaning against the counter. The suit, the confidence, the power, the money—all wrapped up in a fuckable package. Or so Audrey hopes, I'm sure.

She rakes her long nails down his arm as she speaks, and he looks up. I'm about to rush over to make sure he doesn't send her to hell, but he actually smiles, and before I blink, she's pulling out her phone and pursing her lips, raising her chin and leaning her head toward him.

A wave of something bitter swoops over me when he smiles for the photo, the sex god personified. I asked him to be more personable, but Jesus.

They talk, while Audrey continues to touch him here and there, and I have enough. Three minutes my ass.

"She has no shame. It's embarrassing," Audrey's friend mutters behind me.

"I think it's your turn." I wink at her. She has more followers, after all. This is all professional.

"Audrey, let me show you the Italian collection." I smile at the eager woman beside Gio. "We have a piece from everything, and you can't get it anywhere else, not even in our other locations. We work hard to offer a collection that is truly exclusive. Let me introduce you to our store manager."

She pouts, but her friend seizes the opportunity and introduces herself. I continue working the room, making sure everyone gets a piece of the big boss, and after three hours I'm ready to take off the stupid heels and wrap everything up.

"I didn't expect we'd make any sales today, but these girls didn't take just the swag." Tully approaches me. "It's good when my crew can make a commission. I still don't understand why money was spent on a new logo, but I got a flavor of what we're trying to achieve, and there are some good pieces involved."

"You and your crew are natural, none of the guests today felt they were sold to. They were simply offered a glimpse of a lifestyle and they wanted it."

"You brought the right crowd in."

I grin. God, I'm a glutton for praise. "Tully, that's my job. I can't take credit for much more though, I've been with the company for a week."

"Really? But you two"—she beckons her head toward Gio, who is talking to Audrey again—"work so well together. There is a natural rhythm, you complement each other, and he clearly respects you."

I almost spit out the water I've just raised to my lips. "I don't know about respect, but Gio is fair and results-driven. When you deliver, he lets you breathe."

"He's cold, and definitely not a people person. But

he's smart, and I'm pretty sure he values you. And perhaps fancies you as well."

My eyes widen. "Tully."

"My lips are sealed. But if you ever need to report him to human resources, I'll provide testimony."

"Oh, I ensure you there is nothing to report." Oh my God, I need to keep my distance, because people see things that don't exist.

"Okay." She cackles and leaves to join her coworkers.

I pack up my things and decide I'll just go to the hotel and wait there for Gio. We don't need to do everything together. Especially not after Tully's words.

"We can have a quick dinner tonight before you leave." Audrey's husky suggestion carries to my ears, and I roll my eyes. I guess he doesn't need me to wait for him, anyway.

I rush to the exit, escaping his response, but his voice stops me in my tracks.

"Mila!"

I face him, heat spreading from my cheeks to my ears. He grabs his things and storms in my direction. Moving to avoid him, I stagger outside and almost collide with a pedestrian. Gio yanks me away from the man, but that causes me to crash against him.

Solid muscles. Intoxicating scent. Deep brown eyes. And flared nostrils.

"Where do you think you're going?"

"I-I..." Why is he upset with me? I fucking clear the decks for his date, and he's pissed I didn't ask for permission to leave? "I was going to wait for you at the hotel."

"Why?"

"You were making arrangements for a date." Jesus, that's what I lead with?

"No, I wasn't," he grinds through his teeth.

He's still holding me, protecting me, though it's not necessary. I wish he wasn't so close. His breath mixes with mine, and it's so hard to think with him taking over all the space. All the air. All my mind.

"You're right, Lydia does that for you." I've never been a spiteful person, but here I am. Gio Cassinetti turns me into this woman I don't even recognize.

"Do you have an opinion about my lifestyle?" he spits.

"I do, actually, but I also have self-preservations skills, so I'm going to keep it to myself."

A sly grin makes me swallow hard. "Are you jealous, Princess? Would you like to get on Lydia's list?"

The air escapes me in a stunned huff. Is he for real? Never. Not in a million years. He might think I'm slutty, but there is no way I'd ever consider getting on rotation.

So why am I not saying anything?

Princess. Does he want me to become more? Is that why he asked? That's not flattering at all. Or respectful. Why is my brain non-existent right now? *Stop this, Mila.*

"Let me go. People are already talking."

He drops his hands, as if I've burned him. The loss of his touch sends shivers down my spine. If looks could kill, I would probably be seriously wounded. If not dead.

"Tully suggested—"

"Get in the car, Mila," he growls. "Now!"

Chapter 7

Mila

We don't speak on the way to the hotel. For some strange reason, I feel like I've done something wrong. Jesus. The uneasiness this man's behavior injects into my veins will give me an ulcer.

"Let's get dinner." The clipped tone leaves no room for argument as he turns toward the restaurant in the lobby of our hotel.

I sigh and follow. Because I'm hungry, I tell myself.

We get a table and order. Gio pulls out his tablet and starts working. Willing him to look up and talk to me, I glare, but the man is immune to my attempts at engaging him. With a sigh, I pull out my tablet and phone to monitor the media coverage we receive.

Our meals arrive and we both eat in silence, working. It's not the way I'd like to spend my evening, but there is a benefit to getting all this work done.

"People talk, Mila. Gossip, scandal, sensation help many to take their attention from their own problems, or deal with their own insecurities. I apologize if the boundary may have blurred between us. I've known you since before you started working here, so I guess I might have acted more familiar than our current relationship warrants. Have I made you feel unsafe or uncomfortable?"

His words drop between us like a boulder, crushing me under the weight of his genuine worry. Jesus. Is this what has been bothering him? That I would report him?

I mentioned Tully's remark to save myself from him, not because I feared he'd abuse his power or coerce me into something I don't want to do. I used that as protection, because there is so much I want to do. With him. To him. Under him.

His eyes are intent on mine. Dark brown pools of concern, and something sour, disappointment perhaps.

"No." One simple word, just a whisper, hangs between us. He assesses me with a skeptical look, and I search for something to say, to explain. To reassure him.

He's stepped into my personal space with the predator look at least twice since I started working for the company, but neither time did I feel he was doing it because he was my boss.

"We will finish the next three events and then the project will be taken over by Portia Krane. She'll be coming here with you for the other events before Christmas." He returns his attention to his tablet.

It pisses me off. As he said, people like to gossip, and I hate how that has changed everything between us. He wasn't overly open with me or warm, but we've established a decent rapport, and now it's gone.

Perhaps for the better. We are only coworkers. He's my boss. Let's work then.

"We're trending really well on Instagram, and I expect several blog posts by prominent lifestyle influencers. I've just emailed you the highlights of the coverage. I think the messages are coming through nicely." I push away my plate and continue typing away, making notes for a report for Marnie and Portia.

My skin crawls with recognition. I don't have to look up to feel the intense gaze. To know Gio's attention has shifted from the laptop to me.

"What?" My eyes remain on the screen.

"You've been working this whole time?"

Now I look at him and he's staring at me with his typical impatience, but there is something else ghosting his face as well. Respect? Awe? Surprise?

"Did you think I was just mindlessly browsing

while you chose to work during dinner?" He flinches at *chose*.

"I like efficiency, and eating seems like empty time." He flinches again, responding to my gasp. "And I didn't want you to feel obliged to have a conversation with me."

"Yet you practically ordered me to have dinner with you." I cock my head. Gio adjusts his cufflinks. I've learned already it's his tell. He wants this conversation to finish.

"It's dinnertime, and you worked all day without as much as a snack." He closes his laptop.

And there it is again, that flash of care he casts but pretends to have only logical grounds for. It warms me inside, and I give him a break.

"Gio, have you met me? When have I ever felt obliged to converse? Half the time I'm driving you crazy with my questions and opinions."

"Just with your abiding need to express them." His lips quirk.

"Oh, I see, so you don't mind my opinions, you just mind that I'm offering them."

"Too liberally." He leans back in his chair, and I'm unreasonably pleased to get relaxed Gio back for a moment.

"I'll ask for permission next time I feel the annoying need to talk."

A grin springs across his face. "Don't. You've been very helpful with... peopling. I appreciate it. You've done a great job so far."

Oh, those dimples. And those words. Warmth spreads through my bones, and my smile eases wider. "Thank you, Gio. I really appreciate it."

He pushes his chair back and crosses one leg over the other. "I'll be recommending to Marnie, or her successor, that we offer you a permanent position. Would you want to work internally on our social media team?"

"No." Shit. "I mean yes. I..." Jesus, of course, I need the job, but I've never seen myself in a large corporation.

"Be honest with me, Mila. I don't want to pry, but I got the impression freelancing wasn't really meeting your needs. But I understand some people don't want a regular paycheck."

"I appreciate your interest, and I'd love to work full time in your company. I need the job and I'd enjoy it, but to be honest I've always seen myself having my own agency. Event planning and social media management."

"You'd be very good at that. Why is it still a dream?"

God, how much can I safely share with him? Most of it is purely humiliating. I don't want him to know all the gory details of my circumstances. Not right after he showed me professional respect.

"It's just a series of unfortunate circumstances that derailed me." Now I sound like I can't take responsibility and blame others. "I need a regular paycheck to get back on my feet, and then I'd pursue my agency."

I avert my eyes, because his gaze is too much. His genuine interest is too much. I don't deserve it. I'll fuck it up. I'll disappoint him. I shouldn't care, but I do.

"Even setbacks teach us a lot." He leans forward. For a man who struggles with peopling, he is suddenly all approachable. Understanding. Jesus.

Emotions tickle the back of my eyes. Brian never saw failure as a learning opportunity.

"I understand you don't think I'm a suitable candidate, knowing I don't plan to stick around for too long, but I'd still appreciate the opportunity." *And need it desperately.*

"Of course. You've been with us for a week and your contribution is undeniable. I don't expect people to sign away their lives to us."

If he doesn't stop right now, I'll start crying. "So you didn't want to have dinner with Audrey?"

He jerks his head at the change of subject. "You could step up your segue game." He shakes his head, but one of his rare grins lights up his face. "I don't think there is a respectful way to describe her... lack of boundaries."

"Look at you, that's quite diplomatic, though you could have fooled me. It looked like you were enjoying the conversation." Wanting to change the topic away from me, I've stumbled into equally precarious territory. Why can't I keep this professional, and on the project itself?

"Things are rarely what they look like." Gio motions for the check.

His words ring with a raw finality. With experience. *Not everyone has the freedom to do things like normal people.* Somehow, these two statements are related. Or I'm just reading into things without the right context.

"Is that your personal experience?" Of course I won't shut up.

"Mostly."

The waiter interrupts my inquiry. Probably for the best.

Gio signs the bill and we make our way to the elevators. We ride up alone in the small car. It didn't feel this small when I checked in. Gio fills the space with his impressive stature, but it's the energy thick with electricity and unsaid words pushing me into the corner.

I fix my eyes on the numbers above the door, but all

I can focus on is him. His masculine scent in my nostrils. His confident breathing in my peripheral vision. His solid arm brushing against my sleeve.

"This was nice," he says.

"Yes, thank you for the dinner, and for your compliments." I smile, but my stomach is clamped with... what is it? Desire? Hope? A bit of discomfort? Delicious discomfort.

"Mila, it wasn't a compliment. It was an earned assessment of your work. And make no mistake, the dinner was a company expense on a business trip. A working dinner." His voice is clipped now.

He started by saying *it was nice.*

Chapter 8

Mila

"**G**ood job, Mila. Yesterday's coverage is not exactly viral, but the volume is impressive. If we continue like this at the other locations, the brand is going to get the boost we planned for." Marnie pushes herself higher in her bed. "I'm going to sign out now, but discuss the details further with Portia."

She ends the call and Portia's face stretches across the screen. "Okay, so externally we are meeting the expectations. How are the employees?"

I lean back in my chair, fidgeting with the sash of my robe. It's only six o'clock and I didn't have time to dress before an impromptu catch-up with my managers.

"Honestly, I think it helped that we invited them for drinks. I don't think they don't buy into the new concept—it's more they feel they were completely absent from the process. And with the new management, they are more focused on potentially being replaced. At the end they were incredibly professional, and found the day itself beneficial."

"A good call on the drinks and other internal meetings. We missed the mark on that one. Sometimes we look at these acquisitions as numbers on a spreadsheet and forget there are those who actually forge the success on the ground. How is Mr. Cassinetti handling it all?"

Mr. Cassinetti? This is not the first time I've heard people addressing him this way, even when he's not present. I knew him as Gio before, so it has never occurred to me to call him differently.

Maybe I should. If nothing else, it would put the rumors to rest. Not that there are any. I'm sure Tully voiced her concern only to me. I hope.

"He's not the warmest person—"

Portia bursts into laughter. "No argument there. I know your focus is media, Mila, but I need you to humanize him as well. With all the shit thrown his way, he has removed himself from personnel interactions, but with Marnie on bed rest and me tied up here... Well, I know he is rusty in that department."

"I thought he just doesn't enjoy peopling." I shrug.

"There is that, but after the lawsuits he's just not

interested in dealing with employees. He's more the numbers guy, and lets others manage people."

"Lawsuits?" I straighten up, a bit too eager probably.

"I'm not the one to gossip. Anyway, please make sure he turns on some charm. Or leadership, I should say." She shakes her head, as if annoyed by herself.

"Okay. I have to get ready—we're flying out soon. I'll send you a quick update after breakfast, before the event starts."

"Great. Good luck today."

I dress quickly and apply a little makeup before tossing my hair into a messy bun. Throwing my things haphazardly into the suitcase, I end up with ten minutes to spare. Internet search it is.

What skeletons do you have in your closet, Giovanni Cassinetti? I roll my eyes at the social media posts, and gossip site photos of him with a socialite, model or influencer on his arms.

Even Audrey posted yesterday's catch. Argh. Oh, and Claudia, his latest fling, responded. Cat fight!

Finally, I scroll deep enough, and bingo! Three years ago, several women came forward claiming sexual harassment. There isn't much coverage for such juicy news. Someone did a good job cleaning up the mess.

All I find out is that no evidence was found, and

Gio settled out of court with all these women. He paid them off? Is this where Tully is coming from? Portia didn't seem concerned at all.

He has his dates set up by Lydia. He is rude more than anything else. I run my fingers over the keyboard.

I just found out about Gio's sexual harassment cases. Do you know anything about it? Xoxo Mils.

I pace for a moment, but Gina must be busy. As I push my carry-on through the door, my phone rings.

"Well, stranger, you don't as much as call me about your fabulous job, and now this text?" Gina says.

"I'm sorry. I was a bit upset you got me the job. It made me feel—"

"Don't go there, Mils. You wouldn't have the opportunity if you didn't deserve it."

I sigh. "Thank you. For the job as well." I hit the elevator call button with my elbow.

"I asked Massi and he says it was all a scheme to get money out of him, but he didn't give me more details. Is everything okay?"

The door opens and I barely squeeze in. Where are all these people going this early? "Yes, yes. It just surprised me, that's all. Listen, I have to go, but I'll call you later."

As I step into the lobby, my eyes meet with Gio's, the impatient tick in his jaw prominent.

"You're late," he growls, and turns to leave.

Good morning to you too.

✳ ✳ ✳

The employees in Santa Barbara are somewhat more welcoming than expected, and the breakfast goes off without a hitch. Gio is stiff and aloof, but he answers all questions, awarding people with the respect they deserve.

Well, everyone besides me. I deserve only growls and glowers today. Seriously, the man is exhausting.

I can't help but connect the dots I might be just imagining.

Not everyone has the freedom to do things like normal people. Things are rarely what they look like.

Should those two statements stem from the false harassment accusations, it would explain a lot about his behavior. It wouldn't excuse it, but I can't help the wave of compassion I feel.

I can't imagine anyone misinterpreting his behavior as anything but crass. But after having a few glimpses of the caring, interesting beekeeper, I'm starting to believe this is a mask.

Intensified by his severely impaired—or completely

lacking—communication skills, but still a protective mask.

It must be so lonely to know that any relationship, professional or personal, might not be motivated by who you truly are, but by what you represent. How much people benefit from knowing you. Just like those socialites. People like Audrey.

"We have four hours before the event. We can work from the hotel's business center or our rooms. I'm sure an early check-in can be arranged." Gio closes the pouch of his tablet.

"I think we should go for a stroll on Stearns Wharf." How much more normal can a visit to Santa Barbara get? We're not tourists, but still.

He couldn't look more shocked if I had puked on him. "Come again?"

Oxygen barely reaches my lungs as my heart hammers against my ribcage, but I can't back up now. "We've been working nonstop since Sunday, I think we need to clear our heads, so we can continue functioning at top level."

His eyes tighten at the corners, and I expect him to fire me or to leave me there. Call me on my bullshit. He drags his tongue over his top teeth, and I suck in my breath. Not that again.

"Okay."

Jesus. Wait. What? "Okay?"

"That's what I said," he enunciates, annoyance lacing his voice.

"That's what you said."

"Are you just going to repeat everything I say?" He crosses his arms over his chest.

"No, I'm going to get the driver to take our things to the hotel and call us an Uber." I grab my phone before he can change his mind.

* * *

"Seriously? In years?" I dig into my triple scoop chocolate mint ice cream. "How is that even possible?"

He shrugs. "It's not like I didn't have any ice cream. There is always a sorbet served at functions." He scoops up a tiny amount of his mango ice cream and leans forward slightly before he puts it into his mouth.

I haven't stopped grinning since we arrived at the shore. Gio has been teetering between being perplexed and enjoying himself. This not yet relaxed, but definitely less guarded side of him is appealing.

We have strolled up and down the wharf and we're heading toward the park now. I'm balancing my shoes and the ice cream in one hand, regretting that I went for a cup instead of the cone. The feel of sand under my feet compensates for that well.

Gio walks beside me on the boardwalk, having categorically refused to take his shoes off.

I lift my face to the sky, feeling the gentle waves of heat on my cheeks. Stifling a contented sigh every time my soles dig into the soft sand, I inhale the ocean air. The breeze ruffles my hair, carrying with it the scent of palm trees and salt water. And a bit of traffic, but still so much better than the current frigid conditions of New York.

"Why do you call me a princess sometimes?" Shit. Why did I go there? Now, when I know about the lawsuits, I feel like any conversation is a potential minefield.

He chuckles. "When I saw you the first time at Massi's restaurant during the shit event nobody showed up for, I was impressed by the poise and peace you carried yourself with, despite the crisis. You paced making calls, but you smiled at the staff, talked Massi down at one point, breezed through it all. You carried yourself like a queen."

A queen is the leader, but she knows her role without interfering. His words when I was at his house flicker through my mind. I can't believe he remembers that much about the first time we met.

I certainly didn't feel composed. Two weeks of prep for nothing, let alone the drama between Gina and Massi. I remember the stress. And my less than favorable impression of Gio with a long-legged blonde and his phone stealing all his attention. I guess I was wrong.

"Then later I heard you blabbering and giggling at some other time," he continues, smirking, "and I—"

"Not quite a queen." I shake my head and grin, I don't even know why. He shrugs, with a silent apology on his face, and I decide I like being a princess. To him at least.

We continue to the end of the beach, focusing on our ice cream. Thousands of thoughts pass through my mind, and at the same time a peace descends on me. It might be the familiar sunny neighborhood, but I think it's the company as well.

"Where do you know the vendor from?" Gio catches my elbow as I lose my balance on the soft surface. He helps me jump onto the wooden path, so we can cross to get to the intersection.

"I used to have ice cream here more than my hips would ever admit. I can't believe he still remembers me though. It's been a year now." A wave of melancholy washes over me. I didn't realize I missed this place.

"I doubt anyone forgets you."

I'm not sure I heard him correctly as a convertible roars past us. I'm not even sure if it's a compliment, but it warms my insides.

I don't put my shoes on, padding across the busy

street carefree, biting my bottom lip because Gio's discomfort is practically clouding the air.

We get to the park, throw away the empty cups, and I drop my shoes and sit down on the perfectly manicured grass. "Come on, join me."

He shifts from one foot to another, eyeing me with that face he makes—a mixture of disdain and disbelief, with a dash of disgust. I used to hate that face, but I'm starting to enjoy it. It's like he's suffering at the mere thought of doing something trivial.

"I don't sit on grass," he pushes through his teeth.

"Don't be ridiculous." I lie down—probably not a good idea if my dress should last for the day—to demonstrate what a delight it is to lounge in the grass. "You're a beekeeper. Didn't you tell me something about connecting with nature?"

He frowns and fidgets for a moment and I almost give up, but he takes off his suit jacket. Placing it carefully beside me, he lowers himself down.

"Are you afraid of ants?" I squint against the sun at him.

He's sitting on half of his ass only, minimizing any contact with the ground.

"No, I'm not," he snaps, but relaxes a little.

This is ridiculous. I pull him down. Catching him by surprise, I actually move his firm body and he collapses beside me.

I close my eyes and sigh in delight—well, the closing of my eyes is more to avoid his glare. I assume he's glaring, but he is not moving, so I guess I won.

We lie there, the sun kissing our skin. The sound of a tennis ball from the courts to the side interrupts the silence with a rhythmic thump, but otherwise it's just our breathing. Simple. Vital. And somehow connected.

"So, no ice cream and no laying in the grass. Are those things too common for you?" I tease.

"It's not like my lifestyle allows much time for these... normal things."

Again, he refers to normal as unattainable.

"But your lifestyle is your choice. Even a busy businessman can stop for a cone of delicious treat."

"I don't have time."

"You don't make time."

A shadow blocks the sun's rays, and I open my eyes and meet his gaze. He's lifted up on one elbow, watching me with interest. A softer look than his usual annoyed glare. "To be honest, I haven't even thought of going for ice cream."

"I have a feeling you got a taste now just to remember how trivial and unnecessary it is." I push up on to my elbows, our faces closer now.

A bit too close. If I move a couple of inches, my lips would brush his.

As soon as the thought flickers through my mind, it

spreads like a virus, taking over my brain. My eyes drop to his lips. My lips part of their own accord. *Look up, Mila, look up.*

I do. I shouldn't have. His gaze is heated now. Our chests heave. The tennis ball bounce is deafening and non-existent at the same time.

I want him to kiss me. No doubt he wants to. Yet he can't. I sigh, and a shadow passes over his face.

I jerk up to sitting. No point in torturing ourselves with something that can't happen. Not while he's my boss. I dust my dress with unnecessary vigor, regretting the silly idea of bringing him here.

When he sits up, I can't look at him. Jesus, I never hold myself back in these kinds of situations. Though this is impossible, the realization of how much I want it rattles through my bones, shaking me with regret and ever larger, unsated want.

"Why did you move? You seem to love it here." His voice is gruff, with a frustrated edge to it. Or maybe I'm mirroring my own feelings. At least he's diverting the attention from the moment we've just had. Because we definitely had a moment.

"It was the only way to escape an unhealthy relationship." The words are out, true and uncensored, before I can stop myself. Jesus, he doesn't need to hear that pathetic story.

"Do you miss it?" He picks a stalk of grass and rubs

it between his fingers. It's a mindless move, but something about it makes me smile. A moment in time, away from his busy schedule and my problematic situation, filled with innocent simplicity.

"My family is in New York." I give him a vague answer. All I'm willing to offer now.

The next words from his mouth break me into shards. "I hope he knows what he lost."

Chapter 9

Gio

"Okay, Marnie, I trust your judgment on this. Offer Portia the job and start listening to your doctor's advice to take it easy." I fix my tie and adjust my collar.

The sun, not yet fully awake, creeps through the window, casting cones of lights across my hotel room.

"Thank you. The events exceeded our expectations and we're seeing an increase in revenue just from the publicity alone. Are you leaving soon?"

"I have a vineyard to look at in Napa Valley and then I'm back in New York. Have a nice weekend." I'm about to click on the screen to disconnect the call, but Marnie is not done.

"Gio, before you go, I want to apologize for fighting you on the new hire. I didn't like you meddling in my affairs, but Mila hit the ground running and delivered above my expectations. Where did you even find her?"

I adjust my cufflinks. "Believe it or not, at my brother's restaurant. She handles his social media." I set my luggage by the door.

"I know it was me who insisted on a six-week contract, but I would like to extend an offer to her. Hopefully she can let go of her other clients."

I tense. Mila deserves this job, and apparently needs it even more. Fuck, I promised her the opportunity myself.

"Let's wait and see how the rest of the events go. Move on Portia's promotion to take your position in interim and then she can chime in on hiring Ms. Ward."

I'm a selfish bastard. How can I tell Marnie that I don't want to hire Mila because I fucking want to ask her out? It's not fair to the team, or to Mila. For fuck's sake. I thought I was a better man, but spending time with her, watching her work, smile, eat, talk to others—talk to *me*—making me do shit like the beach walk in Santa Barbara, has changed everything.

"Okay, Gio, you're right. I need to allow Portia to make these decisions." Marnie interprets my suggestion in a completely reasonable yet very wrong way, but I won't fight her on that. Her version is more noble.

We disconnect the call and I stare out the window.

I should have had Mila book a commercial flight home, but I didn't. I also didn't tell her we're going to Napa. It will be a surprise detour.

I want to spend more time with her. Even though I can't touch her, these moments we share are the most normal I've had in years.

She's a breath of fresh air. I thought she hated me, but that heated moment in the park and how flustered she was afterward—a blush coloring her beautiful, soft skin—confirmed she might be as interested as I am in exploring this further.

I need to tread carefully. Fuck, when she mentioned Tully suspecting something in San Francisco, I almost lost it. What is it with fucking people making up shit to get a piece of me? Though in this case, Tully was just fucking observant, seeing things the two of us didn't yet recognize.

I hate that I can't just ask her out like a normal person. The irony doesn't escape me—I have experienced more normal with her in a short week than I have in years.

While she works for me, we can't discuss the growing attraction. I need to find her another job. An idea sparks and I grab my phone.

"Hey, asshole, have you seen it yet?" Conrad pants on the other side. The pounding and squeaking of the belt suggests he's at the gym.

"No, I'm flying there today. I thought running was for girls."

"Are you calling to spoil my mood?" He swallows, probably chugging down his electrolytes.

I chuckle. "Could you ask around and find me a social media/event planning company to buy?" I stand up and walk to the window.

He scoffs. "What would you need that for? Don't you have in-house people to do those jobs? It's not the type of company you could turn around for a reasonable return."

"I have my reasons," I growl. I don't need his business advice.

"Okay. I'll look around. At least you won't tease me about my pet projects."

"Fair enough, asshole. I guess we're old enough to spend on things for reasons beyond profit. Anyway, make sure the company is financially healthy."

There is a clunk and commotion before he comes back. "I fucking almost fell off the treadmill. Why would you want to buy a financially healthy company? You buy them, you heal them, you sell them for a shitload of money. It's been your jam for years now."

I sigh. I'm usually very open with Conrad, so why do I feel I can't tell him? Because it's not a business decision, and no way I'm admitting that. "As I said, I have my reasons. Just find me one while I'm wasting my time scouting your stupid vineyard."

"I think the California sun melted your brain." He chuckles.

I exhale, but my exasperation lingers. Not because he's challenging me, but because I fear he's right. "Don't you worry about me. Say hi to Nora and we'll talk when I return."

"Oh, before you go, Nora wants to go to the Alzheimer's Society gala. I'm thinking about getting a table. It's at the end of January." He exhales, and a few short beeps followed by silence suggests he's finished his run. "Nora would love you to join us."

"I didn't know you're staying for another month. Sure, I'll be there."

"Great, but don't bring one of your usual dates. Nora hates most of them. They don't talk, just purse their lips and take selfies."

"Thank you for your opinion. I'll make sure my companion meets your demanding wife's requirements." If I have my way, Mila will be on my arm by then.

We hang up, and as I pack the rest of my things, I catch myself whistling. What the fuck?

If I can eliminate our working relationship without impacting Mila's ability to make ends meet, I will ask her out.

Hopefully she will agree to the terms.

* * *

I exit the elevator, and for once Mila is not late but waiting downstairs. Or laughing with the fucking photographer. The asshole has been documenting all the events and is awfully friendly with her, but I assumed he was just ensuring his paycheck.

What the fuck is he doing here? Red edges around my vision as I take in the cozy scene. They are leaning on the back side of a sofa in the middle of the lobby, looking at pictures. He's too close, leaning in.

Her laugh ricochets off the pillars around the room, grating on my nerves. It's sweet and genuine. What is so damn funny?

I storm across the lobby. "What are you doing?" I growl at the man I've seen four times. I should know his name. Dead. That's what he'll be called soon.

He jumps up, his smile fading, but Mila doesn't read the room. "Gio, look, Fabio made a portrait of me and had it printed. Isn't it beautiful?"

She pushes a frame toward me, and I look down at a black-and-white close-up of her beautiful smile. Her hair is in her face, but the mess only emphasizes the natural beauty. It's a snapshot stolen without her awareness, lending it truth.

The fucker did a good job, but why was he even looking at her? "I thought you were hired to document the events."

"And you'll be pleased with the results, I'm sure." He smirks.

Mila presses the photograph to her chest. Her protective move snaps me back to reality. What the fuck am I doing?

"Let's go. The helicopter is waiting." I don't wait for her and jerk my carry-on. Annoyance spreads through me like poison. At Fabio. At Mila. But mostly at myself. What kind of a caveman behavior was that?

"Helicopter?" Mila breezes behind me.

Fuck. There goes my lovely surprise invitation to Napa.

Chapter 10

Mila

"**I** could have taken a commercial flight." I'm annoyed Gio didn't tell me sooner about his plan to visit some vineyard in Napa. It would be different if it was for fun, but he's dragging me to assess a property.

Every time we take a step forward and I feel like our relationship has reached some normal, respectful ground, he drags us ten steps back. What the hell did he just pull in the lobby?

And now a detour to Napa. Annie has been home alone with the kids for a week, and I need to get back. She puts on a brave face, but I know the flare-ups can completely incapacitate her, or at least her ability to take care of the kiddos.

"Sorry, I forgot to mention it. It will be a quick

stop." He moves fast, as if getting to the stupid helicopter will make this unexpected detour faster.

I almost trip, typing and walking. I'm firing twenty questions at Annie, assessing if she is lying about handling things just fine.

Besides, I have never flown in a helicopter, and I'm not sure how I feel about spending ninety minutes in that small globe.

"When will we get home?" I don't look up and almost collide with Gio.

The deep ridge in the middle of his forehead complements the stony jaw. What does he have to be annoyed about? Jesus, the man is impossible.

Since our moment in the park, we have both focused on the job, more or less avoiding private moments. I would enjoy more of them, but it won't happen. Gio is too guarded to even attempt anything, and I need this job too much to risk coming on to him.

But this morning has just reminded me that there is nothing to risk. More headache perhaps. Asshole.

We glare at each other, and I wish his scent wasn't interfering with my need to be annoyed with him.

He is wearing a chocolate brown suit. I would have never guessed that anything outside of the black to navy' scale could hug a person in such a favorable manner.

He's edible. Minus the firing eyes. Deep brown

abyss of... well, I don't even know what it is today.

"Are you in a hurry to return?" he snaps and I raise my eyebrow. A shadow passes over his face, and then he shrugs, a grin almost ghosting his face. "It could be a fun trip."

Is he placating me? Really? Fun? Not with you, mister. I shake my head and continue toward the chopper, jumping between two apps to message Annie and draft a final report from this week.

"Is there someone waiting for you?" He catches up with me.

I jerk my head toward him, studying him, and then I roll my eyes. He really has no notion of other people having a life outside of work. "Yes, there is someone waiting for me." I march to the pilot, leaving him behind. Selfish prick.

"I'm Aldo, your pilot." The man is tall and handsome in a boring way, but what strikes me is his age.

"Hi, Aldo. I'm Mila. Don't take this the wrong way, but you look—"

"Young to fly Polly?" He laughs.

I bite my lip and shrug in apology.

"Mila, I've been flying Polly for five years, and I've been a professional pilot for almost ten years. This face is just genes." He winks and I giggle, slightly reassured the metal bird will get us wherever it is we're going.

"Ready?" Gio growls behind me, and I roll my eyes

again, earning another wink from Aldo.

I check Annie's response and, hesitantly satisfied with her wellbeing, decide to enjoy the flight. It might be the last time I'm in a helicopter.

I feel Gio's eyes on me. He's not even hiding his glowering, or observation—who knows with that prevalent frown of his. Every time I challenge him with my gaze, I expect him to look away, to hide his open attention, but he doesn't. What the hell?

I force myself to stare out of the window. The landscape below is beautiful, but I can't relax enough. I guess helicopters are not my thing.

An hour and a half into our flight, Aldo's voice carries through the intercom. "We're almost there. We'll be landing in—"

A loud clattering sound fills the cabin. I whip my eyes toward Gio, and his face mirrors my surprise. The feeling is short-lived as the helicopter lurches violently, and every fiber in my body tenses.

Another jerk and I clutch the seat in front of me as we drop. Like a roller coaster ride we free-fall, and I think I scream, but the sound is eaten by the clatter and roar of the machine and my pulse throbbing in my ears.

"We're losing altitude quickly." Aldo's voice sounds removed, far away. "Hold on tight."

I dig my nails into Gio's thigh, and he wraps his hand around my palm. I focus on that point of contact, only catching *autorotation, landing,* and *brace for impact* crackling at me from the intercom.

Our eyes meet for a moment before I make the mistake of looking outside. The ground is rushing toward us. I gulp down breaths. We're still hundreds of feet in the air, the whooshing of the rotor blades deafening in my head. Is this going to be the last sound I ever hear?

I need to block the outside, so I look at Gio again.

My heart hammers against my ribs.

Panic licks at all my senses.

I want to scream while being completely muted.

But I find comfort in his eyes.

A strange sense of hope.

"It's going to be okay," he mouths, and despite everything I believe him.

Somehow, the rattling of the rotors becomes almost calming. Proving we're still in the air, still alive. Everything seems to slow down as we glide toward the ground. I don't dare to break the eye contact with Gio.

The dark brown abyss of safety. In this moment, he's my anchor, my lifeline.

The entire cabin shakes, we're thrown to the side, and then skidding forward on the ground until we stop.

The communal exhalation soars through the cabin. Before I have time to form a thought, Gio is over to me, jerking off my seatbelt and wrapping me in his arms.

Half-carrying and half-dragging me, we stumble out. The feel of the solid ground under my feet is exhilarating.

I shiver, desperately trying to pull myself together, but remain frozen in horror. My mind rebels against me, cheering that the terror is over, while my consciousness can't yet absorb the reality.

But then there is the solid wall of muscles, tugging me into an embrace, wrapping me in his masculine scent. I shiver against his warm torso, both with relief and fear, and a sob shudders through me.

Without thinking, I snake my arms around his waist, squeezing for dear life. Like we're still in danger. His hand, warm and heavy on my back, stroking me gently, makes things only worse, giving me permission to let go. So I do.

Gio murmurs, "I'm sorry. I'm so sorry. I'm sorry."

His voice spreads a sense of comfort through my suddenly exhausted limbs.

I don't know how long we stand there, frozen between the fear of the past few minutes and the normal ahead of us. When my crying fades, his words register, but not their meaning.

I look up at him and my breath hitches. Something flickers in his eyes, and then his lips capture mine, our mouths crashing together in a desperate dance, channeling the fear and ordeal of the past moments.

The kiss is sloppy and brutally honest. Somewhere in the back of my mind, I acknowledge we're both seeking release from the angst cruising through our veins. Solidifying the gratitude.

Still, the feeling of his lips against mine tears something in my chest, infusing more reckless adrenaline into my veins, fueling my actions as I dig my fingers through his hair, desperately seeking more connection.

I didn't know a kiss could make me light-headed—and perhaps it's the adrenaline after-effect—but I invite the feeling like a junkie needing his next hit.

Intoxicating. Delirious. Dizzying.

I welcome his tongue with frenzy and urgency, as if this was the only way to recharge and move forward. Our bodies are tangled, seeking refuge and relief. We're pressed together so tight, our frantic heartbeats sync in a wild harmony of mutual catharsis.

When we finally pull apart, he rests his forehead against mine, stroking my still tear-soaked cheek with his thumb.

"I'm sorry," he whispers, repeating the words of comfort he murmured before.

"It wasn't your fault." I reach up to stroke his cheek, but he recoils. The previous connection frays and then disappears with Aldo's voice.

"Okay, folks, help is coming. We're not far from your destination."

Our eyes remain locked for a beat longer in a silent duel of indecision and confusion, but I see the moment when Gio retreats into his usual efficient mask.

I imagine a glimpse of reluctance in his eyes, but then he gives in, turns away and starts talking to Aldo. The bubble of tentative closeness bursts.

I try to follow the conversation, but my mind swims with everything other than the post-landing activity.

The kiss. The apology. The withdrawal.

Tires screech, breaking through the fog in my brain.

"That was some landing." A woman in her fifties jumps out of a Range Rover, two younger men following her. "I'm Danita Crawford. Are you okay? Any injuries?"

Aldo takes over and talks to the woman, and the next two hours are a blur of me trying to act logically, but really I just let people take care of me while I continue on autopilot, hoping to meet Gio's eyes.

At one point, everyone forces me to go to the hospital, but I don't want to. I want to forget the whole thing. To find my safe place and reassure others I'm not in shock, I babble about how fine I am, and thank God for Danita who is more than willing to indulge me.

It turns out we landed in a clearing near the vineyard, and our first rescuers were actually the family Gio came to see.

Danita offers us a meal, but I need to wash away the sweat and the feelings.

"I'm not hungry, but would it be okay to take a shower? I think it might—" I hear my voice going, but I don't particularly care what I'm saying. Anything to cloud the thoughts of the crash—technically emergency landing—and the kiss.

Danita leads me out of her kitchen and down a hallway. Aldo talks on his phone in the entrance and raises his finger when he sees us.

He hangs up. "My boss is sending a car for me and a team to recover the bird. If you don't mind, I'll go take care of that. I'm sorry. There will be an investigation and we'll inform you about the results. For now, I can only say it was an inexplicable engine failure—"

"Don't worry. You landed us safely. I'm sorry I doubted your experience." I give him a hug. He awkwardly pats me on the shoulder, and I fight tears. "Thank you."

"I'm glad everyone is okay." He steps aside, looking over my shoulder.

Gio stands behind us, daggers shooting from his eyes. "Thank you. I'll make sure you get properly compensated for your skills today." Somewhere between the helicopter and now, Gio's voice has gone robotic.

"Okay, I'm going to take a shower." I smile at Aldo

and turn to Danita. "So, are you living in this house? It's beautiful."

"It needs a lot of renovations." She opens a wooden door, the hinges crying with effort.

"It might need some love and investment, but it has charm."

"You're too kind. This is the only habitable bedroom. The shower is clean, but nobody has used it since this summer when we had students working with us. The bathroom is that way, and there are clean towels on a shelf there, too."

She leaves, and I sink into a comfortable armchair by the window. A pond glistens on the horizon, surrounded by row after row of currently bare vines. It must be breathtaking in the summer.

I close my eyes, finally able to digest today's events. Thoughts, regrets, memories, abandoned plans and those not-yet planned attack me from all different directions with various intensity. Scattered and shredded, with little sense, they don't really connect into anything concrete.

And then the kiss—

I jerk awake with a jump, goosebumps covering my skin. The fog in my head fights with the darkness before I focus my eyes. Outside, the sun is low on the horizon. Inside it's even darker. Where am I?

My vision adjusts along with my recollection. Shit,

I must have fallen asleep. I check my watch. Three hours! Jesus. I shuffle to the bathroom and take a long shower, letting the hot water melt my tense muscles.

When I find my way back to the main room, it's empty. I venture outside and spot Gio on the veranda, sitting in a white rocking chair, his legs propped on the banister and his laptop in his lap.

"You're up." His eyes are full of something, but it's not his usual annoyance.

"Do you ever stop working?" I challenge him like on our way to California, which feels like years ago. The point seems even more urgent now.

"I enjoy it." He drops his feet and puts the laptop on the table beside him. "You fell asleep, so I used the time."

"We could have died today." The words surprise me and Gio flinches. "And you go on and work. It seems... I don't know."

"It helps me to bury myself in work, so I don't have to think about other things." He steps closer, reaching for his wrist. But his sleeves are rolled, and he can't adjust his cufflinks. He clenches his fists. "I'm really sorry."

"It wasn't your fault."

He shakes his head, as if I misunderstood.

"Oh." A realization hits me like a freight train. "You're sorry about the kiss! Don't worry about it. It was two people channeling the trauma." *Oh, ground, please swallow me now.* "And you don't have to worry, I won't tell anyone. It was completely consensual. You don't have to worry." I blabber, heat spreading across my cheeks. "Really, Gio—"

"Would you shut up," he growls.

Tears prickle behind my eyes. "Of course. My lips are sealed. As if it never happened." I turn and lean against a wooden post to hide. To avoid his eyes. To avoid his expressive face. "It's such a beautiful place. Are you going to buy it?" Let's move the conversation somewhere safe.

Gio lets out a long breath. "It's my friend who wants to buy it. Conrad Hermann wanted my assessment. He has a talent for sniffing out potential, but I'm good at assessing numbers and seeing business opportunities often hidden behind red numbers on a spreadsheet."

"Sometimes it's about more than numbers, though." I think of the Wings employees who work hard, and for months they have been only a number on a spreadsheet. I guess that's normal for Gio.

"Often it is. Not even the best business proposition can succeed without people. Sometimes I lose track of that, as you may have seen this week. But places like this, a family-run business, remind me of the value of passion and dedication."

I chance a look at him. He doesn't meet my gaze, his focus on the horizon, deep in thought, but his consideration again confirms there is a soul behind his aloof behavior.

Part of me can't wait for this business trip to be over, so I can regain my senses, and part of me wishes we can continue this mutual discovery, and maybe, just maybe, explore it more.

Does he regret that kiss because of HR, because he's my boss? Or does he regret it because it's me?

"There is only one bedroom here." Gio's soft voice interrupts my thoughts. "I'm going to call Danita, so her son can drive us to Napa to get a hotel."

"Is it far?" The idea of traveling anywhere spreads dread and painful exhaustion through my bones.

"Yountville is closer, but there is a wedding and some conference happening and they're booked out. The other option would be calling the estates around here, but we may as well go to Napa."

"Or stay here. I'll leave the bed for you and sleep in the armchair. It was actually quite comfortable."

He narrows his eyes, probably worried he's going to expose himself to an HR investigation. Jesus.

"Gio, the idea of entering any vehicle again today makes me want to cry," I plead.

He nods. "Of course, we'll stay. Me on the sofa in the tasting room. It's okay. My jet will wait for us first thing in the morning at the county airport, only 40 minutes from here. Let me call Danita and ask where we can get dinner."

I smile, but it's not an effortless movement, my heart still shuddering from the helicopter and Gio's rejection. "Thank you." I run my hand down my face as if I can wipe away the bitter taste. "Jesus, I don't know why I'm so shaken. I should be exhilarated that we survived."

"I don't think there is a right or wrong reaction to a situation like this. I'm glad you're okay. I'm sorry I dragged you into this." He puts his hands in his pockets, awkwardness stretching between us.

He really is ridden with guilt. I don't have the capacity to analyze this at the moment. "Do you think I can have a glass of wine?" I sag against the post, rubbing my hands over my arms.

A sad smile tugs at his lips. "Definitely. We're in a vineyard after all. Let's go inside and call Danita."

While I search for wine, Gio gets the fire started in the tasting room. I sit on the sofa and take a sip.

"I didn't know you could make a fire."

His eyes widen. "Well, Princess, I learned tricks from my *keepers*."

Princess.

We stare at each other, the awkwardness from moments before melting away. Or perhaps the shadows are not as obvious in the room lit by the flickering fire. It's cozy here, and sitting down, I allow myself to relax.

Gio takes his glass without breaking eye contact with me. Unspoken words hover in the air. I wish the professional boundaries would blur away and we could just move out of this vacuum of suppressed attraction. God, if only I wasn't making it up.

"I put you in danger, Mila. You could have been home with whoever is waiting for you, and instead you're here and—"

"Hello," a voice from the entrance calls, killing the conversation. Gio rushes outside and after a few minutes he comes back with a picnic basket.

"Danita's son got us dinner." He puts the basket on the table. "I'll get the plates."

I gulp down the wine because I'm buzzing with nervous energy. Something has blossomed in my chest on this trip, but I need to be realistic. Yes, Gio is not who I thought he was, but he dates tall, skinny arm-candy women who belong to his society circles, or at least aspire to fit in with their followers, modeling contracts and inheritance.

The kiss between us was amazing, but it resulted from the adrenaline rush. Did he feel more, like I did? Fuck, this is so frustrating.

By the time Gio returns with plates and cutlery, I've riled myself up. This day is like a roller coaster ride. My body immediately recalls the sudden drop of the helicopter earlier.

Wine sloshes over my wrist, the glass slipping from my quivering hand and shattering into pieces on the stone floor.

"Are you okay?" Gio's eyes scan me with curiosity and worry.

"Sorry, I'm such a mess today."

"Come around carefully. If there was a day to be a mess, it's today."

The glass crunches under my soles as I approach the table. "I should clean it up."

I shuffle to the kitchen and find a broom. Despite my long nap earlier, every move requires enormous effort. While Gio prepares two plates for us, I sweep up the glass.

The choreography is strangely domestic and comforting, as if we've co-existed like this regularly.

Gio gets me another glass of wine and I take a generous gulp, the heat and heaviness spreading through me.

"Eat." He beckons to my plate, and something snaps in me.

"Don't fucking tell me to eat." I stand up and my glass topples, the dark red stain spreading quickly across the table's wooden surface.

Gio's chair screeches as he pushes away from the

table. "For fuck's sake, Mila, you haven't eaten all day. I don't want you to faint like you almost did at the gala for some vain reason." He winces at his words.

"I don't want to eat. Fuck you with your stupid protein bars and your pretense of care. You dragged me here and I almost died, and I'm going to miss a weekend with my family," I yell. Not necessarily at him. Or maybe at him. I don't know. All I know is it feels good to release all these stupid emotions.

"And at the gala? You thought I was starving myself on purpose? For some fucked-up reason? Maybe that's how your tall-legged girlfriends operate, but I didn't get a chance to eat that day..."

Oxygen is hitting only the top of my lungs. Gio is staring at me wide-eyed, but he's not stopping me. He isn't rolling his eyes, or rewarding me with the dose of annoyance and contempt so often written over his face.

"... they screwed up my rental order and I got an ill-fitting dress." I pant. "And it might be hard for you to understand, but I couldn't afford to tell London I have no dress, so I suffered through the night. I might be desperate to pay my bills, and fuck up occasionally, but it's none of your business."

I turn and storm away, but stop at the door. "And for the record, I enjoyed the kiss. I wish it had happened under different circumstances, but don't worry—I won't report it to fucking HR."

Chapter 11

Mila

"Mila." I hear Gio's voice, but I don't stop.

The guest room is only a few feet from the tasting room, but even the short distance is enough for the painful realization to sink in. Today's events may have sparked my attack, but I unloaded too much, and perhaps some of it was unwarranted.

And I just admitted to my boss I liked him kissing me. Poor man has been mortified by that particular event, and I just made it worse for him.

"Mila."

I didn't hear him approach, but he's close. I lean my forehead against the wooden door. God, I can't look at him, embarrassed to the core. "I'm sorry."

"It's okay. It's been a long day."

We remain silent for what feels like an eternity. I crave the closeness, the heat and the safety I discovered in his embrace after the landing. But I understand it was just a figment of my imagination, or rather a natural reaction to the adrenaline surge.

"I'm sorry I kept you away from New York," he apologizes again.

"It's my sister and her kids. She is sick and needs my help," I explain, not sure if I really want to show him this side of my existence. We had a few beautiful moments over the past week, but I don't know if I can afford to uncover more of me. I trust him, but I'm still hesitant.

Somewhere, somehow, I've lost the boundaries our professional relationship should have, and now I'm scrambling to find my footing while the ground under my feet slides away.

For all I know, I might be making shit up and the connection is in my head only. Giving him a piece of my private reality seems like a big step. Am I going to make him uncomfortable?

After a fortifying breath, I push off the door to face him.

His features are contorted, and now I'm sure I'm over-sharing, but he says nothing, and a part of me is hoping his reaction is related to his guilt over keeping me on this side of the country.

"I'll call the pilot and have him get organized so we can leave immediately." He steps closer.

His solution is fast and efficient, and I don't know if it's compassion or guilt driving it. Does it even matter? "That's unnecessary. We can leave in the morning. I'm sorry I unleashed on you."

"I didn't quite understand half of it, but I think I deserved it. Come, I'll get you *another* glass of wine."

A smile tugs at my lips, but I'm too exhausted and overwhelmed to let it blossom. Or to decide if returning is a good idea. But my feet shuffle away. As I pass him, the smoke and spice scent awakens all my numb nerve endings, and I remember I also told him I liked that kiss. *Please, universe, now would be the time to get me a time machine.*

"For the record, I liked that kiss as well. But I can't—"

"I know. I know, Gio." The last thing I want is to cause problems for him. If I accept an official position at the company, we can't date. If I want to date him, I would have to look for other opportunities, while increasing my credit card debt or having Annie miss her meds again. Fuck.

"I'll figure it out, Princess."

My poor heart decides to train for a marathon as hope blooms inside me. He wants to figure this out.

We return to the tasting room.

"Tell me about your family." Gio sits down and tears off a piece of baguette.

I guess if there was a time to scare him off, it would be now. "Annie has chronic arthritis with a multitude of complications, including constant pain, and it severely impacts her life. Her son, Aidan, has several issues, including learning disabilities and epilepsy. And she has a two-year-old girl. Her husband bailed after Ellery was born. She relies on me, and I'll be gone for most of the next two weeks again."

"I'm sorry I didn't consider you when making the plans. I just assumed you'd tag along. And then I put you in danger."

"For the hundredth time, it wasn't your fault, but I accept your apology for the lack of consideration." At that my stomach growls, and Gio shrugs, barely stifling a grin.

I roll my eyes. "Okay, I'll eat something." I pull the plate closer and take a bite of cheese with the bread. "Oh my God, this is good."

"Homemade." He takes a sip of his wine and crosses one leg over the other. "I'm sorry I misjudged your behavior at the gala. I-I had a woman faint on me once during dinner, and I guess—"

"Yes, your charm is legendary." I tease him because I need us to go back to relaxed and superficial. And I don't want to talk about his women. It's a stark reminder of what I'm not.

"Touché. She was really skinny, but still starving herself. I saw you sway at the gala and, fuck, I was sure I diagnosed the symptoms."

I smile this time. "You cared, which gives you some smiley points."

He chuckles. "I'll take that."

Silence descends on the room, but this time it stems from companionship and comfort. I finish my plate and yawn. "I can't believe I'm still tired."

"It could be your body dealing with the influx of adrenaline." He raises the glass to his lips and watches me from behind its rim with hooded eyes.

I'm hyperaware of my breathing.

A tiny scar marks the smooth skin above his left eyebrow.

The room grows unreasonably hot.

I swallow.

When was I ever cognizant of my swallowing or breathing?

His shirt hugs his shoulders, a promise, teasing me with all the muscles I wish to discover underneath.

"Why do you have your assistant arrange your dates?" My brain must have been damaged during the incident. *Why did I ask that?*

His gaze drops and he studies the table for a

moment before he sighs. "I haven't realized how diffi-cult it would be to keep this professional."

I'm not sure what he means. Am I overstepping with my personal questions? But it's pain, not his typical annoyance, skimming his face. Sharing is a struggle for him. So, of course, I don't shut up. "Let's agree that for this one night we are just two people stranded in wine country."

His eyes snap up, assessing me like a dangerous object he wants to touch, but is wary of at the same time. My stomach sinks. He doesn't know if he can trust me. "Don't answer, Gio. You're right, you have no reason to trust me."

He narrows his eyes. "That's not... I'm not... I—" He sighs and drags his hand over his face. "One night in wine country where we're just us? Wine honesty?" He chuckles humorlessly.

"Without the alcohol-induced loose tongue." I grin.

The heavy sigh confirms how hard this is for him. "People—women—want to be with me for my money and influence, so that's what they get. I spend time with them, so they can post a photo with an eligible, rich bachelor and increase their public profile, and they agree to my terms, mostly covered by a non-disclosure agreement. That's why lawyers and Lydia are involved. It's an arrangement."

The proud man I know sounds defeated, his

posture slightly bent. Whatever prompted him to look at relationships through the prism of a cynical business deal? I'm sure the lawsuits were a part of it, but it just seems so sad. "But what's in it for you?"

"I need a woman in my life to accompany me to events, to keep my mother from matchmaking, and to keep the other hunters and gold diggers at bay."

"So it's like a series of fake relationships?" I can't wrap my head around this.

"No, they're not fake. They are real. Maybe not conventional, but—"

"You can't have normal." I look away, trying to reconcile what he's just told me. "But doesn't that prevent you from finding the one?"

He shrugs. "Just because my screening process is unorthodox, it doesn't mean I won't meet her. If the boxes are checked."

I widen my eyes in disbelief. He can't disregard relationships like this. He has wedding pics of his friends and family at home. Doesn't he want the same? "You're such a romantic, Gio," I tease. "Isn't it lonely to operate from a place of such control?"

"It is what it is. I accepted it. It's certainly less of a headache than the other, *normal* way." He pops a grape into his mouth. "I did get some normal with you this week. Though sitting on the grass might have trauma-tized me."

I laugh. "Did your mother give you shit for staining your pants?"

He throws his head back and laughs. "Okay, you're right, the trauma happened before you. She was always so mad at us, and with four boys, you can imagine grass-stained clothes were only a minor offense."

"Yet it stuck with you." We grin at each other.

He runs his tongue across his upper teeth and my heart contrasts his languid move with a spooked gallop. "Is your reaction earlier a ghost of the past?" he asks.

My smile freezes. I busy myself with the uneaten food on my plate.

"Mila, wine honesty, remember?" I feel his gaze on me, heating my skin. I'm sure I look like a ripe tomato by now, trying to sort through my hesitancy.

"Winesty then?" I avoid his eyes and hope to avoid his question as well.

"Winesty. You don't have to tell me." It's more a challenge than a statement. He shared, after all.

How do I tell him I'm this weak, insecure woman who let her boyfriend control and manipulate her? How it took months just to make me realize who the failure was in that story. How I might act like an easy-going, mostly happy, strong woman, but really I'm a mess.

"A controlling father and a manipulative ex with narcissistic tendencies. I used to crave his praise and tried to please him so much that I let him stomp all over me. Honestly, I don't know why it rushed out earlier. When you told me to *eat,* I just felt like you were trying to control me. To manipulate me. Tell me what I should do. I know you were just caring, but—"

"I understand. The events of today could trigger a reaction out of character."

My eyes fall on his lips and then meet his gaze. I'm pretty sure we've just both remembered the kiss.

* * *

The razor-sharp metal cleaver plummets through the air and connects with a violent clang against the wooden surface, splitting it. Panic courses through my veins, and I scream. My lungs burn with the effort, blurring my vision, but there is no sound emerging.

I sit up abruptly, the cold sweat dripping down my face and seeping into the fabric of my shirt. I pant as the dream fades away slowly in the frantic beat of my heart. Shit. I haven't had this nightmare for months now.

"Mila." Gio knocks on the door. "Are you okay?"

No.

My disoriented mind, still lingering in the darkness of my sleep, can't form an answer. Is this a dream as well? "I'm okay." I think I say that, but Gio knocks again.

"Mila, I'm coming in."

The door squeaks. I lean forward, dropping my head between my sheet-covered legs.

"You screamed."

My mind is still fighting the fog, and the bitter aftertaste.

"Mila, you're scaring me. Can I come closer?"

"Yes, please."

My sob rolls through the air and Gio is by my side immediately, wrapping his arms around me. I try to fight the tears, but they rake my body anyway. I don't know how long it takes before I finally fully register the situation.

Gio runs his hand up and down my back, his palm warm and safe. He murmurs soft words of consolation into my hair.

"I haven't had that nightmare in a long time."

He loosens his grip and leans back to look at me. I'm a mess, my face wet with tears and more.

"It wasn't about the helicopter free fall?"

I shake my head. "Half a year ago, Massi's business rival threatened me and Gina. He wanted to cut my fingers off with a meat cleaver." Another broken sob shudders through me.

I flinch as Gio's fingers dig into my arms for a

moment. Something dark passes through his face before his eyes soften, focusing on me with so much care that the terror melts away slowly.

He pulls me back into his arms. "Fucking hell. Massi mentioned something, but I didn't realize it was this serious."

His masculine scent surrounds me, awakening butterflies in my stomach. Cradled in his solid arms, I feel safe. It's a strange concept after years of worrying to please someone and then worrying about taking care of someone. And failing mostly.

"I'm sorry. I'm usually not such a mess. It's just—"

"Stop it, Princess, you have every right to be a mess. You're a beautiful mess, in any case."

We both tense at his words, boundaries blurring, need and want coursing between us.

"Sorry. I-I—"

"Gio, stop, let's apply the winesty to the rest of this night." I don't even know what I'm asking of him, but before I can stop myself, I kiss him.

It's a chaste kiss, soft on his lips, but I don't break it immediately, just lingering against his warm breath, waiting. The air of anticipation mingles between us. We both tense, but he doesn't move away.

Our faces are only an inch apart, and in the shadows of the room I can't see his face, but I can feel the war in him. I hesitate and hope. Is he going to pull away or lean in?

I'm about to collapse back and hide under the pillow when he groans, and oh my…

His hands rake through my hair, pulling me closer and angling me for better access. He takes over with such confidence that I let go of all inhibition, allowing him to savor me. This kiss is different than the first one. It's still urgent and desperate, but it's also decadent, like a dark chocolate with a sweet but bold promise.

I moan and Gio lets out a deep, masculine guttural sound. If sin had a musical score, it would be this sound. He thrusts his tongue, deepening the connection, and I swear I feel lightheaded again.

This is an oxygen-stealing kiss, and I can't get enough. My skin tingles with desire, my heart pounds with lust, and my core clenches with need.

I pull him closer and Gio twists us both. My back hits the sheets and the bed groans under our combined weight. He leaves a trail of kisses and bites down my neck, hitting a sensitive spot under my ear.

My back buckles, my body responding with urgency, purely driven by my senses—the essence of him, his sounds, his touch, his masculine presence.

His erection presses into my thigh, and I grind myself shamelessly against him. Seeking friction, reveling in his touch, grasping at all the decadence he offers.

I find the hem of his T-shirt and scrape my nails up his back, his shoulder blades wonderfully solid in my palm. It finally registers that he's only wearing underwear.

Oh, how I wish I could see him, but I erase the thought. I don't want to be thinking, I want—I need—to feel only.

He stills and lowers his forehead to mine. The non-existent clock in the room ticks away with dread, all the excitement evaporating as I wonder what's going on.

"Sorry, Princess, I can't."

Chapter 12

Mila

I open my eyes and groan. The bright sun dances around the room. I must have fallen asleep after what was the most humiliating night in my life. And I dated Brian, so I've experienced my share of shame, as my therapist's bills can attest.

Gio's face when I asked him to leave—threw him out really—haunted me for most of the night. The remorse in his features. The memory alone pisses me off. He rejected me, and he looked like the wronged party. What the actual fuck?

I check my watch. Yeah, after just two hours of sleep, being pissed will probably become the theme of the day. Throwing the sheet over my face, I groan.

My mind immediately returns to last night and I decide I better get moving. Keeping myself busy is the best remedy for all the problems. If only I didn't need to face my *boss*.

Argh! I shuffle to the bathroom, wash my face and try to fix my appearance in the best way possible, but given our suitcases are God knows where, there isn't much I can do. I take a fortifying breath and venture out of the room.

Following the noise and the divine smell of freshly baked bread, I get to the kitchen and stop in my tracks.

Gio, with his back to me, is mixing something at the stove. The planes of his shoulders strain beneath his white undershirt, and my mind slides down the slippery slope of delicious fantasies.

As soon as last night flickers through my mind, the fantasies dissolve into a bitter aftertaste. Annoyance takes up their spot. Why does he have to be this gorgeous? Or rather, why do I have to be attracted to him? Just two weeks ago I disliked him.

I attempt to mentally list the reasons I never liked him, but it frustrates me because it's gotten pathetically short. I can't even blame him for dating bimbos because now, when I know the background behind it, it makes me sad. How lonely his life is to believe this is his only option.

What else?

He's often arrogant, but this past week showed me it's a combination of not being a people person—we can't all be—and of having built a wall around himself. We all have them. In his case, his life has created experiences to reinforce those walls.

Not that I condone his overall attitude, but understanding what's behind it taints it a different, less harsh color.

I don't dislike him as much as I used to. In fact, I'm more intrigued by the caring man under all that bravado. And that makes his rejection sting even more.

"Good morning." I pad toward a coffee pot on the island.

Gio turns to face me and we both still for a moment. If I thought I looked like shit after the sleepless night, we could both go to a zombie convention. The dark circles under his eyes are profound. The dark brown abyss. But this morning I don't understand the gaze.

He looks worried. Is he worried I'd report what happened yesterday? Jesus, I didn't even think of that. Consumed by his rejection, I licked my wounds with no regard to the circumstances.

We stare at each other, the unspoken words hovering in the space between us. I need this business trip to be over, because this tension and unresolved desire is destroying me slowly, painfully.

A charred odor drifts through the room and Gio whips around and lifts the pan.

"I made breakfast. Do you feel like mildly burned eggs?" He raises one eyebrow and I swear even that simple gesture is sexy. Yes, this trip needs to end.

I want to refuse and tell him I'll wait for the ride outside, anywhere but near him, but my stomach growls. He doesn't wait for my answer and distributes the scrambled mess onto two plates.

"I guess I'll try it." I climb onto the stool by the island, and he pushes the plate toward me. He leans down and pulls out a tray from the oven. So that's the bakery scent filling the house.

"I reheated the baguette."

He transfers a few slices to my plate. It's grilled with cheese on top, and when I take a bite, I moan.

"It's like a fresh one."

"Yeah, you need to pat it with water so the oven doesn't dry it out, but it makes it crunchy."

"How do you know that?" I take another bite, even the slightly burned eggs are scrumptious.

"I told you I picked up a few tricks from my keepers." He shrugs and swallows a spoonful. "My granny used to make it that way."

His phone chimes and he looks at it. "The car will be here in twenty minutes. Are you ready to leave?"

"Oh, I couldn't get out of here fast enough."

He studies me again, the silence stretching between us. I forget the tasty breakfast, trying not to fidget under his stare. Why does he have to make things worse? After last night, he could either pretend it didn't happen or at least try to make things less awkward.

A clock ticks somewhere in the house. A truck roars in the distance outside. My heart thumps in my ears. I swallow around the lump in my throat. If he is waiting for me to say something, he's crazy.

"Let me do the dishes." I collect the plates and put all my frustration into the task. It's hard with Gio's eyes following me like a hawk. Goddammit.

I finish and leave the kitchen. Collecting my bag, I make my way to the veranda and sit down, letting the shy winter sun warm my skin. My private moment doesn't last long because Gio comes out.

He bores his eyes into me again, and this stupid staring contest is getting tiresome. Though I guess nothing is pleasing after a sleepless night. I'm cranky and dejected, and he's the only person I can channel my feelings at. And the only reason for them, frankly.

Danita comes over and we thank her for the hospitality, and shortly after a limo pulls up. A limo. For fuck's sake. At least I can sit as far as possible from him.

The drive isn't long, but it fills with pent-up energy. Or perhaps it's just me, because Gio keeps working on his phone or his tablet without lifting an eye.

I have only myself to blame. My strange infatuation with this man sprang out of nowhere. Just because he was nice to me. Kind of. Because he told me I'm good at my job. Because he shared a few private moments with me.

Can I be any more naïve? I never thought I was, but here we are. This man draws something from me that is needy, and frankly not very appealing.

"How many hours a day do you spend on the screen?" I challenge him.

"As many as needed." His focus remains on the phone.

"Interesting you don't wear glasses yet."

He lifts his eyebrow, giving me a disapproving look, and returns to his work.

"I'm sure you wouldn't be able to function without it. You're addicted." I'm not even sure why I'm pursuing the topic. It's not like I don't spend godless hours on the screen. It's my job, after all.

I just want to rile him up, as pitiful as that may be. I'm tired, which leads to being less than mature.

"Thank you for your unsolicited diagnosis. I can function without the screen. I choose not to. I like my work, and I care little for small talk," he deadpans.

Argh! Here I thought he felt bad about last night, but I was wrong. He's just his usual self. The few glimpses I got earlier were a fluke. Or wishful thinking on my part.

"I challenge you to go without it over the Christmas break." I truly don't know why I care or insist on this.

He looks up. "And why would I want to do that?"

"To win a dare?" I shrug.

He licks his lip, his eyes tightening at the corners. I'm sitting in the far corner of the car, but I can see his jaw tick. "What would I win?"

What? I didn't expect him to go along with this. I didn't even think it through. I was just being... well, I guess a glutton for his glare and growl. Now what?

"Confirmation you're not addicted," I say lamely.

He studies me, and I barely stop myself from squirming, but I withhold his scrutiny with my chin high. Those dark eyes. A strange feeling coils around my stomach, a cocktail of dread and thrill.

"I stay off the screen during the social occasions of the season and you grant me a wish."

My eyes widen. This feels oddly personal for the uncomfortable morning-not-after we've just had. "What kind of wish?"

"Anything I name." He shrugs.

"What's in it for me?" The driver must have turned up the heat because the interior of this car is sweltering.

"I'll grant you a wish."

My eyebrows jerk up. "Any wish?" Why is my poor heart struggling to find a healthy beat?

He nods. "I'm a law-abiding citizen, but otherwise, yes, anything."

There is innuendo in his tone, and I don't know how to reconcile that with his rejection. Or does he think I'm so desperate for him? Bastard. Yet the challenge is intriguing. What can he want from me?

"How would I know you complied?" I tap my fingers on the leather of my seat. How did we even get here? I wanted to rile him up, but I'm the one taut like a string here.

"I'll send you a screenshot of my phone use every night." He shrugs.

I smile at him, unsure of anything anymore when it comes to this man. "I have a feeling I'll regret this, but okay."

"Good." And with that, he returns to his work.

We reach the airport, and the same crew as last weekend greets us. I plop into the seat and pull out my phone and start working. Isn't that what my boss would expect from me?

He sits across from me and does the same. He seems to concentrate fine, but I can't. The last twenty-four hours were eventful to say the least, and I'm exhausted on top of it.

The flight attendant offers us lunch, but I refuse. I can't eat right now. Gio looks at me, but doesn't dare to suggest I should eat.

I close my eyes, hoping to sleep off this funk I'm in. A few more hours and I don't have to see him anymore. I keep fidgeting, unable to settle.

"You can use the bedroom," Gio says.

I fling my eyes open. "What?"

He points to the end of the plane. "There's a bedroom there. You'll be more comfortable."

I look over my shoulder. "Okay. Thank you."

He's being kind, but it's fused with this surgical precision, like he's executing the motions but making sure he acts as detached as humanly possible. Which, in his case, is almost inhuman.

I open the door and barely swallow a gasp. The queen-sized bed reigns in the small space. What's lost in square footage is lavishly compensated by the design. I don't think I've ever been in a more luxurious bedroom. The soft lighting soothes around the beautiful finishes of silk, fine wood and leather.

I drop onto the bed and cover myself with the gazillion thread count sheets.

When I open my eyes, I'm slightly disoriented, but the plush bedding reminds me immediately where I am. My watch says I only slept for two hours as my tired mind tries to find its way out of the fog.

While this was the most luxurious sleeping arrangement, the sleep was deep but not refreshing. After a sleepless night, two hours are not enough, but I don't feel comfortable staying here longer.

My boss is working outside. And while I would prefer staying away from Gio for the rest of the flight, the professional in me wins. I wash my face and return to the main cabin.

Gio is sprawled on the sofa along one side of the plane, his feet crossed at the ankles. His tablet is on the floor. It must have fallen down when he fell asleep. I take a moment to admire his peaceful face.

The relaxed features are more breathtaking than the scowling or glowering ones. His jaw is loose, and I wonder if he ever drools. He must, otherwise life is not fair.

I sit on the sofa across from him and pull out my phone to check the media coverage and start on a final report from this round of events. I'm returning to California on Tuesday, so I might as well get started on it now.

Gio startles and sits up. "Oh, you're up." He picks up his tablet and runs his hand down his face before he stands up and heads toward the bathroom.

As I watch his retreating ass, I can't help but admire the firm muscles. He enters the bathroom, and my beat of voyeurism reminds me of last night again. I groan.

"Did you get some shuteye?" He returns and sits opposite me.

"Hm." I pretend to be working, but I can feel his gaze.

"Do you feel better?"

What the hell is he asking? I snap my eyes at him. "Yes," I spit. I guess the shuteye didn't improve my mood either. God, I just want to be home.

"Mila." It's a demand, and I find myself immediately drowning in his gaze.

He opens his mouth and then closes it. He adjusts his cuffs. Here we go, he is bracing for... what?

I don't want to rehash last night.

I don't want to think about the connection I felt with him.

How his kiss made me feel cherished. How his urgent hands on me felt deliriously amazing. Him losing control, even for a moment, made me feel like a goddess, gave me a needed jolt of self-confidence.

Then he stomped all over it.

I don't want to talk about misinterpreting the whole thing, because clearly for him it was a moment of insanity he quickly corrected. And now he's probably worried about legal consequences.

He suggested he would figure this out. And used

that stupid Princess name, so I just assumed we wanted the same thing.

There is a reason I stay away from relationships and focus on occasional hot hookups. I don't understand men. And Brian left me so wounded, I misread the signs.

I might be attracted to Gio Cassinetti, my boss, but he's pulled back several times, and stupid me, I haven't gotten the message. I chose to ignore it each time.

And yet, there is a distinct predatory look in his dark eyes, drowning me in a pool of self-doubt and confusion.

Gio clears his throat. "Winesty moment, Princess."

His voice is darker than his stare, and I realize I'm too weak to survive this man. I'm already too deep in this need to unravel the mystery of him. The weird curiosity to find all his hidden parts, parts he almost allowed me to see but still hides really well.

I exhale. "I would rather not." My voice is an octave higher, floating through the cabin on a breeze.

"Too bad, because I need to explain," he says in a matter-of-fact way, but the urgency of the delivery is unmistakable.

"I don't want to hear it, Gio. Can you spare me?" I should have stayed in that stupid bedroom.

"Winesty, please." He uses please, but it's a demand, not a plea.

Clearly he's worried about last night, but fuck if I didn't have enough humiliation to last me a lifetime. It's not like he has to see me ever again. Why does he need to discuss this?

"Mila," he urges.

"Okay. Say what you need to say and let's get it over with." I fold my arms across my chest and raise my chin. I can pretend.

"I didn't want to take advantage of you last night, after the accident and the nightmare."

Wait? What?

He erases the distance between us and leans in, caging me between his arms, his palms digging into the leather of my backrest. He's too close, mere inches from me. My body immediately reacts to his heat, a tingling sensation rippling through me.

"Look at me."

I obey his demand, even though looking him in the eyes is a life-threatening endeavor—surely my heart is developing a chronic condition.

"For the record, Princess, when I fuck you, it will be because you crave it as much as I do. Not because you need release after a shitty day and three glasses of wine."

"Oh" is all I manage. His words spread through me like hot chocolate, all heat and decadence.

It wasn't a rejection.

It was a consideration.

He treated me with respect and care.

He didn't take advantage...

He glares at me for another intense moment. His eyes drop to my lips. Anticipation snakes up my spine. His Adam's apple bobs up and down, and then he stands up as abruptly as he landed above me.

"Besides, I'm still your boss. I told you I'll take care of it, so stop sulking. It doesn't suit you."

"How?" I croak, still whiplashed from his words earlier. The dominance, the undeniable need, the confidence. I think I need a fresh pair of underwear.

"Let me deal with that. In the meantime, you think really well, Mila, about my conditions."

"Conditions?" I widen my eyes. Oh, he is talking about the NDAs. Goosebumps cover my skin as I realize he sees me just like those other women. "I don't want to be treated like one of your... I'm not a trophy date."

He runs his tongue across his upper teeth. "It's not such a bad thing, but I promise you'll never forget a date with me." His voice is dark with promise and sin.

We stare at each other again today, but this time the energy zaps with electricity, need, and a promising thrill.

I definitely won't survive Gio Cassinetti. Oh, but I can't wait to succumb.

Chapter 13

Gio

I take a screenshot and hit the send button, smiling like an idiot.

Tedious. The holiday season has been tedious, but these moments at the end of the day are worth the suffering. I look forward to my nightly chats with Mila.

Acquisitions, crises and takeovers get me excited. They are my personal adrenaline boosts.

And now I'm daydreaming. Jesus.

Whoever invented small talk hated mankind. I've suffered through so much of it in the past two weeks, I ended up canceling at least two engagements because I couldn't go through more hours of torture.

Today was the cherry on top of many social engagements. The worst one. Christmas lunch with my family at London's. The pretense was palpable as we all tried to ignore the fact my stepfather has been undergoing cancer treatment, and might have celebrated his last holiday with us.

Paris was awfully quiet, and London's boyfriend has been charming my mother as if he needed her approval. London scowled as usual, but at least she didn't coerce us out of all our money for her charity.

I love them all, but getting them in large quantities, all concentrated in one event, is not exactly my jam.

Under normal circumstances it would have been survivable, but without the shield of my phone, the minutes stretched unbearably.

My phone beeps with Mila's response.

MILA

Merry Christmas. You really want that favor. I wonder what I have that your keepers can't get you.

I can't put that in writing, but I can't wait to tell you in person.

Oh, keeping me on my toes.

Or your back, your knees, against the wall... I delete all of that.

How was your day?

I catch myself grinning. Simple joys like asking someone about their day. I haven't done that in years.

MILA

My day was great. The kids loved their presents and my sister is feeling reasonably well. I splurged on a whole huge turkey but it didn't fit into the oven. LOL.

Fuck. She buys a turkey for Christmas and calls it splurging? Do I pay her that little? Are those medical bills so steep? And her oven is too small to fit the bird? Where the fuck does she live?

Red edges around my vision. At her situation. At my inability to help her out. Fuck me.

Who's your sister's doctor?

The three dots blink across the screen. Then they disappear. Then reappear. How long does it take to type a name?

Dr. Christensons in Chelsea. Why do you ask?

I guess this conversation isn't as playful as the other nights, but I can't cope with this feeling of uselessness.

I might have someone better.

Gio, her doctor is good.

I'm sure he is. Anyway, I'm on a screen ban, so good night.

Good night.

I look up Dr. Christensons and shoot a message to London who knows this world better.

Then I email my concierge and pour myself an inch of whiskey. I sit by the fireplace and spend the last moments of the day as I have been every night since California.

Fantasizing about Mila Ward.

Her infectious smile. Her annoying chatter. Her defiant chin-ups. The toss of her silky hair. Her rapid typing on the phone. The way she challenges me. The way she doesn't take shit from me. The way she tackles her work and still spreads kindness, even though life hasn't been kind to her. How she looks at me with those huge eyes.

The way her lips burned mine, and how her body melted into me. Those curves and subtle responses to any accidental touch. Nothing about my thoughts—or our texting every night—has been appropriate and will probably get me in trouble.

It's wrong.

Yet I can't stop.

My thoughts quickly turn into what could have been if I hadn't bailed that last night in Napa. How would she look screaming my name?

As every night, my cock hardens. I take another sip of whiskey and consider a cold shower. Not that it's been helping me. Fisting my cock and finding release to images of Mila is not enough.

I don't know what the woman has done to me, but I need the real thing. I need her. I want her.

Self-control is something I've never struggled with, and here we are. I'm fucking pining after a woman.

What the hell is wrong with me?

A lot of things.

Because lately, even jerking off leaves me frustrated and lonely. And I have no interest in any of my regular dates. None at all. The mere idea of a quick, mindless fuck is as appealing as walking on hot coals. Fast, with a fleeting satisfaction at the end, but I would rather stare into the fire.

Mila Ward has ruined sex for me. And I haven't even slept with her. She's ruined my perfectly curated relationship scheme.

Merry fucking Christmas.

"Why have you been extra grumpy?" Paris plops down on a chair across from me. My club is buzzing with its usual morning activity.

"Good morning to you too, sis." I look up from my newspaper. I fucking read newspapers now because of a woman. And I don't mind it either, which annoys me slightly. Okay, minus the fucking ink on my fingers.

"Sorry. I've been a bit on edge lately and exhausted." She sighs.

"And I've been extra grumpy because I'm off the screen and frustrated." The frustration stems from more issues, but they are all related, anyway. I won't give Paris the details. Or maybe I should.

"Why are you off the screen? You hate interacting with people. I'm not saying your phone use is healthy, but the current state is concerning. Bianca wants to know what's going on." Paris smiles at the server.

Of course, my mother sends one of my sisters to find out what's going on.

I wait while Paris orders and lean back in my chair, studying her. This would be a great time to check the markets or scan the prospectus for the Singapore development. My phone is burning in my pocket.

She touches her hair. "What? Stop staring at me and turning the conversation."

"Was there a conversation?" I deadpan.

"You, no screens. Why?"

"A bet." I don't know why I decide to answer. This no screen policy is having all sorts of side effects. Like I actually talk to people, opening cans of worms.

At least Paris is the only woman in my family who is a helpless romantic. Not that I'd ever confide the whole situation to her, but if I was to discuss my current obsession with someone, it would be with her. Massi and Andrea would just laugh at me. And Conrad—since he's been pussy-whipped, he's lost perspective.

Paris smiles. "No way. You have everything you need and can buy everything you ever wanted. What can possibly entice you enough to drop the phone shield?"

"Hey, it's not a shield. I work a lot and my phone is a good tool—"

"Yeah, yeah. What's the bet?" She rubs her hands in front of her and wiggles her shoulders.

"A date." The shock on her face was worth the confession.

"Oh my God, oh my God." She tries to contain her excitement and whispers her scream, but the energy radiating from her is hard to hide, and several people turn to look at us.

"Behave, Paris, or I will revoke your access to my club."

She holds her breath for a moment, her fists clenched in the air, practically vibrating.

The server brings her plate with an extra-large full breakfast.

"Hungry?" I raise my eyebrows.

"Don't you dare... it's winter, I'll get back in shape for spring. Who is it?" She digs into her hash browns, stuffs her mouth, and then freezes. She straightens up and starts eating like a lady. Thank God.

"It doesn't matter who it is."

"It does, because she clearly is worth the suffering." Paris points her fork at me.

She is. She fucking is. Mixed feelings coil around my stomach. The desire for Mila has been all-consuming. I don't like it. Especially since it's been ruling over my willpower and self-control.

"You don't know her, anyway," I lie.

"How long before you win the bet?" She forgets the manners again and eats like a lumberjack. She stops her fork halfway to her mouth, because my thoughts are probably showing on my face. She drops the food.

"Enjoy, just don't attract attention." I shake my head.

"Back to you, bro. So, what happened to all your *dates?*"

"I'm hoping to get her to agree to my conditions."

Paris is the only one in my family who knows about my dating arrangements. Not by choice. Just one drunken night when she came to drown her sorrows over a man, and I talked.

"Gio!" Paris wipes the corners of her mouth with the napkin. "You clearly care enough to agree to drop the phone act for her. You can't treat her like a business arrangement. If she was one of those women who wants you for the prestige or your money, you'd have signed her already. You can't scare her with your stupid schemes."

"She knows, and she understands those are the conditions."

"Gio, if she wants you for you—not the billionaire, not the most eligible bachelor in New York, not for an Instagram moment, but for you—she would want the same from you. She would want you to trust her enough. Not put her on your contract rotation."

"That's not what that is. I've had enough bullshit to deal with over the years. As much as I try to be low-profile, I'm not. There is always someone trying to get a piece of me. I have a process in place to deal with that."

Paris's shoulders slump and she sags into her chair, frowning. "Oh, why are men so oblivious?"

"I'm being considerate. You should understand. All that shit three years ago impacted you as well. You lost two of your high-profile clients."

Maxine Henri

She pouts for a moment longer and then sighs. "Signing an NDA and having conditions laid out before a first date is the opposite of romantic."

"Well, some of us need to be pragmatic."

* * *

MILA

Do you know something about the Four Seasons Christmas dinner delivered to my house today?

Depends. Are you happy?

Gio, I can't accept this.

You wouldn't let them throw it out, would you?

No, the kids are too excited. Thank you. How did you know where I live?

I have access to the HR files.

Thank you. You made my family happy.

What about you?

I know texting can be deceiving, but why do I feel she is less than happy? Annoyance crawls up my spine.

I don't want you to see me as a charity case.

170

. . .

Fuck me. I offended her with a gift. But how am I supposed to improve her life if her pride doesn't let her accept small presents? Paris's warning from this morning flickers through my mind. She pissed me off with her romantic notions.

All the women I've dated have gushed over every gift. Jewelry, spa certificates, flower arrangements, trips. The turkey I sent to Mila was a fraction of the price compared to those. Not that I know. I didn't put a budget on it when I called my concierge.

MILA

Gio, I'm grateful, I am. It's a thoughtful gift after our turkey disaster. I just... I don't need you to buy me.

I stare at her message, unsure how to interpret it. If I even attempted to date this woman in a *normal* way, I'd fuck it up.

A moment of winesty.

The moment stretches as I stare at my phone, suddenly feeling uncomfortable in my own skin. I know she might be taking care of something before responding, but for fuck's sake, it's a yes or no question.

Okay.

I don't want to be texting anymore.

Another endless beat of silence from her and I stand up to pour myself more whiskey. I'm about to dial her when her response comes.

Oh, okay. We should stop. I understand.

Okay, now I'm pissed. I don't even know at whom. Not at Mila, but at the fucked-up situation.

No, you don't. I miss you and I'm solving that problem right now. See me at the office in two hours.

Chapter 14

Gio

"You'll need to get Portia looped in on this," Fatima, my legal counselor, warns.

"Okay, I'll do that, but it can wait till after the break. Let's just get the paperwork signed now."

"Everything is prepared. You don't have to stay for this. I'll take care of it." Fatima takes the folder from my desk.

"No, I want to be here to make sure..."

Her hawk-like gaze stops me. "Gio, has something happened between the two of you already?"

I stand up and adjust my cufflinks. "Why would you ask that?" I don't want to lie to Fatima, but I can't tell her I almost fucked an employee. Consensual or not.

She narrows her eyes at me. "I need to know. You

pay me to protect you, but frankly you always let me deal with your ladies and your eager involvement has me worried."

Fuck me. I hate every minute of this. I wish I'd never hired Mila. None of this is normal. I can't even explore the attraction without being questioned.

"There is chemistry. We kept it appropriate and within the company policy."

Fatima's smile stretches across her face, full of smirk. "She is special."

"And now you're inappropriate," I growl.

"I've been running your dating scheme for long enough to have the right to—"

"Stop right now," I warn her, and she laughs.

Sometimes I wish the humiliation would have ended with the financial settlements, but here we are. I'm still a source of entertainment for some.

A knock on my office door stops her, and she immediately puts on a business-like face. I like that about Fatima, she is relaxed and fun, but ruthless and professional.

I didn't drag Lydia to work as we're officially closed for a week, so I go to open the door.

My eyes meet with the light blue sparkle. God, I haven't seen her for a few weeks and my memories of that beautiful face were completely wrong. She is even more beautiful. Her long hair is in a ponytail on top of her head, and I clench my fist to stop myself from wrapping it in my palm and pulling her to me.

She smiles at me and it hits me in the chest, spreading sunshine through my cynical soul. We stare at each other for a long moment, just absorbing the sight.

"Hi," she breathes, and it makes me unreasonably happy to have this effect on her. Thank fucking God, since there is a lump growing in my throat that shouldn't be there.

I'm electrified by the mere vision of this woman. *Jesus.*

Bundled in a thick black jacket, she looks smaller. I want to peel away every layer of her winter clothes to inhale the essence of her mixed with lavender.

"Hi," I rasp, and smile at her.

Fatima clears her throat and we both jump. Right, I fucking forgot about her. Mila jerks her head and steps back, her eyes darting between me and the lawyer.

"Ms. Ward, I'm Fatima Ayad, Mr. Cassinetti's legal counsel. Please come in."

Mila doesn't move, frozen with her gaze on me. She shakes her head. The slight gesture sucks all the air from my lungs. Fuck, I should have taken Paris's advice.

"Mila, hear me out." I extend my hand to her, but she doesn't take it.

"I told you I'm not one of your—"

"Ms. Ward, let's take this conversation inside. Or you're free to leave," Fatima says.

"No, she is not." I whip my head to my lawyer, and she rewards me with a glare that could kill a man.

"Gio," Fatima warns.

Mila sighs and flails her arms in an exasperated gesture. "For fuck's sake." She enters and I shut the door.

Two women now glare at me.

"Mila, I told you—"

"And I told you. I can't believe you blindsided me like this. Whatever your lawyer expects from me, it screams at me: lack of trust. How can we ever explore anything between us if you don't trust me? What have I done to make you believe you need to do this?"

"You need this job, and—"

"Ms. Ward," Fatima jumps in. "Due to Mr. Cassinetti's previous experiences, there is an NDA with certain conditions for you to review. I wouldn't call it a trust issue as much as an insurance policy. It outlines a code of conduct, and compensation if the relationship is terminated."

Mila gasps, and the awkwardness fills the room as Fatima holds the folder in front of her, but Mila doesn't reach for it.

In the bright yellow folder hangs my possible

future with this woman. Not even a future, a date. A fucking date. For a moment I consider shredding the damn thing into pieces, pulling Mila to me by that fucking, sexy ponytail and kissing the hell out of her.

The rational part of my brain, which is still recovering from the nightmare three years ago when my family suffered at the attempt to extort money from me, laughs at my romantic notion. There is nothing romantic about these arrangements, but I can make it up to her during the date.

What if she doesn't sign? Am I willing to let her go? Am I willing to risk dating her without strict legal parameters?

Glaring at me, Mila shakes her head again and snatches the folder. "Let me see it."

She sags into the sofa, the leather squeaking. Fatima drops to the seat across from her, elegantly crossing one leg over the other, not an ounce of empathy on her face. That's the reason I have her on my side—in the boardroom it's a valued attitude. Right now? I'm pissed she doesn't treat Mila with more respect.

Mila doesn't look my way, and for a moment I regret staying. Fatima has always handled this with my previous partners.

This doesn't compare. Before it was a social obligation, an arrangement. If those women objected, I wouldn't care either way. The irony is, I fucking trust Mila, I do. But haven't I trusted before? If she only knew how much I trusted. Like an idiot.

Mila raises her eyes. "I understand on principle, but it feels so wrong." She still doesn't look at me, and I'm pretty sure it's just to show me how I made her feel by bringing her here. I wanted the lawyer involved and here I am, a spectator to the situation.

Frustration vibrates through me. "You owe me a favor," I blurt.

Mila snaps her eyes to me, her eyebrows arched. Fatima opens her mouth, but I stop her with my hand.

I don't care about the audience. I look at Mila with all the want and need I've been harboring for weeks now. The initial shock and confusion give way to something new, different. A flicker of excitement sparks in her eyes.

She bites the inside of her mouth as she mulls this over, and this time her eyes don't move from mine. The simple look is filled with suggestion, with warmth and electricity. I have never been drawn to someone like this. With one look, she could have me on my knees.

The realization reverberates through me with a mixed aftertaste. Pure want, and a lot of self-loathing for allowing someone to get under my skin this much.

Her chin up, her eyes burning, she is a fucking queen.

"Remove the termination compensation from the contract," she instructs Fatima, her eyes never leaving mine.

"Gio?" Fatima's voice carries a warning.

"Remove it." I speak to my counselor, but I eat Mila up with my eyes, the anticipation zapping between us. An electric current that will burn us probably, but I don't care. I want to burn. With her.

Fatima murmurs something, her pen scratching across the paper, but it's happening in the background while my entire being is absorbed by the woman in front of me who is doing something she doesn't want to do. For me.

Fatima sighs. "I need you both to initial the change."

Mila blinks and turns her attention back to the papers. We follow Fatima's instruction to initial and sign.

My lawyer shakes her head at me, full of disapproval.

She says goodbye, but before she leaves, she turns to Mila. "This agreement is a personal modus operandi of Mr. Cassinetti, but you're on a freelance contract with this company. Our internal policies apply to you, and we have a strict no fraternization policy in place. You should think about your work here."

Whose lawyer is she? At the same time, I appreciate her warning Mila. Fatima glances my way again, and her eyes say she's not done with me, but I can explain my plans to her later. Now I want to make sure Mila is okay. That our relationship didn't suffer due to this dog-and-pony show.

Mila smiles at Fatima. "Thank you."

Fatima shakes her head and leaves, radiating disapproval. I don't fucking care.

"Thank you," I say as soon as the door closes.

Mila stands up, her eyes narrowed. "A bet is a bet. Did you think of this *particular* favor from the beginning?"

I nod and she shakes her head.

I adjust my cufflinks. "I didn't think owing me a favor would be enough for you to agree to this."

"Oh, so I should have resisted more?" Her eyes glisten with mischief.

"Or you can just do as I say," I say darkly and her breath hitches, but she smiles.

"You're my boss after all," she says playfully, her eyes bright with arousal, but as soon as the words are out, her face falls.

"Yeah, about that. The company is closed till January second. We'll keep this a secret and deal with the rest afterward."

She nods, thinking.

"I'm sorry, Princess. Regretting it already?"

We stand across from each other, the air filled with anticipation, a dash of regret, and anything but normal. I want to remove the short distance and bend her over my desk, but... I might have lost my head for this woman, but the last three years tested my restraints enough to refrain.

That doesn't mean my cock is on board. How do I get a semi just being in a room with her? No fucking self-control.

"Winesty?" Mila takes two steps and I mirror her action. Her scent washes over me, and if lavender ever had calming properties, they are lost on me.

I want to inhale her, consume her, devour her.

We are only a foot from each other, but I'm painfully aware we're in my office. There are cameras —because when the sharks snapped their jaws, I lost the little privacy I used to have here—and we can't be caught. I might have gotten her to sign the NDA, but I can't, in the span of half an hour, ask her to give up her job.

That bridge we cross after the date.

"Winesty." I nod, a smile tugging at my lips.

"Even though your conditions are all sorts of wrong, part of me understands you need the insurance. What made the difference, though?" She licks her lips. "I find it really hot that you stayed off the phone to get a date with me." That high-wattage smile blinds me. I'm a goner.

"Get your things now," I growl, startling her, but she obeys.

I march to the elevator, simultaneously typing a message for my driver and making sure Mila follows.

Once in the elevator, she steps into the corner, far away from the raging caveman I currently am. Smart girl.

"What's going on? Where are we going?" She cocks her head.

I don't look at her. I don't answer, because I'm focusing all my remaining sanity—and let's face it, not much is left—on not pouncing on her.

We get to the underground garage and my car is waiting by the elevator bank, the engine running, just as I instructed my driver.

He holds the door open for us and Mila hesitates for a moment, but then steps inside. She gasps, looking around at the custom-made pale leather interior.

She scoots to the opposite side of the seat. "Wow, this place is almost the size of my bedroom."

I push away the thought of immediately getting her a bigger place, and as soon as the car moves, I drag her to sit across my lap. "I have been waiting too long to do this."

I fist that bouncy ponytail and pull her to my

mouth. She tenses for a moment, but then melts against me, and I devour her like a man starved. Her soft lips feel like the most delicate pastry, exploding on my tongue with a promise and a dash of mischief.

She smiles against my lips, sighing with content. I should find some shred of control, but I gave up on that the minute she signed the fucking NDA.

I cup the back of her neck, angling her, molding her to me, and she fits. She fits perfectly, and a staggering realization rams through me like a tsunami wave.

I need to regain control if I want to survive Mila Ward.

Chapter 15

Mila

"I don't know if it's romantic or just plain wrong," Annie says. "Why did you agree?"

"For many reasons, but when I saw him pleading with his eyes, I thought I deserved better, but so does he. I agreed because that's the only way he believes we can explore this. But I'm going to show him he can have normal without a signed deal."

Annie sighs.

"Are you sure you'll be okay?" I take a dress from my closet and fold it carefully into my carry-on suitcase.

Sprawled on my bed, she smiles wickedly. "You're having a weekend date with the richest man in the city. Don't you dare to think about me. Enjoy every minute. You deserve it, and I need to experience it through you vicariously."

"But call me if you need anything. And he's not the richest man in the city." I search through my jewelry box.

"One of them. I looked up his net worth." A smile softens her face. It's so good to see her filled with a semblance of joy, I might have to date Giovanni Cassinetti just to feed her happiness.

I haven't seen Gio since the uncomfortable meeting with his lawyer and the wild make-out session in his car. I'm still not sure if it was a mistake to agree to his stupid conditions.

Who am I kidding? I haven't stopped thinking about him since California, and even after the post-accident adrenaline wore off properly, I was left with longing and an ache like never before.

It might be simple curiosity after the hot but prematurely thwarted foreplay at Danita's house, but I want to get more of Gio.

I try not to think about the man I got to know in Cali, under all the layers of professionalism and safety, masked by his scowls. Because there is no way a man like Gio would ever want more with me than what he's already offered.

And I'm fine with that. More than fine. He's powerful and controlling, and it would only be a question of time before he consumes me, takes over and manipulates me to his will. And then probably discards me.

For now, I allow myself to buzz with excitement and accept his advances, because for once in my life I can let a bit of selfishness creep in.

And then there are the gifts.

Jesus, the man has been sending flowers and food baskets. I wanted him to stop. He doesn't need to buy me, for fuck's sake. But Annie and the kids deserve every luxury, and then yesterday he won us over with the most thoughtful gesture.

Annie got a call from the office of the most prestigious rheumatologist in New York. Her waiting list is months-long, and Annie will see her in two short weeks.

If I didn't get to know him in California, I'd feel he's conniving, buying his way into my pants. Coercing my gratitude, so I do his bidding. And while I'm more than interested in doing his bidding, no coercing needed, the week we spent together made me believe he's simply generous.

Or really good at wooing. I'm well-wooed. Our business trip primed me like a horny teenager.

After spending time with him, I know these are honest gestures. He's trying to improve my life, and that's not something I want to allow into my heart, or my consciousness.

I can survive his dominance, his power, his general state of annoyance, but I won't survive his kindness if I let it get to me.

"I wish I knew what to pack." I puff air out from my cheeks.

"He hasn't given you a hint?"

"He asked if I have a passport, so I guess we're flying out of the country."

"Maybe he's taking you skiing, or shark swimming." Annie sits up and widens her eyes. "Or on a world tour. Rich people probably do that."

I laugh. "Yeah, I'm pretty sure you can't go on a world tour in two days."

"You should leave me his contact information. What if he brings you to his house and makes you his sex slave for the entire weekend?" she whispers, glancing at Aidan who is drawing in the corner.

"Annie," I reprimand, but my core clenches at the idea.

She grins. "That hot?"

"Stop it." I plop down beside her and we giggle together.

A bell chimes, its sound almost lost in our laughter. I jump up. "Oh God, is he early?"

"Or he sent more food." Annie chuckles and pads to the door while I try to organize my toiletries.

The lock clicks, the door swooshes open, and

Annie gasps. Aidan dashes to join her at the entrance. A low baritone rumbles through the room and I abandon the packing.

At the door, Annie is smiling like she's just won the lottery. Aidan hides behind her leg, peeking at our visitor.

"Hello—" The greeting dies on my lips. A tall, handsome—hot AF—stranger leans against the door frame. "Who are you?"

Annie giggles like a schoolgirl. "He's a nurse." Her voice is a high-pitched squeal.

"My name is Ron Ballard. I work for the Prestige Nursing Agency, and I was hired to help Mrs. Annie Ward this weekend. Is she your mother?"

"Who hired you?" I look at Annie, who is shy of fanning herself, grinning at the Adonis on our doorstep.

"Oh, just a second." Ron pulls out his phone, swipes a few times and then clicks. "We were hired by Mr. Cassinetti. Did I get the wrong address?"

"No," Annie squeals again.

"We were hired for the entire weekend, 24/7, but there is a note to discuss the needs with the client and not intrude. If you let me in, we can discuss your mother's needs."

For some reason I laugh, and Ron eyes me with a wary look.

"Yes, where are our manners, please come in?" Annie pushes me away from the door.

My phone beeps.

GIO

I'm downstairs

For a man who spends so much time on his phone, his mobile etiquette is severely lacking, but then he isn't warm in person. I grin at his message though, and that should concern me. *Pull it together, Mila.*

I'm not packed yet. Give me five.

You don't need anything. Get down here now.

Oh, someone is bossy.

I need nothing for a weekend? Where are we going?

My phone rings immediately.

"Mila," Gio growls without a preamble. "Get your ass here right now. Bring your phone and your passport. You need nothing else."

"But—"

He hangs up.

I shake my head, not even daring to analyze why

his bossiness turns me on. I look up to find Annie mesmerized by the sight in front of her.

Ron is squatting by Aidan who is explaining something to him. This, by itself, is outlandish, as Aidan barely speaks to people he knows, let alone strangers.

"Okay then, Ron, I guess I'll let you discuss Annie's needs with her." I nod at my sister, and Ron's eyes widen with understanding.

I rush to peek at Ellery, sleeping in her cot, and I hug Aidan.

At the door, equipped with my phone, passport and basic toiletries in my purse, I wrap my arms around Annie.

"Oh my God," she whispers into my ear.

"Do you want me to send him away?" I whisper back, concern creeping in.

"Don't you dare." She pulls away and glares at me.

I laugh. "See you soon."

As I push the front door of my building open, I get my second shock of the day.

Gio leans against a red Lamborghini, his legs crossed at his ankles. His leisurely stance emits pure masculinity. He's wearing jeans—jeans!—and a short navy blue cashmere coat, the most casual I've ever seen him. He might be *dressed down*, but the power floats around him naturally. No one would ever doubt he's a CEO.

He looks up and slides the phone into his pocket. His eyes crinkle, with a smile ghosting his face. Licking his upper teeth, he lets his hooded eyes devour me. Dark brown abyss.

His chin sports a five o'clock shadow, another first for him. I got glimpses of a relaxed Gio before, but nothing could have prepared me for this version.

My knees go weak and I stop, savoring the sight of him, overcome with trepidation. Or full-blown fear. I'm a Princess to him, but there is no doubt he's the king. God help me.

"Hi." He pushes off the car.

"Hi." I smile at him, and equally for me. To give myself confidence. "Nice ride."

He shrugs. "That she is. Only appropriate, given my special cargo today." His gaze rivals any predator's in nature, sending delicious shivers up my spine and spreading hot liquid in my core. "Ready?"

I don't think I am. I don't think I could ever be ready for this level of desire. Two minutes into this date and I'm ready to surrender. We stare at each other. Him dragging a languid, hot gaze down my body.

Me? I'm utterly at his mercy. I don't think I can be saved, but what's worse—I don't want to be.

I'm sure he can see my thoughts, because he smirks. "Let's go."

The smirk does it, and I somehow recover my normal human functions. "Wait, did you hire a stripper for my sister?"

He shakes his head. "What? I hired a nurse, so you don't have to worry about Annie all weekend."

He remembers her name. A thousand butterflies soar in my stomach. "Yeah, but they sent a male nurse. He doesn't even look like a nurse. She's fanning herself upstairs. He's so hot."

Gio grabs me around my waist and jerks me to him with a smirk. "Don't you fucking mention another man being hot in my presence."

Oh, the dominance oozes through his eyes, and I let it wash over me with a tremor of anticipation. He seizes my lips, possessive and urgent. Claiming me.

"Do you want me to cancel the nurse?" He pulls back, leaving me breathless.

"No, Annie would kill you."

He chuckles and opens the door for me.

"What is this place?" My feet sink into the plushest carpet I've ever stepped on. Soft wooden paneling mixes with silver silk padded walls in this luxurious room that could be a living room, if it wasn't for the glass displays of jewels and watches.

When Gio threw his car keys to a valet, I wasn't paying much attention, but we were at—or rather beneath—the flagship Saks Fifth Avenue store. Though I was pretty sure the store doesn't have underground parking.

We took the elevator to the top floor and a woman —who was clearly expecting us—took our coats and ushered us to this room. A living room? I would sit on one of the soft-looking white leather couches, but the carpet is light brown, and it seems ridiculous to stain it with outdoor shoes.

I wipe my hands on the side of my thighs and consider taking off my boots. Gio doesn't share my concerns and walks right to the double seat and makes himself comfortable.

"A store." He shakes his head slightly, probably annoyed. This version of him I know and can handle better.

"Obviously," I deadpan, and cross my arms over my chest. He doesn't elaborate, but before I can tell him what I think about this date so far—okay, minus the Lamborghini ride, that was cool—another woman enters.

"Mr. Cassinetti, so nice to see you again." She doesn't acknowledge me.

She's wearing a flawless blond bun at her nape, a haughty expression, and a black dress that looks simple but is clearly more expensive than anything I own.

Gio growls a greeting, frowning at her. "This is Ms. Ward. Open a file for her and get her packed for a weekend in the Caribbean."

She still doesn't look at me. A bitter taste spreads through my stomach. Gio's indifference and her ignorance roll around undigested. I have half a mind to storm away, if I knew which way to go to escape this humiliation.

What? The Caribbean?

"Any formal occasions?" The Haughty Bun asks.

"No, it's a casual weekend."

"I'll be right back." She gives him a perfect, blinding smile, and without sparing a glance in my direction she leaves.

Gio's eyes snap to me as soon as the door clicks behind her. "Come here, Princess." He pats the seat next to him.

I trudge across the room to join him, no longer worried about the carpet. The Haughty Bun can clean it, bitch.

"You don't enjoy shopping?" Gio pinches my chin between his finger and thumb and forces me to look at him.

Deep brown abyss. Full of softness.

I sigh. "I don't enjoy being blindsided and treated

like an accessory. She didn't even look at me, and you didn't really care to explain why we're here."

His eyes flicker with something while he takes in every inch of my face. His gaze is a gentle caress on my skin, and my apprehension melts against my will. God, this man sparks the entire scale of emotions in me, and he doesn't even have to try.

"You're a breath of fresh air, Mila." He pulls me closer and captures my lips with such possessiveness that I gasp against him.

He eats the sound and angles my head for better access. Both his hands hold me in position. His calloused skin ignites my cheeks.

You're a breath of fresh air. I worried about not matching up to his other women, but his words and this reverent kiss delete all those stupid preconceptions, shredding them into the stupid plush carpet.

A tap on glass pulls us from the stupor of lust, and Gio backs away but keeps bracketing my face. He lowers his forehead to mine, ignoring the audience. "Do you want us to leave?"

I shake my head no. This is his world, and I might feel like a fish out of water, but I want to experience his domain. All the other women he brought here were probably dazzled. I can't blame him for assuming I'd feel the same.

He touches my lips lightly one more time and

turns. Spreading his arms across the backrest, he leans back. He might be sprawled on the sofa casually, but there is nothing casual about the power he emits. A king in his court.

He assesses Haughty Bun, who keeps tapping her nails on the glass vitrine and then pulls his phone out, his expression utterly bored.

"Let us take your measurements and we'll bring out some pieces for you to try." She beckons a young man with tailor tape around his neck in my direction.

I stand up. "I'm size ten. Get me a swimsuit, beach dress, casual evening dress, two T-shirts and shorts. Let's get this all done in under fifteen minutes please." I smile at Haughty Bun, and she blinks several times.

"Shorts?" gasps Tailor Tape.

"Mr. Cassinetti?" Haughty Bun's question comes with a high-pitched edge.

Gio doesn't even look up. "You heard the lady. The clock is ticking." And while his voice carries his typical aloofness, a slight smile pulls at his lips.

Haughty Bun loses all color from her cheeks and jerks her head to her assistant, who scurries away. "We'll be right back, Ms. Ward."

While Gio continues to work, I peruse the glass cabinets. The pieces on display are elaborate, clad with stones of different shapes and sizes, but my eyes catch a simple chain with an intricate butterfly pendant of rose gold wires and tiny emeralds.

Tailor Tape wheels in a rack of clothes. Ha! The plush carpet is not very practical. He stops at the edge of the room by a door I didn't notice before. He pushes the rack inside of what looks like another living room and looks at me expectantly.

"The changing room," he stutters.

"Thank you." I smile at him. As awkward as this is, he's only doing his job. "I don't think I need to try anything. Let me see."

I prance over to him and start swiping through the hangers. I don't think the poor man has ever been so shocked, and I bite the inside of my mouth to stifle a laugh.

It only takes me two minutes to choose a few items. "I guess I would need sandals."

"And lingerie." Gio surprises us both. My eyes widen and heat spreads over my cheeks. I'm no prude, but Jesus...

"Of course." Tailor Tape runs away.

I put my hands on my hips. "Gio."

He looks up from his phone.

"You could have just told me we're going to the Caribbean and I could have packed all I need. This is ridiculous, and such a waste."

He flinches and crosses the room so fast I can't even react. He snakes his arm around my waist and yanks me to him. His solid muscles envelope me in his masculine scent, and I almost moan from the sheer explosion of sensations.

"I wanted to treat you, and for future reference, you will always let me treat you." The dark undertone in his voice rumbles through me, settling with heat in my core. My breath hitches and I nod. "Besides, nothing is a waste when it comes to you, Princess."

* * *

"Thank you, Tarek, that will be all. We'll see you tomorrow." Gio dismisses the personal chef who has just prepared a four-course dinner for us.

"Actually, if it's okay, I'd like to cook tomorrow." I bite my lip.

I can't really cook, but I was hoping to spend time alone with Gio. We were alone in the Lambo, but that's about it. The personal shopping assistants, the flight crew, the driver, the chef, the housekeeper. Ever since we've arrived in this paradise, someone has been around.

I want to experience Gio in his own domain, with all these comfortable and at times annoying luxuries, but this is our first date. Call me selfish, but I want the man for myself.

Gio raises his eyebrow and quirks his lips. "You heard the lady. We won't need you tomorrow."

Tarek leaves and we're finally alone, and the awkwardness settles. In the middle of a Caribbean paradise, I feel slightly out of place. I'm not even sure why, but I guess with all the *catering*, I haven't digested where we are. Or who I'm with.

An infinity pool glistens, with flickering lights illuminating the large terrace. Below us a private white-sand beach stretches into the waves of the Atlantic. The bungalow—as Gio called it—is a huge U-shaped structure of white walls and glass. In fact, the terrace, surrounded by the house itself, feels like a part of the interior.

It's beautiful, luxurious, and bursting with decadence everywhere. I'm in love with the view already, and I could get used to it all quickly. Which only reminds me I shouldn't.

I don't know how long Gio will indulge me, so I need to force myself to enjoy with restraint. The last thing I need is getting over the man *and his lifestyle* at the same time. God, I'm shallow.

Gio snakes his hands around my waist, his heat caressing my back. He kisses the crown of my head and pleasant shivers tingle my skin. "Penny for your thoughts."

I chuckle and lean into him, enjoying the feel of him. The breeze. The smell of the ocean mingling with his smoke and spice scent. "I thought you dealt in more zeros than that."

He snorts. "That doesn't mean I wouldn't value a penny."

Butterflies. Heat. Weak knees. This man. Jesus.

I turn around and cup his face. He's breathtaking. Especially this version, with relaxed features, crinkles around his eyes, and the dark brown softened into delicious chocolate.

"It's beautiful here. Thank you for bringing me." I rise on my tiptoes and kiss him.

He tightens his embrace, spreading his large hands across my back, pulling me to him as he deepens the kiss. We both moan at the same time.

"I'm glad you're here with me, Princess. Winesty?"

I lift my eyebrows. "Oh man, this date hasn't even started, and you have something to confess?"

He laughs, and I take a mental snapshot because Gio confirms why rare things have increased value.

"I want your winesty, Mila."

I frown and he kisses my forehead. "You say you're glad to be here, but ever since I picked you up this morning, I've yet to enjoy the carefree woman I spent time with in California. What's going on?"

I sigh and lower my head to his chest. I thought I was hiding it well enough. I look up and scrunch up my face, but that has never made things easier.

"Gio, I don't want to sound ungrateful, because everything you planned for me today was wow and dazzle, but I wanted to spend time with you. I appreciate all the gestures and luxuries, I really do, but it's also hard to accept, and I want you, not the things."

He captures my lips with an urgency that takes my breath away.

Heat. Grace. Reverence.

"Jesus, woman, we need to find a compromise. I want to treat you."

"Maybe fewer keepers and more of you, the real you, would be a compromise." I lick my lips.

"Just you and me for the rest of the weekend, Princess."

I grin. "Thank you."

He dips me and I yelp as we fall onto the sofa, kissing. It's a playful kiss, a tease really, but as Gio finds the hem of my dress and his warm, possessive hand scorches the skin of my thigh, I sigh.

He doesn't travel farther, just devours my mouth, digging his fingers into my flesh. We have done nothing beyond kissing yet, but somehow I feel like he's claimed me already.

His touch.

His kiss.

His gaze.

They are possessive, all-consuming, and I don't mind any of it. Somehow, I know I won't survive resisting, and I probably won't survive surrendering.

But as the trail of his kisses down my neck leaves goosebumps on my skin and ignites an inferno in my core, I know I can't stop anymore. The only way to take my next breath is to let this man guide me to it.

Broken walls, shattered pretenses, cracked masks and all.

Gio pulls away and studies me with a piercing look. I don't know what he sees, but his gaze is softer than I've ever seen, and yet somehow harder, as if an internal war was brewing within him. I feel I'm at the center of that battle, but I have no idea if I'm pointing the gun or waving the white flag.

"We should eat our dinner."

I blink a few times. "What? I'm not hungry."

Gio chuckles and the cloud disappears from his face. "Of course you're not. You're going to fight me over every meal, aren't you?"

"Are you going to push a protein bar on me?" I bite my lip, leaving the strange darkness behind.

A shadow erases his smile. The predator is back. The glare hits me right in my center. "I can think of better things to thrust into that pretty mouth of yours." The timbre of his voice reverberates every single fiber in my taut body.

"Promises," I breathe.

And then I scream.

Chapter 16

Mila

My scream is the only reaction I manage as Gio jumps up and hoists me over his shoulder. "What are you doing?"

He slaps me and I squeal and—

Splash!

I inhale before the water swallows me. Bastard. The buoyancy propels me back up, and I flail my arms before I finally gain the grace to float. I dip my head backward to tame my hair.

Wiping my face, I look up just as a wave sloshes over me, almost taking me back under. He jumped in after me.

The brief annoyance with his silly antics dissipates, because the playfulness of the moment squeezes at my heart. This side of the growling boss, always annoyed and short with people, is fun and carefree.

And it's not the behavior that swells inside my chest, it's the fact he chose me to see it. To be a part of it.

Gio reemerges in front of me, wrapping his arms around me, fusing his lips with mine. The water stills around us. He discarded his shirt and pants. I wish I could admire his almost naked body.

I wrap my legs around his waist, and he digs his fingers into my behind, supporting me, but also claiming me inch by inch. Oh, and I'm more than willing to give it to him.

My short, yellow summer dress clings to me, an annoying barrier between us. I need to feel him completely, his velvety skin against mine. I start yanking at my dress and Gio chuckles.

"My beautiful Princess is needy. Desperate," he rasps, approval quivering through his tone. "Let me help you." He grips the neckline, rips the dress in two, and pushes it off my shoulders.

I gasp and laugh. Leaning back with my arms stretched, I let the water take the remains of the fabric.

Sunset colors the sky in all the shades of orange. The air is warm, but my nipples react anyway, pebbling with need.

Sun-kissed. Gio-kissed. Completely blissed.

"You're perfect," he says. I float as Gio runs his hand between my breasts, down my navel into the waistband of my underwear. "Fucking perfect." He leans in and kisses my belly button.

His words lick at my center, liquid heat and tantalizing desire. His cock twitches against my core, and I realize he is completely naked.

He lets go of my behind. The water and my legs around him hold me as I coast. I want to see his face, but I love how without watching him, every touch, every kiss, every move is a surprise.

His hands are all over me, kneading, squeezing, caressing. His warmth radiates through me, pooling at my center.

"I need you," I moan.

"Patience, Princess," he growls, but his erection hardens against me. Knowing I have this effect on him makes me smile. Patience, my ass.

My skin is so sensitive, so primed, that a slight breeze of ocean air could make me come. Gio walks backward to the corner of the pool, pulling me with him. I outstretch my arms, the water threading around me.

I'm weightless. I'm fearless. I'm a goddess.

He reaches the rounded corner stairs and scoops me up. I straddle him, our bodies flush against each other. Gio takes my nipple between his teeth, and even through the fabric of my lacy bra, the sensation is a pure ache, spreading down.

I gasp and arch my back.

"So responsive," he grates, and gives attention to my other nipple. He unclasps my bra and leans back, his eyes full of lust and wonder. The way he looks at me is... I don't know, it's like I'm the only woman in the world. Like he cherishes the chance to savor this view. This moment.

"Fuck." The rumble of his voice is primal. Carnal. Almost dangerous, but instead of scaring me, it draws me closer.

"Let's," I breathe, and he lifts his gaze.

Burn. Scorching coals. Dark brown abyss.

He cups my neck, yanks me closer, and eats the gasp I utter. His kiss is punishing, as if I dared to rush this with my *let's fuck*, and now he'll kiss me senseless. It's not like I have any sense left, anyway.

Or senses are all that's left of me.

I reach between us, desperate to be filled with more of him. But Gio grips my wrist and somehow flips us over. In one move, the dynamics have changed. I'm on all fours and he is behind me, his cock digging into the flesh between my thighs.

Gio spreads my knees apart, and several sensations explode at the same time. Somehow I ended up with my ass above the water, and the ripples are now stimulating my clit through the thin fabric of my panties, cold and hot. I'm on my elbows, and a similar pleasure tortures my nipples.

Gio covers my back with his solid form and nuzzles my neck, inhaling me, licking and biting. When he rears back, I groan at the sudden loss of contact, and he chuckles. His hands caress my behind, just a feather touch that drives me crazy.

I swear I'll come from the breeze and water and pure anticipation. The man has no mercy.

"Please," I beg, practically whining.

The bastard chuckles, sinks his fingers into the waistband of my underwear and yanks, tearing them apart.

"Are you going to destroy all my clothes?" My question ends on a whimper as he slides his fingers through my folds.

"I'll replace them."

He grips my hips, halting me as I try to lean into him, yearning for him shamelessly.

"Don't move," he demands, and then his hands are gone, and a splash of water sends more ripples toward my sensitive center and I whimper again.

"Gio," I growl, and get his laugh as a response.

It comes from a distant angle, and I look back to find him floating two feet away.

"What the fuck?"

He laughs again. "I said don't move. I fucking need

to admire that beautiful pussy of yours."

I turn and launch at him, but he clamps me in his arms before I manage to sink him. I wrestle for a useless moment. I have no chance against him.

He hurries back to the stairs, sits me on the top step, hoists my legs over his shoulders and leans in.

He spreads my folds and blows. His breath, the breeze, the water, the ache he hyped up, it all collides into a shudder that rakes through me, ending on a gasp.

"Is this what you want, Princess? My mouth between those beautiful legs of yours?"

I nod, and he smirks.

"You only need to ask, sweetheart."

Our eyes lock. When I remain silent, he quirks his eyebrow.

It's not lost on me that he gave me a new wardrobe, a weekend getaway in the Caribbean, a nurse and a doctor for my sister, Christmas lunch, and God knows what without me asking, yet he wants me to beg for the one thing we both want. We crave.

Our silent duel stretches, and I fight the urge to moan as every ripple is getting me closer to the precipice. My chest heaves and my arms shake as I lean onto my elbows more, trying to gain some control.

His dominance sucks up all the air. Everything has been going according to his rules. His expectations. His limitations. Even wild with desire, I can't let him win this one. I'm not begging, even though my body screams for him.

"Maybe you should ask nicely if I'll let you eat my pussy." My voice is not as confident as the request itself, but the question empowers me, regardless.

Something dark passes through Gio's face, and for a second I almost beg, fearing that instead of fucking me, he'll drown me. But then something akin to admiration settles on his face.

"Would you allow me the honor of fucking you with my mouth, my fingers, and my cock, Princess?" The need in his voice spreads through me like a wildfire.

"I thought you'd never as—" I lose my voice, my sanity, my thoughts. Myself. As he dives in and eats me like I am the most decadent dessert on Earth.

His firm hold on my hips. His talented tongue. The gentle splashing around us. The soothing sun. My mind offers only disjointed fragments of this moment as I become liquid.

Only feelings. Only heat. Wanton desire.

He sucks, licks, grazes his teeth in all the right places. I writhe and thrash, trying to escape the sensual overload. The last rays of sunshine tickle my skin, but it might as well be the middle of a cold night because nothing else exists, just this man.

His name leaves my lips as I scream my way

through a steamroller of an orgasm, but Gio doesn't stop prolonging my pleasure.

He kisses me gently on my thighs, up my navel, around my nipples as I slowly come down, completely languid, limbless. He scoops me up with care and easily walks out of the pool.

I bury my face in the crook of his neck, completely blissed out.

"Where are we going?" I murmur.

"To get condoms."

He pads through the living room down the hallway to the master bedroom, leaving a trail of wet footprints. Without finesse, he drops me on the bed.

"Hey, I'm wet."

He pounces on me. "I hope so."

We grin for a moment, the heaviness of his body on me comforting and safe.

"Fuck me senseless, Mr. Cassinetti."

He smirks, reaches to the nightstand's drawer and pulls out a large box. My eyes widen, but I don't ponder over the quantity of condoms. I snatch one from him. "Let me."

I rip the package open with my teeth and sit up.

Gio's gaze slides over my skin like a honeyed wrap. I sheath his cock, slowly sliding the condom over the impressive girth. Okay, he's fucking big.

"Don't worry, Princess, we'll fit perfectly." He picks up on my hesitation.

We'll fit perfectly. I don't think he meant more than fucking, but somehow it feels like he did. Might have. I don't get a chance to explore the statement further, because he lays me back and hovers above me before he hooks his arms under my knees, raising them over his shoulders, and fills me to the hilt.

We both groan. He was right.

We fit perfectly.

"So tight. Such a perfect pussy." Gio thrusts and continues whispering smutty words of praise. I swear the man hasn't said this much to me in weeks, but his velvety timbre complements his ravishing and piston-like tempo perfectly.

I didn't think I could get there again after the pool, but another explosion coils around my center as he increases the tempo. I'm sinking into oblivion again when he withdraws.

"Please," I whimper, which earns me another chuckle.

He flips me around and pushes between my shoulder blades with one hand while jutting up my hips with the other. He plunges into me and sets a punishing rhythm.

The pool water and our sweat soak into the silky

sheets, the slaps of our naked bodies reverberating around the room as we both chase release.

He reaches around me and pinches my clit. "Come for me, Princess."

"Gio!" His name on my lips does it for him, and as I clench around him he lets go, pulsing inside me.

We collapse, tangled limbs, erratic breaths, and satisfied grins. He rolls over and leaves. The water runs, the lid on the waste basket claps, and then he comes back with a wet cloth.

He flips me over and kisses the insides of my thighs, before he places the warm cloth between my legs, wiping me clean and ripping my heart out with aftercare I never would have expected from him.

He throws the towel to the floor, lies on his back and gathers me to him. He kisses my forehead. "Give me a moment and we can go again."

I laugh, raising my chin. His eyes are full of mischief.

"If I only knew your workaholic tendencies stretch to the bedroom..."

He fists my hair and drags me to his lips, kissing me with fervor and urgency as if it was our first kiss.

The air explodes with joy, and I'm almost scared that coming down from this high would be a life-threatening endeavor. Hopefully my heart is strong enough.

Something scratches my shoulder and I pull away.

Gio got another condom and he's tapping my shoulder with it.

"Overachiever," I quip, and he flips me over and clasps both my hands above my head.

"Are you complaining?"

I purse my lips to the side. "Hmmm…" I pretend to think about it, but my theatrics are short-lived.

Gio bites my nipple hard, and I yelp. And then he delivers enough evidence to squelch any complaints. Not that I had them to begin with. But his proof—multiple times—strips me of any doubts that this man is shallow.

He's deep and profound in everything he does. Fucking included.

I'm humming with contentment, sprawled in the most comfortable bed. Gio draws lazy circles on my thigh. We're lingering somewhere between sleep and wakefulness, both of us too spent to continue the orgasm marathon, but refusing to succumb to the darkness.

I don't know how long we've been lying here. We don't even talk anymore, just a few lazy words here and there.

The bedroom isn't large, but it has two glass walls and feels—as the rest of the house does—like an extension of the outdoors. We haven't drawn the shutters. On one side, the dark ocean glimmers on the horizon with a few lights from the yachts anchored around for the night.

The pool lights flicker behind the glass, lending the room just enough light to cast shadows around.

"Is this your house?" I turn to meet Gio's eyes.

"No, it belongs to my friend Conrad and his wife. I've only been here twice before. For a weekend when Conrad thought he lost his girl and needed to get drunk, and then again for their wedding." The mindless caress of his calloused fingers is hypnotic. I might meow.

He narrows his eyes. "Why are you smiling?"

I bite my lower lip.

"Winesty, Princess." He pinches my chin between his thumb and index finger, locking me in his gaze.

I groan. "I'm the first woman you brought here. It makes me feel ridiculously accomplished." I show him my tongue, to soften the neediness.

Gio laughs. "Princess, you're accomplished for many other reasons. And I assure you, you don't need to be jealous of anyone."

I know it's just words. I know that I'm so blissfully and thoroughly fucked, my mind is missing common sense and rationale, but somehow this date feels special. More special than he's had with his other women. I wish there were no other women. I don't want to think about them.

"Mila," he growls. "The winesty continues. I can see the war behind those beautiful eyes."

"The NDA..." Am I really going to go there?

"What about it?" He stops drawing the circles. I haven't even said anything and the air in the room has shifted. Gio's shoulders tense. He's studying me with hooded eyes, but his jaw is rigid.

"It doesn't mention exclusivity..." I recoil as if the words were poison despite my uttering them. I don't know why I'm so insecure about this. I don't want to see Gio withdrawing now when we've just woven a fragile net of understanding and togetherness.

"I didn't particularly care." He shrugs and rolls on to his back, covering his eyes with his forearm.

I guess that's that. Deflated, I admire his tensed features for a moment, and then turn my back to him, hoping I can fall asleep. I don't make it halfway before his strong hands grab me.

I yelp, my back sinking into the sheets as Gio's weight pins me down. The fire in his eyes is intoxicating. I know it would burn me, but I can't help leaning into it. Flames. Inferno. Pure lava of lust.

"I didn't care. Until now." He kisses me roughly. "And make no mistake, Princess. You as much as look at another man and I'll destroy the fucker."

There is no doubt in my mind that his threat is serious. I should recoil and run, but instead my lips stretch into a smile. I've just gotten a vow of exclusivity from Giovanni Cassinetti. I can't claim it was the most conventional declaration, but then he doesn't really do normal.

"There is no one else, Gio."

He seizes my lips and things escalate quickly. Who needs to sleep anyway.

Chapter 17

Gio

"**O**h my God."

Mila's squeal penetrates my sleep, and when her foot painfully connects with my thigh, the awakening is complete.

"What's going on?" I push up on to my elbows, the pleasant breeze tickling my naked ass. When was the last time I slept naked and woke up next to a woman?

And what a woman! Mila's mussed hair and swollen lips, her silky face irritated from my whiskers are adorable. She clutches the sheets, covered up to her neck, and stares beyond my shoulder.

"Mila, baby, did you have a nightmare again?" I get to my knees and try to gather her in my arms.

"Put something on. Someone is by the pool," she shrieks.

What the fuck? I turn and chuckle, plopping back

to the bed and pulling her to me. "It's just Conrad's security. I guess they do the rounds at this hour. Why aren't you sleeping?"

"Why are they here?" She tries to arrange the sheets around us in a desperate attempt at decency.

A memory of my weekend here with Conrad pre-Nora flickers through my mind, and I'm pretty sure that the guard has seen my ass and more. Not that I want those memories here right now.

"Because we're here. He has a firm to handle the security, so I didn't bring mine."

She lifts her head, still clutching the sheets under her chin. On the second thought, fuck my ass, I hope the guard didn't ogle Mila's naked body. Annoyed, I look outside and push the button by my nightstand.

The engine hums and the shutters roll down.

"Come back to sleep, Princess." I wrap her in a tight embrace. Another first. Since when do I cuddle?

She pulls back, frowning. "What do you mean you didn't bring your security?"

"Just that." I shake my head, tired as fuck. I indulge her twenty questions more often than is reasonable, but not now.

"You have bodyguards?" Her voice is too awake for... I glance at the clock on the nightstand... for three o'clock.

"I'm glad you're catching up, but can we sleep?" I

growl. Usually when I growl, people shut up. Of course, that's not the case with Mila.

"How come I've never seen them?"

"I pay them a premium to be invisible." I pull her head into the crook of my neck, hoping to smother any further inquiries.

"They were with us in California?"

"Yes. Have mercy, woman, let's sleep. I'll give you a full brief on my security in the morning."

She mumbles something unintelligible, or my brain is half-asleep already. But her whisper jerks me back to reality.

"It's good we closed the shutters. The sunrise would wake us up."

I chuckle. "Yes, genius, though I guarantee you can't see sunrise from the same window you watched the sunset."

Mila tenses in my arms before she dissolves into laughter. It rings around the room like a symphony, and even my tired brain catches the melody and I laugh, I'm not sure why.

"Gio Cassinetti, it's official, you fucked my brains out." She leans in and kisses me, the laughter still reverberating through her soft lips.

Okay, perhaps there are women who are worth sleep deprivation. I deepen the kiss and decide I won't get up in an hour to work. Fuck the routine for one day.

Fuck the work. I have much better things to do. To fuck.

* * *

"I still can't believe I didn't notice them." Mila shakes her head.

I explained to her how my security team flew to Cali the day before us to familiarize themselves with the event locations, and how I gave them a day off for the Napa visit because the helicopter was booked under an alias, so it was deemed low risk. I should fire them. Even though I know they didn't cause the chopper's malfunction.

"That means they do their job." I run my hand up and down her shoulder, reaching down over her chest. I give one nipple a tug and Mila arches into me.

We are on a lounge bed by the pool, and I enjoy having her between my legs, leaning her back into me. Somehow, the cuddling has stretched unnecessarily past the bedroom. And strangely, I don't mind.

"But what's the threat?"

"Once you have a lot of money, there is always blackmail, crazy shit, but nothing serious." Jesus, is she scared? I nudge her chin up to look at me. "You're safe with me, Mila. Trust me. I'll talk to the guards to make sure they do their rounds more discreetly. I promised yesterday this weekend would be just you and me."

I kiss her, and my cock salutes, poking at Mila's back. She giggles. I'm a fucking teenager. Cuddling, and unable to control the lust.

"About that... I really appreciate that you dismissed Tarek and the housekeeper, but I don't really know how to cook." She bites her lip, grinning.

"You lied!" I mock my horror. Playful, horny teenager. Kill me now. "I'll just have to feast on your sweet pussy and feed you my cock."

She laughs and flips to her knees, dropping her hands on the armrest on each side of me. Wiggling her ass in the air, she leans down to my lips, but without as much as brushing them, she leans back. A wanton smile splitting her beautiful face.

I suck in sharply when she cups my cock. "Perhaps I should have a taste first."

I fist her hair and drag her in for a kiss, smarting her lips with my teeth. She's delicious, the innocence in her eyes in such contrast with the free personality. "You do that, Princess. We need to make sure you don't go hungry."

Dirty talk is part of the game for me, but I swear I haven't talked this much in years. It's official—Mila Ward, with her smile, annoying chatter, and body made for sin, has ruined me.

She hooks her fingers in the waistband of my briefs and looks down. My dick springs out and her eyes sparkle. The woman is genuinely excited to see and taste my cock.

It's not pretense or quid pro quo. The need and want in her eyes make me groan when she takes me into her beautiful mouth. I went down on her yesterday in the pool without even expecting her to reciprocate. Another rare occasion. Yeah, definitely ruined.

She hums with pleasure, and I almost blow from the sound.

A different sound brings things to an abrupt halt. Mila's eyes widen and she lets go, my cock popping out of her mouth. "Is someone at the door?"

"Yeah, let me get it." I stand up and put on my robe, my erection tenting it. I lean down and kiss her, and she groans.

"If it's another keeper to do God knows what, I'm packing up and spending the day on the beach." She pouts, and oh, I want to spank that pout off her face.

But I know who is at the door, so I file that idea for later.

When I return with the package, Mila sits at the edge of the pool, tracing the water with her feet. I don't know what got into me when I threw her in there yesterday. Fuck, another out of character behavior.

When I was making my coffee this morning, I started tallying up all the unusual behaviors, starting with sitting on the grass in Santa Barbara, or perhaps even before. But then she came out of the room, all wrinkled from sleep, and my mind sank into my briefs.

This should concern me, but I haven't felt this uninhibited, this liberated in so long, I can't help but appreciate the recharging it offers. Perhaps there is something to slowing down.

"Who was it?" Mila looks up, smiling.

"Delivery for you." I drop the package to the lounger.

"What is it?" She frowns, stands up and pads across the tiled floor to get to the box.

Snaking my arm around her waist, I stop her with a kiss. "It's new underwear and a few more dresses."

She raises an eyebrow. "Why?"

"Number one." I kiss her. "I destroyed your underwear and the dress yesterday." Another kiss. "Number two, you were annoyingly frugal when I took you shopping, so I needed to rectify that." Another kiss. "Number three, I plan to destroy more of your clothes."

"Is that so?" She beams. God, that high wattage smile of hers is addictive.

"Yes. Until I figure out how to keep you permanently naked." I seize her lips. "Now, let me call Tarek to make sure we don't starve."

"I was hoping we could go into town." She cocks her head, biting her bottom lip.

"Town?" I frown.

"Come on, Gio, please." With everything I've paid for her, given her, gifted her, the idea of discovering the small, touristy town makes her eyes sparkle.

"Okay, Princess, I'll wine and dine you in town tonight."

"And let's stroll the streets." She bounces with excitement. Fuck me. "It's probably my last time in St. Martin, I'd like to see the place."

I chuckle, her joy rubbing off on me. "We'll come again." I kiss her forehead.

She beams at me.

Fuck. Did I just make a commitment?

There is no way I'm going dancing. I said that an hour ago, and here I am, twirling this beautiful woman around.

Mila is tipsy, and she shimmies around me with that look of adoration as if I'm the only man on the planet. She grinds her hips against me and then spins again, all innocence, smiling seductively.

We're at a small club, with a bar on one side and several booths around it, but all the guests are on the dance floor. Sin and sex fill the air, and I'm pretty sure several couples left already to fuck in the dark crooks and crannies of this dingy place.

I would have never stayed here, but Mila dived onto the dance floor the minute we entered, so here we are. A first for me.

One of many today. I didn't work. I ate fish pastries on the street. I walked, for no apparent reason but to look around. Though most of the time I was looking at Mila.

She drank in the whole place with all her senses. Touching colorful tchotchkes in front of the souvenir stores. Inhaling the ocean air as if she could store it for later. Tasting way too much food from the street vendors.

Chatting with them about their day and listening to musicians on the small square as if it was a symphony concert at Carnegie Hall.

And I did all of it with her. Okay, I didn't touch anything but her and the food.

"It's so nice..." she whispers to my ear, but then moves away, teasing me with her swaying hips.

I yank her closer, and this time I snake my arms around her, not letting her float away again. "What's so nice?" Whispering into her ear, I inhale the scent of her. Fucking lavender will be the death of me.

Mila tilts her head, her mouth almost brushing mine. "To see you smile."

I kiss her, grasp her hand and push her away, twirling her under my arm and pulling her closer again. I execute the dance move to give myself time to assess her words. I'm fucking smiling.

Mila Ward is going above and beyond to give me a taste of normal, and I'm not sure I want that. Once she's gone I might miss this, and that's not an option for me. She is a satisfying distraction from my life, but I can't get used to this.

Can I? I better call Conrad to get an update on that event company.

Mila gyrates her hips against me, shimmying up and down, and my cock stirs. Fuck it.

I pull her up roughly and she yelps, her eyes wide.

"We're going home. Now."

She laughs, throwing her head back and losing her balance. I catch her, pulling her closer. "What's funny, Princess?"

"I'll go home if you ask me nicely."

"Or I can throw you over my shoulder and punish you for defying me."

It takes a second of her irises dilating with dark desire before I hoist her over my shoulder and carry her out of the place. Caveman-style.

* * *

"Okay, gentlemen, that's good progress. Send me an update later today and let's offload the dead wood. Thank you, everyone. Let's schedule another catch-up in a week's time." I end the conference call with my European associates.

"You're working," Mila's hoarse voice comes from the opening to the pool. She is wearing one of my shirts, and fuck she looks delicious, her nipples begging for my attention through the white fabric. Her skin is slightly tanned already, the crease from the pillow case making her look young and innocent.

"Good afternoon, Princess." I walk across and kiss her.

She rubs her eyes. "Have I slept too long?" She yawns and I chuckle, kissing her forehead.

"No problem, I needed to get some work done."

"Aren't you hot?" She runs her nails around the buttons of my vest.

"I'm not wearing my suit jacket."

She shakes her head. "I can't believe you worked while in this paradise in the first place, but why would you dress up for it?" She runs her hands over my chest, and lust pools between my legs.

"Not wearing a suit jacket is as casual as I'd go for a conference call."

She raises to her tiptoes and kisses me, just brushing her lips against mine. Her scent of lavender and me drifts to my nose, spreading in my chest.

"You'd get the same amount of work done, and I bet have the same authority in a T-shirt. And perhaps people would get more relaxed around you. Not that I don't love your vest. It's hot."

I don't see myself working in a T-shirt, like ever. But I don't ponder that, because the way she breathes out *it's hot* hits me right in my groin. Shame there is no time. "I'll make you coffee and you go and pack. The car is picking us up in two hours." I kiss the top of her head.

Her shoulders sag and her face falls, and I'm gripped by an urge to fix that. She turns, but I grab her arm and pull her to me.

"What is it?"

She looks toward the ocean, avoiding my eyes. With my finger, I nudge her face to look at me.

"Winesty?" She bites her lip and I nod. "It's so beautiful here and we don't really need to go back, so I was hoping we would stay. Maybe celebrate the New Year here?" A blush spreads across her face.

"I have work." It's out before I think about it. I've never taken more than a day or two away. Aside from Lake Como every summer, where I work for a month.

She studies me for a moment, all the joy gone. She

nods, but then stops herself and rises to kiss me again. This time she teases with her tongue while running her hand down my body. She cups my cock and I hiss.

"Tell me, Mr. Cassinetti, will someone die if you stayed three more days?"

She works on my belt, and I want to stop her, but... well, I don't want her to stop. "No," I croak.

"Will you break any social engagements that would fall apart without you?" She unzips my pants.

My nostrils flare and I fist her hair, forcing her to look at me. I shake my head.

"I see," she croons. "Will you lose a lot of money?" She puts her finger into her mouth and licks it, before she lowers it down and draws circles at the tip of my cock with her saliva.

I breathe in sharply. Little vixen. "Perhaps."

"Hmm..." She scrunches her lips to the side and continues to tease my cock. "I wonder, Mr. Cassinetti, how much is time with me worth to you?"

Is she going to negotiate with me? Fuck me. Clever girl.

She pulls down the waistband of my briefs and fists my length. "No one dies, no one will really miss you, so how much are three more days worth to you?"

I wouldn't really lose any money if I stayed. Not much would change if I moved a few things, and probably some of my coworkers would enjoy unexpected free time. I'm used to working because that's my happy place. But right now... only three days.

Fuck me. I grip Mila's ass roughly and hoist her up. She wraps her legs around my waist. My pants fall to the ground and I shake them off. I turn with her in my arms, and the brilliant sun reflecting off the water blinds me. But I'm probably blind already.

Mila yelps as her back hits the glass wall. "If you take care of my cock, Princess, the three days are priceless."

Chapter 18

Mila

With my eyes still closed, I turn and sigh, sliding my hand to the side. The silky sheets are cool and smooth under my fingers. I frown. There are just the sheets, and Gio's side of the bed is cold.

I sit up. Six o'clock in the morning. The man doesn't stop working. Ever. I pull my ridiculously useless—in terms of coverage—nightie over my head and pad out of the bedroom.

In the last two weeks, I've discovered Gio's house pretty well. I even met most of his staff despite the fact that we're still keeping our relationship a secret. I guess they have NDAs as well.

The light seeps under his office door and I can hear his deep rumble. He must be on a call with Europe or Asia. I turn to leave him to it and perhaps start coffee, but then I bite my lip and turn the door handle, pushing the door slightly and squeezing through.

He sits at his desk across the room by the wall of windows. Talking to someone on a video call, he doesn't notice me. He's wearing a crisp white shirt, but no tie, and under the table he is in his flannel pajama pants. The image tugs at my lips. This is way too casual for him.

His broad shoulders are tense, and I doubt myself for a moment. Perhaps I shouldn't interrupt an important discussion or presentation.

I step back and end up knocking the door closed. *Click.* Gio flicks his eyes to me, and they widen before he gets back to the screen.

"Could you explain their conditions to me again?" He frowns at the screen. I'm intruding, so I turn to leave, but his next words stop me. "I'm sorry, I'll have to turn off the video, I'm having problems with the connection. Do you believe the negotiations are still salvageable?"

The person on the line answers and I pivot around slowly. When my eyes meet with Gio's, shivers explode all over my skin. He is far from me, but the heat reaches me with delicious intensity.

He leans back. The king in his court, his eyes eating up every single part of me, leisurely admiring and taunting at the same time. He is daring me to make a move. He killed the video and now he wants to see what I'll do.

"Of course. That's an excellent suggestion." His words jerk me out of my lusting indecision. And while he's having a conversation with the person on the other side, he continues to fuck me with his eyes.

The man can multitask.

Two can play that game. I drop to my knees and Gio hisses. The person on the other line doesn't seem to notice, droning on about leverage, assets, liquidity.

I lick my lips and lower to my hands and knees. Gio's eyes burn now, scorching my body, while an inferno swirls between us.

His desk is a large glass surface with four chrome legs. His PJ pants are tented with his solid response to me. I smile at him, and his Adam's apple bobs up and down. He answers a question on the line.

I don't really hear the words, but I take it as a challenge. I want him to lose control. The thought propels me forward. Slowly placing one hand and knee forward, I crawl to him, my hips swaying. Not for a moment do I leave his gaze.

I make it to his desk and hesitate for a moment, but his eyes on me are like an aphrodisiac and I don't want to break the connection, so I raise to my feet. Gio pushes his chair back, making room for me.

I can walk around, but that wouldn't be fun. I

push my knee onto his desk and hoist myself up, crawling toward him. He inhales sharply but doesn't reach for me. We're not touching, but his gaze grazes me with reverence, and lust so strong my skin burns.

Slowly, elegantly, I lower my ass to his desk and pivot, so I can glide my legs to his side of the table. I stay seated at the edge and find his raging erection with my foot.

Gio stifles another sharp breath and the person on the other line has to repeat a question. I rub my foot against his hard cock, and he grits out the response. It sounds astute, but I focus on rubbing my foot up and down his raging erection.

"I sent you the slides, so you can follow the presentation since your video is not working. Did you get them?" the voice on the other side says. Oh shit, there is still a presentation to go over?

"Yes, I have it here." Gio lies because he hasn't even moved, let alone checked his email. "Do continue," he says, probably to both of us.

I push myself off the table and get to my knees again. His eyes darken, mixed with warning and encouragement.

The presentation hums in the background as I slide my finger into the waistband of his pants. His cock springs out and Gio fists my hair. He leans down and seizes my lips, with ownership and need that empowers me in so many ways.

When our lips part, I'm a mess, ridden with lust and desire of my own, but it only mirrors what I see on his face.

I wrap my hand around his base and lick the tip. Gio watches me with hooded eyes, and I realize that the best part about getting down on my knees is seeing him undone, vulnerable and in awe while needing me so badly he forgoes work.

It feels like a minor victory, not that I was keeping score, but this man has been busy and always distracted, and having his full attention is the best treat ever.

I flick my tongue and Gio hisses, but swallows the sound. God, I love that he's losing control. I take him in and start sucking, licking and moving my hand and mouth in the same rhythm. His muscles tense and both his hands rake my hair, fisting painfully.

He's too big, and as I hollow my cheeks, tears spring into my eyes. Gio swipes a tear with his thumb and mouths, "Touch yourself."

He doesn't even say the words, but the scorching command is palpable, and I immediately drop one hand between my thighs.

Gio inhales a deep breath through his nostrils and takes over with a punishing tempo. He fucks my mouth, and I'm so wound up that just a mere touch of my swollen clit edges me over the precipice.

It only takes a few moments before we both fall apart. I swallow as much as I can before he jerks me up, spins me around and pushes me to his desk, my butt jutting out. His warm, large hand is like a vice between my shoulder blades, holding me without the option to move.

His other hand travels up my thighs and I pant, trying desperately to stifle my moan. Gio hikes my knee up on the table, spreading me for him. He plunges into me and fills me to the hilt, and I sink my teeth into my forearm, hoping the audience on the other line won't hear us.

He lowers himself over me and moves his hand to my mouth, covering it completely, almost cutting off my air supply.

His other hand and the edge of the table bruise my hips, but the discomfort vanishes as quickly as my mind gets fogged by the feeling of him.

I'm floating on a cloud of lust, nothing matters, just this: the cool glass grazing my nipples against the heat of the man bringing me to the brink of nirvana. I bite his finger hard, but being completely at his mercy, I can't think of any other way to retain some control.

He hisses. Loudly. I tense, but he doesn't stop his punishing tempo. Jesus. A scream tears from me as the freight-train of an orgasm rams through my body. As much as I want to stay silent, I can't. I dissolve into a rag doll, melting into the glass surface.

Gio follows me shortly after with a roar, and my lusty mind snaps. Did we just silence the presenter? Oh my God.

Gio feels my tension and chuckles. "I disconnected the call."

"You bastard." I exhale.

He chuckles again and slaps my butt cheek. "That's what you get for interrupting my meeting." He hasn't pulled out of me, still pulsing inside my center.

His body, hot and large, covers me completely as he nuzzles my neck.

"That's what you get for sneaking to work and leaving me alone in your enormous bed." Not that he was the only one getting some.

"If this is the result, I might just work a bit more." He bites my shoulder.

I groan. "You missed your presentation."

"And I don't regret it, Princess. You might fuck me out of my workaholic ways."

I laugh, and it earns me another slap on my ass. Gio pulls out, cleans me with tissues, spins me and sits me at his desk.

"Thank you for sneaking in," he whispers, swiping my hair from my forehead. "You're beautiful at any given moment, but I adore this just-fucked softness." He kisses my forehead and butterflies flutter in my stomach.

How did we get this far, this fast? The intimacy of this moment is equal parts comfortable and scary. Is he feeling it as well?

There is still the problem of us working together, and the cloud of him footing the bill for Annie's nurse, but this thing between us is growing. For me, certainly.

He stayed with me in St. Martin. He's been working from home more and he's been taking time off —an hour here and there—from his busy schedule. We go for strolls, which I usually spend trying to spot his security service. We go to bookstores, and for dinners in small hole-in-the-wall diners.

We also go to upscale restaurants, and we flew to two benefits together out of town. We mix my normal with his normal and enjoy it. But can I hope for more, or for longer?

"Let's play hooky today." I wrap my legs around his waist.

A shadow passes across his face, but then he smiles, the dimples and all. "Okay."

He laughs when my jaw drops.

"Am I really changing your workaholic ways?" I snake my arms around his neck.

He kisses me, leaving his forehead against mine. "You're certainly impeding my productivity."

We grin at each other, completely engulfed by the closeness we've discovered. I never expected this when I signed the damn contract, and while I hate how this whole relationship started, I don't regret any minute of it.

Uncovering the layers of this complex man who shows the world only his composed, carefully tailored public side has been wonderful. With every new discovery, my defenses weaken. I'm falling. Hard.

Gio tugs a strand behind my ear, caressing my cheek. "Marry me."

I throw my head back, laughing.

"Why is that funny?" he growls, squeezing my hips tighter.

I snap my eyes to him, meeting with his grave expression. Jesus. Is he serious? I hoped for more and longer, but this makes little sense. Too much. Too soon. "I'm sorry, I guess the grand romantic proposal threw me off. We've been dating for two weeks, Gio, don't be ridiculous."

His face hardens, his eyes edge with annoyance, and my laughter dies.

I shiver, and the pleasant atmosphere of the morning dissipates under his stare and his words.

"You're serious?" My heart pulses in my temples,

the deafening pound drowning me. Gio says something. Or I think he does because his lips are moving.

He cups my face, the caress fogging my mind even further. Lowering his mouth to mine, he gives me a kiss. It's a chaste peck, barely brushing my lips, but it's more intimate than a wild, hungry make-out session. What is happening right now?

"I wanted to talk to you about it tonight, but we may as well discuss it now." He opens the drawer and hands me a folder. A bright yellow folder just like the one his lawyer pushed across the table to me after Christmas.

I should move my hand and take it from him, but I'm frozen.

Exposed.

And not only because he's standing between my legs and I'm practically naked. I look at the folder, and then up at him.

The dark brown pools.

Full of hope?

His gaze is soft, his hooded eyes filled with reverence. Or lunacy. This can't be happening. I must still be sleeping. I just can't decide if I'm in a dream or a nightmare.

I inhale a shaky breath and try to lighten up the intensity of this morning. "Usually proposals come with a ring, not paperwork." My words float on a trembling breeze, filling the space between us with awkwardness.

"I blindsided you again, sorry." He kisses my forehead. "Have a look and let's talk." He pushes the folder to me.

I stare at the bright yellow folder as if it was laced with anthrax. It might as well be. Is this a prenup? Is he serious right now? Do I want to become Mrs. Cassinetti?

Jesus. Two weeks of dating. Okay, I've known him longer, and we got close in California. I enjoy spending time with him. I can see myself by his side in the future, but...

I snatch the folder from him and Gio sits back. I slide from his desk, hating that my ass is bare. I round it to sit down on the chair across from him, my arousal-soaked thighs sinking into the soft upholstery.

My vision blurs with tears that I'm trying to push away. My heart beats erratically, and my mind... oh, my poor mind wanders around aimlessly.

I can't accept this proposal, because that's not a story we can tell our grandchildren. That's just one useless thought as I try to tear the rest of them out of my clouded brain.

Flipping through the contents of the folder, I try and fail to refocus. Then my eye catches a name I recognize, and the spiral of confusion somehow, unexpectedly clears the fog, the words forming sentences. The sentences making sense, but with every word I read, I'm more perplexed.

"This is an acquisition contract. You're buying an event planning and social media outreach company. I've heard of them. They are good, the best in the market. I guess it's a good investment, but—"

He smiles, and the contrast between my rigid posture and his relaxed one pisses me off. The king in his court. Am I expected to bow?

As if he can read my thoughts, something unexpected flickers through his expression. If I didn't know him, I would think a moment of regret or fear just grabbed him. It's immediately replaced with the annoyance that's so well set in his pores he can't probably ever wash it out.

"Look at the next document." He gestures toward my lap where the damn yellow portfolio rests, scarring my fingertips.

I don't even know why I indulge him. "This is a title change to transfer the company to... me?"

"We both know you can't work for me. I don't want this relationship to be a dirty little secret, but I don't want to get you into a situation when you'll be scrambling for a job again. You mentioned this would be something you wanted to achieve, and I told you I'd fix our problem." He rolls closer to the desk and clasps his hands in front of him. This is his boardroom posture. Is this a business deal?

My eyes widen and my heart can't decide if it's beating with joy or horror. This is the most fucked-up and yet somewhat strangely caring and romantically twisted solution.

"So you bought a company?"

"Yes."

"And you will just give me the company?"

"Yes."

"That's your solution to the fraternization policy?"

A flash of irritation crosses his face, the habit too strong, but he fights it and smiles.

"Princess, I enjoy your company very much. Isn't the firm what you want? It's established, and you can take it and enjoy the profits, grow it, or whatever you want. It will also help you support your family better. All your problems solved. I need someone by my side, and I've come to believe you're the perfect candidate."

The folder burns my hands with its content, with Gio's cynical attitude, with the manipulation, and everything I shed in California when I finally picked up my dignity and left Brian. I drop it on Gio's desk and stand up.

"I'm the perfect *candidate*? Is this thing between us just another acquisition for you? You can't buy me. I'm pleasant-enough company and a good-enough lay, so you're upgrading my contract? Paying me off?"

"Mila—" He stands up and his chairs rolls and hits the window with a loud thud. "Don't you fucking degrade what we have!"

"*I'm* degrading it? Are you for real? You know what? Fuck you. Go back to your arm candy dates. That's who you deserve. And keep your fucking company."

I storm to the door and fling it open. It bangs against the wall, the entire house reverberating with the sound.

"Mila." Gio's voice follows me.

I run to the bedroom, find my jeans and pull them on. I don't bother with the rest of my clothes and run.

He stands in the doorway, his eyes fueled with anger. The deep whirlpools of his eyes slowly swallowing me.

"Let. Me. Go."

His jaw ticks and a vein mars his beautiful forehead. "Let's talk about this. Let me explain—"

"Let. Me. Go."

The walls of the spacious bedroom where I've spent almost every night since we returned from St. Martin close in on me, suffocating me with every piece of luxury this man has so generously given me without me wanting it.

This is how it always would be. He would keep giving. All the wrong things. For all good reasons.

We glare at each other, my chest heaving. Gio's phone rings, the sound blasting through the large house with urgency. "Mila." He reaches for me, and I flinch.

I can't think when he touches me. I can't be here. I need to leave and think. Or forget. Or anything but this right now.

He jerks his head as if I slapped him and steps to the side. I push around him and rush away. I'm not letting him see my tears.

He's moving behind me, but he doesn't try to stop me anymore.

When I reach the entrance, I push the stupid built-in closet door, grab my coat and stumble around, putting on my boots. Turning to him, I'm hit with his confused, painful expression, and I almost stop my retreat.

His whole body is slumped, beaten. I've only known him proud and greater than life, and as I see the broken version of the king I close my eyes, desperately trying to find the silver lining.

This man has never had a normal relationship. I was the closest to normal he'd ever got. But I need to think of myself.

I used to always put Brian first. His feelings. His needs. His wants.

I can't have this man steamroller me into his outra-
geous idea of a relationship. He hurt me. He disre-
spected me. He wanted to buy me.

"Mila," he croaks, and I open the front door.

"I've always been a hooker to you."

Chapter 19

Gio

"What's up your ass?" Conrad asks me as I throw back another whiskey, downing them without finesse. I don't even know why I came to this stupid gala. I guess I thought the more I pretend my life is back to what it used to be, the more it manifests.

It's not fucking working.

In the past three weeks, I had Lydia book and then cancel several dates. Fucking Mila. I knew she would ruin me for other women, and here we are. I gave her everything, way more than I ever offered to anyone, and she...

She didn't understand. It only confirms I was wrong about us working out well. She doesn't understand my life, and as much as it felt liberating to enjoy her simple, normal way of enjoying life, it was just a temporary excitement that doesn't really fit my lifestyle.

Then why...? *Fuck, don't go there.*

"Nothing's up my ass. Can't I enjoy a drink or two?" I gesture for the bartender.

"More like five or six." Nora runs her hand up and down my arm. What am I, some poor bastard? I don't fucking want her sympathy.

"What are you, the drinking police now?" I growl.

"Watch it, asshole," Conrad growls, and takes my glass away. "What's going on?"

I sway a bit, glaring at my friend. Piano lounge music plays in the corner, people are just getting ready to take their seats, and I'm... well, if Nora is right... kind of drunk.

"Nothing is going on," I snap, and reach for the glass the bartender slid my way, but my hand collides with Conrad's and he snatches it from me. "Fuck you."

"Fuck you right back, dickhead." He stares me down. I would win. I always do, but the swaying continues, and besides, I don't give a shit about his opinion.

"I'll go mingle for a moment and the two of you talk." Nora kisses his cheek and looks at me like I'm a lost puppy in need of adoption.

Conrad orders a glass of whiskey and pushes my

tumbler back to me. "Talk to me, bro. Have you lost money, made a wrong move with a takeover?"

The concern in his voice pisses me off. "Not everything is about business and money." I shake my head and the bar tilts a bit. Okay, perhaps I drank more than I realized.

"Fuck me. Now I know something is wrong. Your life *is* your work. What's going on?"

I glare at him, but I need to get this shit off my chest, because it's been fucking three weeks and I can't seem to move past the damn rejection.

I called her, I sent her gifts, I even waited in front of her house, but Mila pretends I don't exist. She doesn't give me a chance to explain. To talk about it.

Women have been squealing over my presents and attention, plotting to get a commitment from me for years, and I fucking propose and she runs.

She quit the job with the Wings the same day she stormed from my place. Now I'm worried about her struggling financially, as much as she's not my problem anymore.

Only she is. I paid for the whole month of nursing support for her sister and instructed the agency to insist that it's non-refundable.

"I bought the event management company." I take a sip.

Conrad raises his eyebrow and laughs. "And it's giving you a headache like the stupid retail chain?"

"Fuck you." I take another swig of my drink. "I bought it for a woman, and she got offended."

The idiot laughs even harder. I should have stayed home. "So, you finally met a woman who doesn't want you for your money. Why are you sulking then?"

"She won't talk to me anymore." I grab his lapels. "Fuck her. I don't need her."

He pats my shoulder. "Based on the state of you, that's where you're wrong. I'm guessing she's the one you took to St. Martin, so let me run the facts. You've never taken anyone to my Caribbean paradise. You haven't spent more than a few hours with a woman since we-know-who.

"Not only did you take this one for a weekend getaway, you extended the getaway by a few more days. Unheard of, given that you never take a break. You bought a company for her, and now you're drinking your sorrow because she's gone."

"Other women would have loved the gesture. I told her she's my equal and took care of her money issues."

"And took away her pride and equated your relationship to a business deal. Yeah, sorry to break it to you, but women don't see it that way."

Her pride? *Here, I pay for your problems, and you stay with me.* Fucking idiot. "I could never be sure a woman wants me for me, and I guess she does. Did. Used to. Fuck."

"Grovel, my friend. It looks like she's worth it." Conrad pats my back.

* * *

"What do you want, Paris? I'm late," I snap into the phone.

Two more weeks have passed, and Mila still hasn't answered the phone. Snapping at people is my current modus operandi. The only way I know how to dazzle a woman is gifts, so I really don't know what the fuck I'm supposed to do. She's hiding from me, and I'm a desperate man.

It's been a month, and this morning when I fisted my cock, I realized jerking off to the memories of her is somehow unfair to her. So now I'm brimming with sexual frustration on top of everything else.

If she doesn't give a shit about my efforts to mend things, I'm giving up. Tonight. I'm going out with Claudia @whatever-the-fuck-her-handle-is. She's dull as hell, but she's decent in the sack. She'll bounce me back, and I can return to my normal life.

"Wow, you're in a worse mood than usual. What's going on?"

"For fuck's sake, Paris, you called me!" I leave my

bedroom to grab my keys. I haven't driven my Lambo since St. Martin.

"Jesus. Okay, could you get me the number of Conrad's wife?"

"Nora? Why do you need it?"

"She is on the board of a foundation that organizes a charity fashion show."

"And? Do you want to get on the board?" This conversation is beyond tedious.

"I want to model, walk down the catwalk."

"What the fuck, Paris? You want to be a model?" I shake my hand and consider hanging up on her. I move to the front entrance and push the closet open.

"Don't be so disgusted. It's just one thing on my bucket list."

"Your bucket list?" I open the cabinet to grab my keys.

"Yes, Gio, could you give me her number?"

I sigh. "Okay, I'll send it to you."

She lets out a squeal that seems disproportionate to the situation. "Thank you, Gio. I really appreciate it. Is your girlfriend coming with you today?" she chirps.

"Drop it, Paris, I don't have a girlfriend." I lower my forehead to the door frame. Kill me now.

"Oh, she didn't sign the NDA? I thought... you seemed—"

"I have to go now." I hang up.

Before I close the closet, I glimpse something on the floor. I pick it up. Mila's glove. Fuck, she is still everywhere. If my housekeeper hadn't been with me for seven years, I would fire her right now.

I break several traffic laws on the way to the new Hunter's Club gym. By the time I park, my newly acquired recklessness courses through me with adrenaline, and a larger dose of annoyance. And then I step into the gym and almost turn around.

Of course, Mila is working the event. Of course, she looks like a vision. Paler and thinner, but still so fucking beautiful it hurts my eyes.

"What is she doing here?" I growl at my stepsister Sydney.

"She's one of the best event planners we know, and was able to get this all together on short notice. What's your problem?" Sydney shakes her head and walks away to greet more guests.

I find myself a spot by the window and pull out my phone. For the first time, I can't find anything to occupy my mind, so I swipe jellies in Candy Crush.

"Oh my God, have you been doing this the whole time we thought you were working?" Gina laughs at my side.

I don't answer. My gaze lifts and immediately finds the blond ray of sunshine. Our eyes meet and Mila's face contorts, and then she looks away and starts rearranging the catering plates.

"What happened between the two of you?" Gina is fucking observant, but she's also Mila's friend, so I wonder what her point is here. She must know already.

"Don't you have a husband to bother?" I snarl.

She raises her eyebrows and puts her hand on her belly in that protective motherly way, and I feel like a bastard. "Sorry."

"I'm going to leave you to your brooding, but the two of you need to talk." She pins me with a vicious glare.

"Don't you think I tried?" I snap.

"Try harder," she pushes through her teeth.

"Don't fucking tell me what to do." Yes, I'm that pathetic asshole who pulls a power play with my brother's wife.

"As someone who took seventeen years to clear the air, I learned my lessons the hard way. Be smart and learn from our mistakes." She waddles away.

I pull out my phone again, but my eyes dart around. I can't find her, and my heartbeat speeds up. Has she left? She's working—she'll be the last one to leave. I look around, ignoring the tightening in my chest and the nautical knot in my stomach.

I'm nearly ready to run around and look for her when Mila walks in, laughing at something Andrea says. My brother fucking misses half of our family functions, yet he comes to the opening of Sydney's boyfriend's new gym and flirts with my...?

I rush through the room, my vision blurred. "What's so funny?"

Andrea's eyes widen for a moment, assessing my mood, and then amusement flickers through his dark eyes. "I was just telling beautiful Mila here how I would like to paint her. Naked."

Mila gasps and puts her hand on my chest. The contact sears me like a propane torch, but it stops me from punching Andrea in the face. I glare at him, and he chuckles and leaves.

I lower my head and inhale. Her lavender scent dulls the ache I've been feeling for weeks. Mila drops her hand from my chest, and I miss the touch immediately.

I lock my gaze on her, drinking in the pain in her eyes. "We need to talk, Princess."

Mila flinches at the nickname. "I think we said enough last time."

"No. I have more things to say." I grip her arm, but she shakes it off and steps back.

"I've heard enough, Gio. Enough to humiliate me for a lifetime. I don't want to hear your further manipulation or atrocious proposals." She shakes her head and blinks a few times.

"Just tell me if you're okay. Does your sister need anything? I can help. Do you have other jobs booked?" I can't see her suffer.

She narrows her eyes. "Leave me alone." She marches away.

There are only a few people in the world I can fully trust. Most of the time, I'm alone, relying on myself. Right at this moment, standing in the middle of a room full of people, I'm lonely like never before.

"Oh, my poor boy."

And here I thought this day couldn't get any worse. "Mother." I don't look at her.

She pats my back in that way she used to when I was a little boy. Now my mother pities me. Wonderful. "What's going on between the two of you?"

"Nothing. I have to go. Something came up at the office." I kiss her forehead.

She looks at me with a skeptical eye. "It's Saturday. I'm sure the office will survive the five minutes you give your mother. Talk to me."

"There is nothing to say. Everyone wants me for my money, and I offered her the best I could. It wasn't —" I almost say enough for her, but I know that's not the issue here.

"The right woman for you wouldn't care about your work, your money. She would stick around to find the real you, behind the walls you built after Kimberly."

My nostrils flare. "Don't mention her."

Mother waves her hand. "Don't be so sensitive. It's been long enough. Mila seems like a keeper."

Keeper. Mila would appreciate the irony. She is a keeper, and among all the *keepers* I have, she is the only one that matters. Too late for that. "I guess I'm not the one to keep her."

"Don't be ridiculous. You rule an empire. I'm sure you can woo a woman." Mother swats at my shoulder. If she only knew how powerless I am in this regard.

"I don't know what to do," I admit. The first bite of humble pie doesn't taste as rancid as I thought.

"Go out of your way. Do something she won't expect, something that would cost you."

More than a now-useless event company?

Reading my mind, she gives an exasperated sigh. "I'm not talking about money, Gio."

"She doesn't want to listen." I need to get out of here.

"Then make her."

Chapter 20

Mila

"**I**'m sure there are options. Funding you can apply for." Ron kisses Annie's head and she sniffles.

I'm so happy my sister has him after the nursing service turned into more between them. But I have a hard time accepting him in our lives. Not his fault—Ron will forever be associated with a man who hurt me.

Hurt me and himself based on the way he acted on Saturday.

I wanted to give him a chance to explain, but I knew he would have manipulated me. I knew I'd have given in because I miss him. I miss him so badly it spreads through me like a slow-acting poison, eating at my organs, leaking bile through my body.

And yet... I know he would plan and execute another

gift. Even within his failed attempt to talk on Saturday at Hunter's Club, he wanted to help Annie and get me another job. I would always be his charity case.

Or worse, he would always go ahead and solve my issues without discussing it or regarding my genuine needs.

Part of me knows—wants to believe—his intentions are good. But that's what I believed about Brian's actions. It's not fair to compare the two of them. Somewhere in the deep dark crevices of my broken heart I know they are nothing alike.

I know that, but I have to be selfish and protect myself from his dominance to ensure I don't drown in it.

"What do you think, Mils?" Annie's quivering voice brings me back to my bleak reality.

"At the end of the day, I don't think they can just throw him out," I offer a useless opinion.

"That may be so, but his teacher's recommendation about him needing a different environment—"

"They are just overworked, and with too many kids. His last seizure scared them and now they are trying to make it easier on themselves." I turn to the window, because I hate myself for suggesting Aidan should stay at his current school when it's quite clear it's not the best choice for him.

"Knowing that doesn't really help Aidan, does it?" Annie snaps. "He needs to go to a school where he can thrive despite his issues. Where they are equipped to help him. He deserves that," she whimpers, and my heart—my completely abused, shattered heart—breaks into more pieces.

"I know that." I turn and wipe my tears. "Annie, I'll try to make more money. I'll beg Portia to give me the job at the Wings back." Even if it means running into Gio on a regular basis. My stomach constricts.

"I can't ask you to do that. You've been doing so much already. My family is not your responsibility." She sobs, and Ron pulls her closer.

"My family is my responsibility, but at this point, between your treatment and the rent, we'll have to keep Aidan in his current school for a bit longer." Now I'm crying too.

"I'll help with the rent," Ron says, stroking Annie's hair. "I've been staying here more, anyway."

Annie raises her head and smiles through the tears. "Are we moving in together?"

He shrugs and wipes a tear from her cheek. "I guess we are, baby."

The scene is gut-wrenching. Love and suffering linger in the air, crushing me inside. Desolation wraps me in a tight embrace, and I go back to watching the street, unable to witness my sister's tender relationship without feeling sorry for myself.

Ron's help would benefit us, but it's still thousands of dollars less than what we need. And with the cost of a private school looming, we're deep in debt before we even solve our current mounting problems.

"We'll figure it out." The two of them kiss on the sofa, and now I feel like an intruder. Great. We can add another apartment to our growing financial needs.

I grab my laptop and make my way to the kitchen where I've been working, because I don't want to spend money on coffee while working in coffee shops. I have a few clients that bring in steady income to cover our basics, but it's not enough. London's next gala is far away...

I flip mindlessly through the mail, and an envelope catches my eye. It's from our landlord. With my nail, I peel the flap open and pull the letter out. The words blur in front of my eyes, swirling another degree of dread in my stomach.

Ellery cries out, waking from her nap. The load of responsibility strains my frail nerves and I sink into the chair, just as Annie walks in with my niece.

"What's wrong?" She stops, frowning.

I study Ellery's sweet face and try to push away the overwhelming feeling that I'm failing them all. The letter drops from my hand.

"Mila?" Annie pulls Ellery closer to her chest. The little girl rests her head on Annie's shoulder, her sleepy eyes full of innocence. I can't take it anymore.

I look down at the last drop of my demise, but I don't pick up the letter. "Our rent."

I push around them, dashing for the front door. Suffocating.

"Jesus Christ, how can we afford that?" Annie's voice catches me.

I stumble, trying to put on my boots.

"What happened?" Ron asks.

"They raised our rent." Annie's voice breaks.

I put on my coat and rush outside. I need to leave. I need to clear my head. Bursting through the stairwell doors and taking two steps at the same time, I more trip and lurch than run downstairs.

The frigid February air hurts my lungs, and I welcome the momentary relief from the other more permanent ache claiming my limbs and soul.

Trying to summon positive thoughts or find solutions, I march down the street. I'm good at silver linings, at happy thoughts. Am I not? But clearly I'm failing again. I can't conjure one positive thought, or find a feasible solution.

I speed-walk through the streets of my neighborhood, assessing the situation from all different angles and coming up empty-handed. Annie's medicine allowed her to return to work as a cashier at a super-market for a few shifts. Too little.

She wants to go to school—something she dropped when she met her ex—to get a better paid office job she can manage with her illness. Too late.

If she goes to school, we will need a babysitter. Too much.

I can, and will take more jobs. Too volatile. Impossible really, because as it is I'm stretched too thin. I can't take new clients because there are only twenty-four hours in a day.

I don't know how long I've been walking. My feet are sore. My nose and cheeks are throbbing from the cold. My chest aches from everything. The worst part is, my mind keeps arriving at the same solution.

I should have accepted Gio's proposal. He offered me a career, a life of luxury, and a permanent solution for my family. I decided to protect my pride, and my heart.

I traded my family's wellbeing to uphold my own righteousness. And what was it good for? Because at the end of the day, I miss Gio so much it's hard to breathe. His absence scrapes me raw every night when I'm crying myself to sleep.

Every day without him stretches the hole in my heart. Every minute thinking about him pulls me into a darkness so profound I can't find my way out of it.

I ignore the feelings in the name of pride. With the notion of protecting myself. Avoiding all his attempts to explain, to talk, because I am not strong enough to survive hearing his voice—regardless of what he would say. Strong enough to survive the dark brown abyss of his gaze.

And now I can't have that conversation anymore, because my family's financial ruin would forever taint any chance of things between us being honest and real. About us. Him and me. A normal couple.

I trudge, one foot in front of the other, my chin buried in my coat's collar. My building is just half a block away. Somehow, I made my way back. Without a solution. Without a cleared head. A bigger mess than when I left.

A familiar car is parked in front of the building. I stop, and my heart flutters while my lungs strain to find oxygen.

The door opens and Gio steps out, his eyes pinning me with a plea, remorse, and something darker. Rage? Anger? Or frustration.

While my body and heart keep falling apart inwardly, I'm pulled to him without a conscious decision. How could I have ever thought we could be equal? How could I have ever hoped we could be normal?

This man owned me before he first spoke to me. I

might have fought it hard, but my dislike was just another pathetic attempt to keep my independence. There is no such thing. I'm completely, utterly, irrevocably dependent on this man. Financially. Physically. Mentally. And, God help me, with all my heart.

I raise my chin, because if I'm going to lose the only thing that's still mine—my dignity—I'll do it with pride. I open my mouth—

"You will hear me out." His nostrils flare.

I chuckle at the absurdity of his idea that I was going to argue and tell him I don't want to hear it. That kind of perseverance died a few days ago, and dissolved completely with the rent hike letter.

My humorless chuckle seems to anger him more. He narrows his eyes, probably wondering if I've gone mad since Saturday.

"Get in the car, Mila." The command rolls down my body into my soul, spreading sweet heat and bitter regret in equal measures.

I inhale my last breath of freedom and get inside, still hoping there is a chance. A chance for us. That he will see past my practical needs and understand I want him for more than his money. It might take time, but he'll see it, eventually. I can make him see it. Can't I?

I take the seat on the longer side of the car, and Gio slides into his usual spot by the door. He runs his hand down his face, adjusts his cuffs and meets my gaze. The air in the car thickens with pent-up, unresolved emotions, but also with primal need.

My body reacts to his presence as if he was the only mate for me on this planet. It's visceral, overpowering, and completely untimely, but as I catch his chest heaving, I'm unreasonably pleased I'm not the only one feeling it.

His scorching gaze eats me up, communicating without words as we try to reconcile the reaction that swept us both. I swallow hard and count to ten. Then I'll surrender. My heart. My soul. My body. To a man who might put more conditions in place.

Ten. Nine. Eight. His jaw ticks, the beautiful sharp edge of his chin covered in two days' worth of stubble I long to kiss.

Seven. Six. Five. He looks away for a moment, adjusting his cuffs again. The chiseled arms bulging in his bespoke suit.

Four. Three. Two. I smile in the bitter-sweet moment before I surrender.

One.

He opens his mouth, but I stop him with my hand.

"I accept." The words rip through the tense air between us like the sharpest blade.

Gio jerks his head and frowns. "What?"

"I accept your proposal." The words barely pass the lump lodged in my throat. "I guess I'm saying yes."

I try to chuckle, but it comes out like a desperate squeal.

Gio's eyes tighten at the edges as he opens and closes his mouth a few times, no words coming out. He licks his upper lip and assesses me with a cold, calculated look.

I push my hands under my thighs, because I'm trembling under his scrutiny. "Please say something." I think of Annie, Aidan and Ellery upstairs, and decide I'll beg if I have to.

"Why?" He shakes his head.

"Aidan needs a private school, and our rent just went up, and I..." I blurt and inhale and tell him about all my financial issues. Months of medications I put on my credit cards, jobs I never got paid for, medical bills, Annie's debt from before I arrived, and all the other fucked-up realities of my life.

Somewhere in the middle of my babbling I realize these issues are not what I should have led with, but he would find out soon enough. He'd believe any other reason was made up to make it all look better. So I don't stop and give him all the gory details of my life. Problems he can solve easily.

His gaze hardens, his jaw sets in that expression of indifference he carries around like a mask. I can almost pinpoint when I lost him. When he filed my motivation along with all the other gold-diggers. So I don't tell him more.

I don't tell him how much I miss him. How he completes me in the most wonderful, unexpected ways. I don't tell him I regretted walking out on him, and that the woman who walked out was the old Mila who still harbored issues from her previous relationship.

I don't tell him I missed his tender care. His rare laughter. His unyielding dominance. His refusal to accept normal and then grasp at it with abandon like he did in St. Martin, or even before in Santa Barbara.

I don't tell him any of it, because I see he's retreated to his cave of solitude, ruled by contracts and well-defined arrangements where he can protect himself. He wouldn't hear it or believe it anyway. So I stop talking.

I don't tell him I'm falling for him. It doesn't matter, because at this moment I know ours can't be a happy ending. With my financial needs, I lost him.

Chapter 21

Gio

"Okay, Portia, let's move ahead with the proposal." I make a note on my phone. "Is there anything else?"

"The Wing project is rolling nicely. If things continue the way they are, we'll be able to off-load the chain with a nice profit." She turns her tablet toward me. "I'm not sure you've seen the latest projections."

I glance at the numbers. So, at the end, the retail acquisition worked out. I should be happy. I should call Conrad and rub it in his face. Instead, I think of the Wing as a venture associated with my week in California. With Mila.

Fuck me. I need to get rid of that chain as soon as possible. I don't want to have good, sappy memories attacking me. It's not like any of it was real. She played me well.

"It looks good." I nod.

"Maybe I can move the project to one of my senior directors and focus more on other strategic leads?" Portia fidgets in her chair.

"You don't need to ask me," I growl. "It's your department to manage." I miss Marnie.

She swallows hard. "Okay, I'll do that. And congratulations, Mr. Cassinetti."

I look up and she withers under my glare.

"I-I mean your engagement." She gathers her things. *Yeah, Portia, get out before I get really pissed.* She stands up. "I miss Mila. She's been a great asset to the team, but now I understand why she left. Congratulations to both of you." She leaves.

I hit my intercom. "Lydia, get Fatima on the line."

I don't know why I went through with it. I keep telling myself she's as good as any other to be my wife. I need one, after all. There are too many social obligations that come with my status, and I need someone to handle that. But even the cynical bastard in me doesn't believe the bullshit I've been telling myself.

A month ago, I foolishly believed she might want me for me. Wrong. Two days ago, that certainty died on her lips as she blabbered about her financial issues. Jesus.

I don't even have a problem helping her out. At the

end of the day, she's a better candidate to become Mrs. Cassinetti than any of my other dates.

She's been upfront about her expectations. With her financial needs. That's an upgrade from fucking Kimberly who took my heart, pierced it with a poisoned knife and stomped all over it. Seven years later, I'm stronger now. Less naïve.

So why does it feel like I'm making a mistake? She's grown under my skin, and I wanted her to be more. Weak bastard.

I should have cut my losses in that fucking car. The air was full of her. The lavender that makes me want to hold her in my arms. Not even bend her over and fuck her into oblivion. *Hold* her in my arms. Make life better for her. Just one look at her distraught face and I turned into a pathetic asshole.

And she didn't hesitate to take advantage of it. I knew it, and still I couldn't throw her out of my life. I got engaged because I couldn't imagine someone else having her. She's mine. She's always been mine.

Only she isn't. She refused to talk to me for a month, and when things got tough, she was happy to accept that damn proposal.

I'm too weak to let her go, but I'm too close to falling for her. I can't do unrequited love. Not again. Kimberly was the first and last woman I let hurt me.

"Fatima is on the line, and your mother called three times." Lydia's voice carries over the intercom.

"Let me talk to Fatima, and tell my mother I'm in meetings all day."

The last thing I need is to deal with Bianca Cassinetti. This morning I had to listen to a cheerful voicemail from Gina. Along with Portia's congratulations, the celebratory mood of everyone around me churns in my stomach like an undigested meal.

"Good morning, Gio. How can I help you?" Even Fatima sounds too cheerful. What is it with everyone throwing confetti today? It's not a good morning.

"I need a prenup," I bark.

"Congratulations." She sounds anything but sincere, and I like her a bit more for that. "Who is the lucky lady?"

"Mila Ward." Her name on my lips floats with lightness. It also deprives me of oxygen. What the hell? I can bark and growl, but I can't snarl the name of the woman who put me in this mood?

"Oh." Silence follows on the other side of the line. It's unexpected, and since I don't understand what the silence is saying, another wave of annoyance swipes through me.

"Do you have anything to say about it?"

Fatima clears her throat. "Not really. I just thought she was..."

So did I. So did I.

"Anyway," Fatima gets back to her business-like self. "Email me the details and I'll have a first draft for you tomorrow."

I hang up and open an email. The cursor blinks, not really inspiring any words. I always thought I'd find an acceptable candidate, outline the conditions and get a partner for life to accompany me to social occasions and be available. Provide an heir.

Why am I now staring at the screen, unable to outline those conditions? Somewhere in my darkened, hardened heart, a tiny spot of softness has bloomed without me realizing. I fucking wanted Mila to be more than a wife of convenience.

I should never have proposed to her. But at least now the cards are on the table, and I know she wants to use me. Maybe that wasn't her plan all along, but I can't nurture any romantic notions about that. It's done, so let's move on.

I pour myself two fingers of whiskey and send an email to Mila, outlining the key points of our agreement. Then I open the app with all the projects of my holding and start firing emails to my team. There is nothing better than work to get me out of this funk.

By the late afternoon, I've drunk three whiskeys, taken over a few projects that were not performing optimally—horrifying the managers—and moved on two acquisitions without the approval of the board.

"Your mother is here. I just got a call from downstairs." Lydia's always calm voice has a hint of panic in it.

Fuck me. I don't even have time to disappear before Mother barges in.

"Why are you day-drinking at work?" She nods at the tumbler at my desk as soon as she enters.

"Hello, Mother." I stand up and kiss her on both cheeks.

She cups my face, her eyes glistening. What is happening right now? Bianca Cassinetti doesn't show emotions. "I'm so happy, Gio. Mila is a perfect wife for you." She pulls my face closer and kisses my forehead.

Yeah, Mila is perfect. Only she doesn't care about me as much as her family, or her bank account. I'm a means to an end for her.

"Jesus, Mom, don't get all sappy on me." I return to my desk. "I can't believe you came to the city to tell me this."

"Well, I came to tell you way more than that." She sits down and glares at me. Now that's more like her.

"Go ahead." I fold my hands behind my head, leaning back and itching for my phone. The monitors on the wall behind her flicker with stock market movements, and I try to focus on that.

"First, I can't believe you didn't call me. Gina told me about the engagement. Seriously, Gio. That being said, what great news. I worried you'd marry one of those pretty trollops you've been so adamant on dating after what happened with Kimberly, but in the end, you picked an exceptional woman. I adore Mila. She's good for you."

Mother's eyes mist again, and I drop my arms to squeeze the armrests. Better than breaking my jaw by grinding my teeth.

"Which brings me to this." She rummages in her designer purse and puts a velvet box on my desk. "I understand from Gina it was a spur of a moment proposal in the back of the car. So, for the real thing, I want you to have Nonna's ring."

I stare at the box like it's a grenade, waiting to burn a hole in my desk. I almost try laughing at the irony. Mila would be the perfect bride, deserving a family heirloom ring. Would being the operative word here.

"I'll get her a ring. Keep this for—"

"Nonsense. I didn't give it to Massi because I was wary of his first marriage with Gina. Too fast, too young. God knows if they're going to have a second wedding now. This ring is yours." She pushes it closer to me, and I fight not to move my chair back.

"It matches your grandfather's cufflinks you wear all the time. It really should be yours. I mean Mila's."

My eyes widen and I look down to adjust my cuffs. I've been wearing my grandfather's cufflinks for years. They would have been my good luck charms if I believed in such shit. I wore them when I struck my first big deal. A part of me wants Mila to wear a matching ring, but the devil on my shoulder reminds me she doesn't deserve it.

"What's going on?"

Great. Now I've planted a seed in my mother's observing mind.

"Thank you, Mother." I grab the box and throw it in the top drawer. I close it and the pens on my desk rattle.

Mother's scrutiny could wilt plants. She sighs and stands up. "Congratulations, darling. And before I forget, I pulled a few strings and we have a conservatory at the Carlyle booked for Saturday."

I frown. "For what?"

"Your engagement party, of course." She chuckles. "Don't worry, I'll take care of all the details. Just send me the guest list. Or it can be a family-only affair."

"Family-only," I say a bit too fast, and she narrows her eyes before she rounds my desk and kisses my forehead.

"I love you, darling Gio. I know you're not ready to give your heart fully, but you'll get there."

Her words linger after she leaves, spurring me to

pour myself another drink. Sipping the numbing, golden liquid, I force myself to focus on my emails.

Mila's name glares at me from my screen. She responded to my conditions.

Of course, looks fine. Whatever you want.

Fuck me.

This is not what I wanted.

Chapter 22

Mila

"No woman should look this sad at her engagement party." Annie pushes the last pin into my simple braided bun and hugs me from behind. Her hands shake, and it's not the arthritis.

"It's just nerves." I try to lighten the mood.

Things broke between me and Gio a week ago in that car. I knew they would, but I had hoped I could make Gio see there is more to my interest in him than just the financial gain. It's like all the connection we had in December and early January melted along with the shitty gray snow in the city.

My hope has been tested by his aloofness and a very practical approach to everything that's happened after I accepted his proposal. That hope has been dying a slow and painful death.

Gio pulled back, and it hurts. But unlike before, I can't even expect that my grief will heal over time. I'm becoming Mrs. Cassinetti in a few months, and all I can do is lick my wounds and hope I survive as they fester. And they will fester if he continues to look at me like I'm the personification of everything he hates in life.

"I can't accept your sacrifice, Mils. There is still time to call everything off." Annie squats and grips my hands with her permanently damaged fingers. It's a firm grip, and it reminds me how much she's improved since getting her treatment regularly.

I cup her cheek and wipe away a single tear. "Annie, this is the best for all of us. I love the man, and he might not love me back, but..." I sigh. "He will get there."

"That's quite a leap of faith, Mils."

"Aidan is in a new school already. You're moving at the end of the month, Ellery has a babysitter to help you out, and you're set to manage your condition and go back to school."

Gio has been very efficient in fixing all the issues. In holding up his side of the bargain. I inhale and fight tears.

"Yeah, and while we all benefit, what about you?" Her tears are streaming freely.

"Don't forget, I got a firm I always wanted." I force a smile.

"I think a marriage of convenience would work if there is no hope or other feelings involved. Mils, there is still time. Let's call it off."

"And then what? I'm exhausted, Annie. I've been doing all I can, and we can't get ahead. This is my chance to relax, so don't you dare think I'm doing it selflessly."

I turn to apply my lipstick, because I won't be able to hold it together if I continue looking at her.

"But at what price?" She stands up. I feel her gaze on me in the hotel suite's mirror, but I refuse to meet it.

The price of my heart.

"Drop it, Annie," I snap. "We don't have other options and I'm doing this willingly. Yes, it would be more convenient if I didn't love the man, but I can protect myself. I'll survive."

He will see past his assumptions. He must.

I stand up and check the clock. "Let's go."

"It's all my fault." She sniffles.

"Stop it, Annie. You didn't ask for the diagnosis. You didn't ask your asshole husband to lock you on the balcony in the middle of winter to get even worse. You didn't bring this on yourself. You didn't ask for the responsibility of taking care of me with no help and support. None of those circumstances are your doing."

Annie was my best friend growing up. She was there to take care of me after our parents died. It felt only natural I came to help her when she got sick.

Our roles reversed in the past year when I took on more responsibility in the care-taking department. Right now, even though I'm helping her and I know deep down she appreciates it, I feel like I'm disappointing her.

A knock on the door breaks the intense moment between us. Annie rushes to open and Gina and Massi come in. "Oh my God, you look so beautiful." Gina shrugs her shoulders and claps her hands.

My dress is a simple navy number, a lacy halter top and a silky maxi skirt. It was delivered to the room this morning. I suspect Haughty Bun at Saks chose it for me. It fits, but it's not a dress I would normally want to wear. I don't care. As far as I'm concerned, this party is just for show.

To make sure the family, the media, and all the eligible-husband-hunters in Manhattan know Gio Cassinetti is officially off the market.

"What can I do? You make the maid of honor job too boring." Gina looks at Annie and cringes. "I know we share the duty, but I'm just so excited."

"I'll make sure you fill all the bathroom help duties." I force a chuckle. "Also, I believe your official tasks are related to the wedding itself."

"Gio asked me to drop his bag here," Massi says and rolls a bag into the bedroom. He kisses Gina's forehead. "Are you coming, Blue?"

"I'll join you downstairs later." She brushes his cheek, and he leans into her palm and kisses it. The adoration in their eyes cuts through me, leaving ugly jealous claw-marks in my heart.

"I'll be right back." I rush to the bedroom and close the door behind me.

I can't cry. I can't cry.

Gio hired a stylist for me, but I sent them away. I didn't want anyone to witness what a mess I've been. Annie helped me get ready, but even my minimal makeup would be destroyed if I cry.

Jesus, why am I such a mess? I pace around the bed and lay my eyes on Gio's bag. Oh my God.

My stomach constricts. The week flew by with all the technicalities of our arrangement and the logistics of the rushed party, but we never discussed what the engagement and then the marriage would look like.

Hope flutters in my chest. Gio needs me to fulfill certain public obligations, but is what happens behind closed doors optional? Gio booked this room. Perhaps if we reconnect on a physical level, we can find each other again. Find us.

A smile blooms, still shy, but real. Perhaps I should just enjoy the day. It's not my dream party and my fiancé is somewhat reluctant, but I can prove to him how much I care. I actually have some control over this situation.

For the first time in weeks, the fog lifts slightly and I let myself dream. I burst through the door with my newly-found confidence.

"Ready?" I practically hop into the living room.

Annie turns from the window, her eyes red. She stares at me, scrutinizing like she used to when I stayed out late and she tried to assess if I was high.

"If you are," Gina proclaims and wraps me in an embrace. "The family is undecided how to feel about this. You couldn't look at each other a week ago and now you're engaged. But I knew it. When Gio said he wanted to fix things, but you wouldn't listen, I told him to try harder. And it all worked out."

Annie lets out a strangled sound somewhere between a whimper and a gasp. I squeeze Gina tighter, trying to steal her positive energy.

I didn't listen. I never gave him a chance to tell me what he came to say, but it's too late. I don't think I'll ever hear those words.

My newly- found confidence falters, but I push the feeling away. There is no point in dwelling on the past. The future is in my hands.

* * *

My eyes mist when Gio speaks, reciting words like a robot. He informs the guests about our engagement without emotions, without a joke or the cute story usually expected on an occasion like this.

He looks at my tears with a mixture of annoyance and something else, which looks more like constipation, and he slides a ring on my finger. It's big and undoubtedly expensive, but it's as generic as they come.

"Maybe at the wedding, let Mila speak, bro. Stick to your phone," Massi calls out, and the room breaks into laughter. It rings in my ears with pretense, but at least the guests bought the charade.

We stand beside each other and I'm hyper-aware of his scent, his heat, his distance. He keeps his hand on the small of my back while people come to congratulate us. The touch is light but charged with ownership. I have a tough time focusing on all the words and questions.

I haven't felt his touch since that morning in his office before the proposal, and while I knew I missed it, I didn't realize how much my body has craved it.

Aside from that connection, Gio keeps his distance. And not just physically. When we entered the room together earlier, without thinking, I laced my fingers with his. His body tensed and he dropped my hand as soon as possible, turning to Massi to say something.

He hasn't said a word to me yet, if I don't count his

uninspired speech. No private moment. No compliment. We're standing beside each other, but the distance can't be longer or deeper.

"Congratulations, darling Mila. I'm so happy for you both." Bianca hugs me and air kisses me on both sides. She lifts my hand and I expect an *ah* or *oh* like all the other reactions. Instead, she raises her eyebrows, unimpressed. "Is this the ring?" she asks, as if it wasn't obvious.

I nod, and she assesses her son who speaks with Bianca's husband, Micah.

"Interesting," she mutters and then smiles at me, patting my hand.

Before she can say anything else, Gio gives her a stern look. "Don't, Mother."

What was all that about? I look at my ring, burning my finger, but then Annie comes to fake congratulate me and I don't have more time to think about the weird exchange.

Later, we have a full tea with all our guests. The weather outside is dreadful, leaking the gloomy mood through the windows and the glass roof. I try to fight the grayness with a smile.

When we move to sit at our table I force myself to eat some, but it doesn't distract me enough from the ordeal. Gio talks to Massi on his other side as if they haven't seen each other for ages.

The fabric of Gio's suit brushes my arm and he shifts his weight, leaning away. This is the third time this has happened, and every time a piece of me dies inside.

"One would think I have a contagious disease. You can't get away from me fast enough." I turn my head, pretending to clean lint off his shoulder, whispering.

He looks down at me. "I better keep my distance, *darling*, if we want to keep this party civil."

His words are a threat, and yet they melt my core while setting my heart into an unhealthy gallop. The dark brown pools of his eyes hold so much resentment, but at the same time something primal.

We stare at each other, the time stretching into a black hole of nothingness. To others it might look as if we are about to kiss, but I'm not so sure. I fear my fiancé might prefer to strangle me.

I swallow, practically choking on the violent disappointment in his eyes, and then I turn away. Fuck him. He can try to punish me for becoming a woman who only wants things from him, but he has no right pretending that's all I've ever been.

My jaw hurts from my fake smile. Annie sits with Ron and the kids at a table to our right, and when our eyes connect, the desolation on her face mirrors the vast hollow planes inside me.

"Your sister seems... I don't know. Is she okay?" Of course Gina would notice.

"It's her arthritis." I grab the glass I haven't touched yet and down the champagne in one swig.

"I can't believe you'll probably become Mrs. Cassinetti before me." Gina pokes me with her elbow. She and Massi haven't remarried yet.

"Well, you were the first Mrs. Cassinetti, if we don't count Bianca." I refer to their first wedding when they were still kids.

"Oh, yeah, our mother-in-law." Gina winks at me.

I glance at Bianca who is talking to Micah, but her eyes are pinned on our table. I don't know her enough, but the woman scares me. She is very nice to me, but the way she looks at me... I feel exposed.

I gesture for another drink, but before I put the glass to my lips, Gio touches my wrist. "Pace yourself." He takes the glass from me and puts it back on the table.

"I'll frame those words along with all the romance of the day. A girl might swoon, dear fiancé." Sarcasm might just get me through this show.

"Watch it, Mila. Just because you got what you wanted, don't make the mistake that I won't hold you to certain standards."

Chapter 23

Mila

How can you love someone and hate them at the same time? Isn't that the fucking definition of love? I don't know. It sounds dumb.

But I know I used to dislike Gio Cassinetti, with his stupid dimples, tailored vests and hot biceps. Tonight, I hate him. Maybe before, when it wasn't personal, it was just a silly game I played in my head to fight my attraction.

Now I know him. I know the man he could be. I know the man he used to be around me. The man I fell in love with.

That man hasn't shown up at our engagement party. That man is buried in his own level of hatred.

Overnight, I became the example of everything he hates about women. I'm an arrangement, a transaction.

Even after I signed the NDA at Christmas, I didn't feel this exposed. Vulnerable. Lonely.

The elevator takes us upstairs. I glare at Gio, hoping to rile him up enough so he talks to me. Yells at me. Growls at me. Anything but this tension. I'm shaking with anticipation.

He holds the elevator door for me. A perfect gentleman. We enter the suite and I turn to him.

He glances at me and walks to the bedroom. I lower my head and breathe. This is too much. He was an asshole when I first met him, and even when I started to work with him, but this is an all-new level. I'm his fiancée now, damn it.

Gio returns with his laptop. "Go ahead. I have work to do for an hour or so."

He sheds his suit jacket and drapes it over a chair before he sits down, lifts his legs onto the coffee table and opens his computer.

I storm to the bedroom and slide the double door shut. The glass panels rattle at the impact. I yank off my dress and kick it under the bed, then take a long shower, letting the water melt my tense muscles and wash away all the tears. I won't cry in front of him.

Back in the room, I take out the red-and-black risqué underwear that I bought, hoping we could rekindle some lust as a first step in this thorny reconciliation. I hesitate for a moment, but then put it on. It's sexy as hell. Provocative, yet classy.

I sit on the bed, not bothering with the covers, and wait.

And wait.

The minutes stretch as I will my fiancé to come to our bed.

Screw it!

I jump up and slide the door open, but I falter, unsure what I want to do. Gio is fully focused on his work.

"Are you going to work all night?" I snap, but the quiver in my voice takes away from the intended effect.

Gio raises his eyes with the same annoyance he bestows on everybody, but his eyebrows jerk up when he takes me in. He looks at me like he can see deep into my soul.

I step forward, not sure why. Mostly to focus on something other than his eyes. They burn. They prickle. They smart.

He slides his gaze down my body, taking in every inch of me and the lacy lingerie. Languid. Heated. Carnal.

And then, without meeting my gaze, he shakes his head as if he realized his ogling is inappropriate or, based on his expression, even unsanitary.

"Do you want a selfie to show the world?" If he slapped me, it would hurt less.

Dejection and anger mix a powerful cocktail in my veins. I have nothing to be ashamed of, damn it. He proposed to me.

"Are you seriously comparing me to all your other women?"

"Are you claiming to be different?" He smirks. "I have a draft of our prenup to prove otherwise. You might be less superficial than them, but at the end of the day you want from me what everyone else does. Maybe not the prestige or the fucking selfies, but the money for sure."

How could he suggest my desperate family situation is anything like the motivation of social ladders climbers? Is he so blind?

"*You* made that proposal." Fuck him. I'm not letting him drag me even deeper into this world of disillusion. "You came up with the whole thing. Why do you pretend that's where my motivation lies? What's *your* motivation for the whole thing?"

"I made a mistake. I offered you a marriage partnership because I thought it was the only way for me. I realized I was wrong to lump you with all those other women. Or so I thought. You didn't fucking let me apologize or explain. But then you had a shitty day and suddenly you were ready to talk. I fucking tried every fucking day, Mila, to reach you and discuss my mistake." He chuckles, bitterness spreading in the air between us. "Ultimately, you *were* for sale."

I flinch at his words. At the tragedy of the misunderstanding. If I had only shut up and let him talk first in the car, he would have helped me with my financial problems without this charade of an engagement. Would I have accepted his help? No point in pondering that anymore. My dignity is gone anyway.

I tremble with the unshed tears and those pushing their way out.

"Fuuuuck." Gio runs his hands through his hair, and then he looks at me again.

Those deep, dark eyes.

We stare at each other, unsaid words and tension filling the room. The heat of his gaze burns my skin.

"Then take what's yours. You bought me, after all. That's the only way you can have a relationship, right?" An eye for an eye.

Whoever said vengeance makes you feel better was an idiot. My words brand us both.

He eats the distance between us and pinches my chin between his thumb and index finger, his nostrils flaring. We pant like hunted animals, desperately needing the escape.

His scent spreads unwarranted peace through me. I want to rebel against it, but his heat, so wonderfully familiar, rips through me like an avalanche. My body yearns for his caress. For his care.

"As you wish, dear fiancée," he grits out, spins me around and pushes me against the wall, covering me with his solid body. He's been dominant, but never this forceful. I should be scared, but strangely I'm reveling in his manhandling.

If only giving him this control would put us on the same ground. Where we can meet and discuss our mistakes, to pass beyond them.

I'm pinned between the wall and his hard body, between the cold and the hot. Both unyielding. I can't move. I can barely breathe, but my body is wrecked with desire so strong I sag into him.

Gio sinks his teeth into my shoulder as if he's going to bite off a piece of me. I yelp. He grinds his erection into my back while he grabs me between my thighs. "Wet already, my dutiful fiancée. Ready for the pre-honeymoon?"

He pushes my thong to the side and flicks his finger around my sensitive bud. I shudder.

"Answer me, Mila," he growls.

What? There was a question? My mind is fogged with an arousal so intense I'm ready to acquiesce to anything.

"Mila," he repeats, his voice laced with the same need I feel.

"What?" I cry out.

"Are you ready for me?" He cups my breast and I lean into him. He plays with my nipple and then pinches it roughly.

I realize he still wants my answer. Is he seeking my consent? Jesus. What is he planning to do? But as his thumb massages my clit, all thoughts leave my brain.

"Yes!"

He plunges two or maybe three fingers into me. I might be wet for him, but I'm nowhere near prepared for the invasion. It burns and I want to recoil, but as he moves with a punishing tempo, the friction creates the heat I've missed so much.

Between his moving fingers and the heat of his body against mine, the inferno unravels within me. I let go of everything and dissolve into the pleasure my body has craved so much.

I whimper when his fingers disappear. I was so close. Damn it. Gio smirks. He lifts me unceremoniously and walks to the bedroom.

He drops me to my feet by the bed, pushes me forward into the mattress. He holds me in place, his large hand pressing between my shoulder blades.

The memory of the last time he took me like this at his glass desk during a teleconference flickers through my mind, and I close my eyes, trying to push the image away.

And hoping he remembers the same thing and it will revive some of the lost trust. Or fun.

Gio rips off my underwear and plunges into me. I gasp at the intrusion. Fisting the sheets, I let him chase his release. He fucks me like he hates me. And at this moment, he probably does. So do I. Him and myself.

It's more punishment than lovemaking. As the pain mingles with heat I surrender, because on some fucked-up level I believe I deserve this retribution.

I've always been good at finding the silver lining in any situation, and right now, as I look over my shoulder at Gio's face, I see the strain.

He's trying to control himself. He could just blow and be done, and yet he's making sure I get there, too.

He cares. That's the last thought before I drop my head again, and he snakes his arm around my hip and pinches my clit viciously.

We both come in unison.

Some things are still *us*.

Chapter 24

Mila

Gio continues moving inside me until we both come down. Then he pulls out, and his absence is a heart-breaking void.

"I have a call with Asia."

He leaves me there, bent over the bed with my naked ass in the air. Thoroughly fucked. And undeniably screwed.

I remember the tender aftercare he treated me with the first time and many other times, and as his cum drips down my tights, I let the tears fall freely as well.

When I wake up next morning, instead of my fiancé, I find a note.

Call Lydia. GC.

The emptiness of the hotel suite spreads through me with finality. I guess sex is not a path to my fiancé's heart and soul. It's one thing that my love is unrequited, but dealing with the loss of respect weighs me down like a lead ball. How long can I remain above the water?

I take a long shower, get dressed and pack my things. As I yank my carry-on from the bed, I glimpse the navy hem of my engagement dress.

I kick it under the bed. Fuck it. I won't play the victim in my own life. Yes, the circumstances would be easier if my heart wasn't the unwanted collateral of this stupid deal. Still, there are lots of positive things I sold my morals for, and I need to focus on that.

Putting my buds in, I dial Lydia's number and walk to the window. The city below bustles. People, events, appointments, meetings, it all seems to flow undisturbed by the loneliness coursing through my veins.

"Good morning, Ms. Ward. My sincere congratulations. Gio apologizes, but he had to leave to take care of business in Vancouver. He'll be back at the end of the week, but wanted to make sure you got everything you need. I have booked the movers tentatively for tomorrow morning. Is that okay?"

Lydia doesn't let slip what she might think about her boss's sudden engagement. She's professional and cordial enough to almost fool me that things are normal.

Normal? What a fucked-up concept. Gio didn't

bother to mention his business trip, but not having him around might be a good thing. It will give me the opportunity to reconcile my new reality. One where I'm no longer lacking money, even though I lack way more.

"Move?" How did I not think about that before? The week leading to the party has been like emotional whiplash, and not once did I think about the living arrangements.

I knew we would, at some point, live in the same residence, but after last night, the gravity has only now truly descended.

"Well..." Lydia sounds perplexed. "You *are* moving into the house?"

"Of course, sorry. I don't really have much. I can be packed by tomorrow morning." I bite my bottom lip. My eyes drop to my engagement ring. I didn't realize I've been playing with it mindlessly.

It feels like a shackle on my finger. A permanent reminder of my failure.

"Great. I'll have a moving van at your place by ten."

I want to scream no. I want to stop the speeding train of my life before it derails. Or even better, I want to rewind time and do everything differently. I need to talk to Gio. I need to explain to him. I need to make him listen.

"Would that work, Ms. Ward?" Lydia is expecting my involvement in all of this. Jesus.

"Please call me Mila. Yes, ten is fine, a small van. I really have very little. When did you say Gio gets back?"

"I don't know yet, but he'll be back by Friday morning for sure. He asked me to make lunch reservations. I will email you the details, along with your schedule for the next two weeks and later events that are already confirmed."

"Okay. Thank you." He asked her to book lunch for us.

"Gio requested I cover the basics with you, so you're more comfortable to get ready for each occasion."

He wanted my comfort? I hang to that sliver of information like it's a lifeline. I know it's irrational. I know Lydia might have chosen those words. I know it's nothing in the grand scheme of things, but it's a drop of water after a week in the desert. A drop of honey to coat my wounded heart.

"Okay, Lydia. Why don't you send me the schedule, and I'll respond with any questions."

"Sure, we can do that. I'll email you the contact information for our concierge as well. And for the gala in May, choose a designer now, so everything can be ready."

I wasn't prepared for this life. Not in my wildest dreams. I experienced luxuries with Gio and with my clients. I experienced things beyond my reach thanks to those connections, but wow, I am completely incompetent at delivering at this level.

"Concierge?"

Lydia clears her throat, but continues with her level voice. I search for a patronizing tone, but there is none. "Yes, think of it as a personal assistant. They take care of your reservations, appointments, shopping, anything you need. Call them with any task at any time and they will take care of you. We have a retainer, so don't hold back."

She talks about *us* as if she's part of the household. I guess she is. Between Lydia, the concierge service, the housekeeper and all the other keepers, Gio's household runs like a well-oiled machine. All his needs and desires fulfilled. An irrational sense of uselessness hits me.

"Provide them with the list of your favorite stylist, spa, etc., so they have it handy and can take care of your appointments. If you feel comfortable, give them access to your calendar."

"I don't have a stylist." Why do I choose to raise that point?

"That's okay. They can recommend someone, but I

think Mrs. Cassinetti might give you more personal recommendations."

The last person I want to call is Gio's mother. She'll see through me immediately. I can't play the happy fiancée in front of her, especially since I don't even know where her son is. She looked suspicious yesterday as it was.

"Okay, I'll do that, but is it necessary to get a designer for the gala you mentioned? Can't I just get something from Haughty..." *Shit.* "From the Saks shopper person?"

"I'll mark in the calendar which events are not necessarily off-the-rack occasions. If you don't have a favorite designer, just get the concierge on it. They might coordinate with our PR department to see who you should wear."

"Yes, I'll do that."

This would be a dream if it wasn't a nightmare. The surreal conversation with Lydia continues for a few more minutes while I get better acquainted with the sharp turn my life has taken.

When we hang up, I force myself to focus on one thing. Gio made a reservation for lunch on Friday. It's not a date, but it's a start. His initiative to spend time together outside of our official schedule.

The knowledge lingers, wrapped in hope as I walk

out of the suite with my engagement dress, my dignity and my heart swept under the bed.

"I don't know why you're such a mess." Annie shakes her head. "It's not like it's your first date."

I prop the phone against a book on the shelf, so she can still see me while I show her the selection of dresses.

"Annie, I want to look my best. Help me here." I didn't sleep all night thinking about today's lunch. I even went as far as getting a stylist, who is coming in an hour to get me ready for my first meal with my fiancé.

It's a daytime meeting, but I'm determined to make him salivate. To make him want me. To remember who we can be together. This time, I won't let him fuck me. He'll have to work for it.

It might be all backward, but I'm going to seduce my fiancé and then let him yearn. Hopefully he misses me enough to remember how good we used to be. Enough to continue where we left off a month ago.

Or I'm just hopelessly naïve. The only one determined to fight for this relationship.

"Why didn't you buy a new dress then?" Annie shrugs.

"It felt weird to spend his money on a dress to have

lunch with *him*." I bite my lower lip, hearing the ridiculousness of my statement. Desperate, I can't seem to find my dignity, or my functioning brain.

"You could use your money. Especially now, when *all* of us are spending his money." She sighs. "But I get what you're saying. I just—" Her sigh turns into a sob.

Ron comes into view and wraps his arms around Annie. "Please, Mila, can you tell your sister she needs to chill about this?" He kisses the crown of her head. "Stress is not good for you, baby," he whispers into her hair.

"Ron is right. It's done, and I'm excited about my lunch today, so can you snap out of it and help me?" I channel all the confidence I don't have into my words. I might be dying slowly, but I won't have my sister suffer. One tormented Ward is enough.

"Go with the red," Ron says, and ambles away.

"Isn't that too bold?" I haven't worn the red sheath retro dress since I arrived in New York. It's classic, chic, and sexy. Ron might be onto something.

"You want bold. That dress shows enough cleavage to tempt, but isn't vulgar. It hugs your ass and suits you well. Go with the red, but tame it down with simple black shoes, and no jewelry. Get your hair done and wear minimal makeup."

I haven't heard from Gio for the entire week. I wrote to him several times, but I've sent none of the messages. I don't want to sound needy and clingy. Staying in touch is not in our deal, and if he wanted to hear from me, he could have at least let me know where he was.

Our communication has been channeled through Lydia or other people on Gio's staff. After my things were picked up a few days ago, I helped Annie pack. She will leave her apartment at the end of the month.

Gio insisted she move to one of his properties instead of sending the increased rent to our landlord. Annie would have been more comfortable staying with the kids where they are, but we lost—temporarily, I hope—the ability to make these decisions.

The worst part is, I know Gio means well. He wants the best for Annie and the kids. Just like with her healthcare providers.

But in his fashion, he forgot to ask, to consider our needs.

Good intentions, wrong actions, again.

Though perhaps at this point he doesn't care enough and just does what's simplest for him.

I carry the dress and all I need from the walk-in closet in the master bedroom to the guest room where I've been staying. Not sure what the staff thinks about that, but I don't have the energy to contemplate their judgment.

When I arrived at my new residence for the first

time, my clothes were already arranged inside the main wardrobe. I hadn't noticed before that there actually were two interconnected rooms for his and hers closets. My side looks pathetically empty.

I'm not sure if it was the housekeeper's initiative or Gio's request, but it appeared I was expected to stay in the master bedroom. The idea filled me with dread. A cruel joke.

There is no way I'd sleep in the bed that used to hold thrilling memories, and now represented only the bitter void of the current state of our relationship. A bond forged on paper only.

I kept my clothes in the master bedroom, but I moved into the guest room. I'm a guest here, after all. Nothing more. Soon to be Cassinetti by name, but nothing else.

I get dressed before the stylist arrives. I've worked with her at several events, and I know she'll deliver what I need.

An hour later, I check myself in the mirror by the front entrance. My face glows with natural makeup, and my hair appears carelessly arranged in waves, definitely a model-worthy mane.

Along with the red dress, this makeover boosts my confidence.

As I leave my house, I feel energized, confident and

gorgeous, and for the first time in weeks I'm genuinely smiling.

Even in late February, New York glimmers with sunshine as the early unexpected spring sweeps through the streets.

New beginning.

Chapter 25

Mila

My smile dies as soon as Gio's lawyer greets me. I wish I didn't have this appointment on my way to meet him, but Fatima couldn't squeeze me in at another time.

"Nice to see you again, Ms. Ward." She looks me up and down. "You look... different."

Now I regret the timing of our meeting even more. The first time we met, I was... me. Now I'm dolled up and dressed to the nines, only validating my motivations behind this marriage. Damn it.

Her office is a corner suite, furnished with efficiency and a lack of personal touches. She offers me a seat on a chair that screams custom-made art, but lacks in the comfort and ergonomic departments. Not that I could feel comfortable given the topic of this meeting.

I adjust my skirt as she studies me. She looks like

she is not sure if I'm her current appointment. Somewhat puzzled and slightly uncomfortable. *Well, Fatima, that makes two of us.*

Without a word, she pushes a folder in front of me. A bright yellow folder. By now, I'm willing to make an animal sacrifice to stop these from appearing. My life has been ruled by these fucking yellow folders.

It's official. I'm stupid and naïve because part of me believed Gio would be here today. Just like the first time when he stayed and made me feel protected from the lawyer and the legalities of his damn scheme, I was expecting—hoping—he'd show up again.

I sigh and flip the front page. "Where do I sign?"

Fatima's eyes widen. Just a split-second reaction that proves she expected me to be surprised. She knew Gio would suggest something like this—and he did—but she didn't anticipate my full collaboration.

"Ms. Ward, as a lawyer I'm representing my client's interests. But woman to woman, I can't help but recommend your lawyer review this before you sign."

"Why? Are there red flags?" I shouldn't be this oblivious to a contract with my future husband, but I've been numbed to the world for too many days now to muster any interest.

"Not necessarily, but this contract is the most

unusual prenup I've heard of. Have you discussed the terms with Gio?"

Yes, that's the only conversation he's had with me. Via email. I know what I'm signing, but I read anyway.

Upon marrying Gio Cassinetti, I'll become a sole owner of the event company he bought, Annie will get a new house, and Gio will foot the bill for her medical care and the kids' education for the duration of our marriage. This much I agreed to.

If I choose to divorce him within five years—what? —he will no longer have financial obligations to my family and the firm will automatically return to his holding. My marital duties include attendance at all of Gio's social engagements, with a right to refuse once a month.

After five years, if we divorce, I get five million dollars. Every stipulation is like a scalpel through my heart. If in five years we remain married, I'm expected to provide an heir.

Tears prickle behind my eyes. "Where do I sign?"

I've been second-guessing my decision for many sleepless nights. The look on Gio's face in that stupid car, the disapproval and disappointment. I don't understand why he went through with it. His reaction makes no sense. He proposed the arrangement. But once I accepted, he seems hurt.

I have Annie and the kids to think about. I can't be

analyzing the fallout of my decision. Yet, here I am, spending day and night doing just that, while Gio has been skillfully avoiding me.

Fatima taps her long nails on the line, and I scribble my name on each copy.

"Well, I guess congratulations are in order. All the best." She stands up and walks to the door.

Done. I signed, and now I'm dismissed. Efficient. Gio would love that.

"I didn't see this coming. I don't judge you, Mila. Good for you. Just... usually I'm an excellent judge of situations, and I really thought you were the one who would pull him out of the shadows of his past into a normal world. Though I always believed I'd be drafting a prenup for one of the selfish women in his life. At least I can see you're doing it for your family. Good luck."

I stare at her for a moment, a war brewing inside me. I didn't ask for her opinion. I didn't want to hear from this stranger what a failure I was. If she's trying to make me feel better by suggesting I'm not like the other women, she's failed.

For some outlandish reason, I feel like I need to stand up for myself and own the deal. "Let's not forget I'm getting a company out of this. Win-win."

I stroll out of her office and find the first toilet. I

lock myself in the cubicle and scream into my fist, so nobody can hear my little personal death.

* * *

If I thought the visit with Fatima was the worst of my day, I was wrong. My nerves are fragile as it is, but when I see what awaits me at the restaurant, I consider running away.

In a busy bistro near to Gio's offices, he sits with his back to me. The hostess weaves between the tables, my heels clicking behind her, my heart thumping in my temples.

His suit hugs his broad shoulders, and my traitorous body immediately pulls toward him. But it's my heart that shatters. There is a woman sitting across from him. Whatever this is, it's definitely not a date with my fiancé.

My steps falter a bit before I stop and take a deep breath. I force a smile to my face as I reach the table and both of them stand up.

"Ms. Ward, so nice to meet you. I'm Hilda Steiner." The woman, in her early forties and wearing a comfortable gray pantsuit, shakes my hand.

She looked vaguely familiar, and now the name connects the dots. She is the owner—the former owner—of the firm Gio bought for me.

This is a business meeting. I push my disappointment as far as possible and focus on my smile.

"Very nice to meet you too. Please call me Mila."

I chance my first glance at him as he steps closer. Way too close. The smoke and spice hit me straight in the chest, closing my throat with a lump.

Our eyes meet, and one thing is clear. My dress and styling fulfilled their intended purpose.

Dark brown abyss.

The glint in Gio's eyes confirms he loves what he sees. That one simple look wraps me in the caress of his dominance.

He lowers his lips to my temple, and I hate that I shudder. That my body immediately screams how much I want him. How much I've missed him.

"Nice to see you, darling," Gio drawls.

Darling? My half-functioning brain kicks in, and I realize this affection is for the benefit of our company. But that predatory gaze is above and beyond, unnecessary for the charade. That gaze is real.

Gio moves the chair for me to sit. His arm brushes mine, and the mini explosions around my body spread heat all over.

"Nice to see you too, *Giovanni*." He flinches at the formal name I have never used before. If I'm a darling... "I hope your trip was okay." I collapse into the chair, grateful for the support.

Gio returns to his seat, glaring at me, but then he focuses on Hilda. "I landed this morning. I was in Vancouver."

The server arrives and we order our lunch.

"Hilda, as of this morning, I transferred the title to the company to my fiancée. Everything else remains the same. You're staying on for three to six months to ensure a smooth transition and minimal disruption for the clients."

Hilda seems momentarily disoriented, but she recovers quickly. "In what capacity do you want to be involved?"

My darling fiancé blindsided us both. As with any business transaction, he keeps his cards close.

I move my chair slightly, so I'm facing her better, but mostly to keep Gio out of my line of vision. I can't show him my back, so the attempt is only mildly helpful, but I force myself to focus on Hilda.

"I intend to be fully involved. I have been working in social—"

"I don't think it's necessary you give Hilda your credentials, darling." Gio squeezes my hand and I almost gasp. The electricity zips through me at the touch. It might be for show and completely insincere, but I still react. "You're her boss."

Hilda's eyes widen and I don't blame her. The patronizing tone and his interruption don't really improve my chances for a reasonable rapport with this woman.

I shoot him a glare and then smile at Hilda. "I'm sure you don't want your company to become just one of the hundreds of subsidiaries of the Cassinetti holding. You built your commendable client list on your personal approach, and I'd like to continue within that business culture, so let me tell you a bit about me..."

I give her my credentials, and soon we fall into a practical conversation about the company, its goals and challenges.

Hilda presents a clear picture and I provide some suggestions. It's all top-level, and I have a long way to go to get to know the employees and the clients, but while we eat our meals, Hilda becomes my ally. I think that before she leaves her baby to me, she'll end up being a wonderful mentor.

Gio doesn't interrupt our conversation anymore, but that doesn't mean I forget about his presence. I don't have to look his way to feel his burning gaze scorching my skin. He hasn't even pulled out his phone.

I glance at him once. Leaning in his chair casually, he looks like the king he is. His focus is solely on me.

It's unnerving and exhilarating at the same time. By the time we get the bill, I'm proud of myself for keeping up the conversation under his blazing scrutiny.

I'm also so riled up I want to storm away, or yell at him for his games. The man is hot and cold, and I just need a fucking break.

We agree with Hilda that on Monday she'll introduce me to the team, and we'll start work on the transition. I'm excited about the opportunity, even though it's tainted by the way I acquired it. I'll prove myself.

At the front door, Gio checks his watch impatiently.

"I have to use the bathroom." I excuse myself to spare my poor heart the humiliation of walking away from Gio without knowing when I'll see him next. Especially in front of an audience. I say goodbye to Hilda and rush away.

As I wash my hands, my reflection surprises me. I forgot how good I look today. All that effort for nothing.

My fiancé stared, but that's about it. Besides, he completely blindsided me with the meeting. On purpose. Lydia would have told me what the meeting was about if she knew.

Pissed at the situation, I yank the door open and freeze.

Chapter 26

Gio

I tug her to me and Mila yelps, forcing me to cover her mouth. Throughout lunch I tried to ignore her scent of lavender and something else. Something primal and overwhelming that pulls me to her against my will. Fucking pheromones.

That curve-hugging dress of a temptress has been driving me crazy since she arrived. Her pretty little nose and pale face with indigo eyes made several men look her way, and I almost bent her over the table right there to show everyone she belongs to me.

But it was nothing compared to the way she put me in my place and took over the meeting. I didn't tell her about Hilda because I didn't want her to fret about first impressions. Well, she wiped the smirk off my face, because she handled herself with grace. I hadn't realized the depth of her experience.

So fucking sexy.

We glare at each other, chests heaving. Pent-up energy from the last weeks zaps between us. I thought the night of our engagement party when I fucked her like I hated her would help me get her out of my system. But there is no forgetting Mila Ward.

She's under my skin, in my bloodstream, on my mind. She's everywhere, and yet we don't spend time together. We can't. I won't let her—or me—get attached. That's not what this union is. It's a transaction.

I relax my hand on her mouth and fist her hair, angling her face. I put my other hand next to her head, caging her between me and the wall. Our lips are almost touching. God, I want her.

"Did you miss me, fiancée?" I nuzzle her neck and inhale. *Mine.*

She braces her hands against my chest, but doesn't push me away. I breathe in the air she exhales. We stand there, glaring and panting.

"Let go of me," she rasps, but she still doesn't push me away.

"Why are you so pissy?" What was she expecting this arrangement to be about?

She narrows her eyes. "I went to see Fatima. It looks like there is a five-year expiration on this marriage, Giovanni."

"Don't be so dramatic. And don't call me Giovanni."

I chance a doorknob to my right and push her inside. It's a service closet, dimly lit. I shut the door and pivot Mila, pinning her again between me and the door.

"Isn't Giovanni your name?" she spits.

My erection digs into her belly, and fuck, I'm losing control here. This woman strips me of all my sanity.

"What's your fucking problem, Mila?" I shouldn't have waited for her. It was a mistake. Now I either fuck her or I walk with a boner for the rest of the day. Pissed at her and myself. At the world. Perhaps fire a few people, the casualties of this fucked-up impasse we've orchestrated.

"Oh, I'll ask Lydia to give you a list. It's too long, and I'm sure you have somewhere to be. A business trip you don't care to tell me about?" Is that what's up her ass?

"I didn't know I'd be leaving. Lydia told you, didn't she?"

"Don't put this on Lydia. A text message would have been a normal way to communicate. Oh, sorry, I forgot you can't have normal." She mocks me. For someone who practically cannot move, she has some gumption. Another sexy quality I hate her for. But she has a point.

"Next time I'll text you."

She blinks a few times, like she didn't expect me to accept a decent communication flow between us. I chuckle. "Anything else you'd like to get off your chest?"

If her eyes were lasers, I'd be dead already. She's been shooting them at me since I accosted her.

"You put a nice price on five years of my life." Her voice falters a bit.

Seriously, she's really going to blame me for protecting myself. Her? A woman who laid her conditions clearly.

"Don't forget, darling, I'm paying for your sister's life, your nephew's education, and your career." I pinch her chin between my finger and thumb, barely holding myself back. Why do I have to be so attracted to her? "Just. As. You. Wanted." I move my hips with every word, poking her with my cock.

I kick her feet farther apart, half expecting her to knee me. God, I want to kiss her. I want to do things to her.

I want to punish her for tainting things between us. I want to reward her for being herself at the same time. I need to warn her to run.

I'm about to step back when she grabs my dick and

with her other hand pulls me to her lips. Our teeth crash against each other. I growl and fist her hair again, making sure I can get as deep as possible, invading her with my tongue.

Mila moans into my mouth and my cock hardens more, if that's even possible. The kiss is full of my anger and frustration, and she takes it all. And gives me more.

"It feels like you missed me, fiancé." She pants, and I bite her hard. She gasps, but it turns into a moan quickly. The sound robs me of all reservations.

I find the hem of that wanton dress and trail up the silk of her thighs to her sex. I cup her roughly. "Hm, Princess, it seems like you're equally desperate for me. Some things have stayed the same."

Our eyes meet, a silent duel.

"Many things stayed the same, you idiot." She fidgets with my belt buckle, and before I process her words, she unzips me and frees my cock.

My chest heaves with resentment and lust. I seize her lips again, and then take her, all against the door of a dingy closet.

This woman who deserves a palace.

I fuck that thought out of my mind. Taking everything I can get from her, which is not enough.

* * *

"You can try that loophole, but sometimes you just have to cut your losses." Conrad shrugs.

The shopping and entertainment center development in Singapore has been driving me crazy. After a series of meetings that led nowhere, I decided to visit Conrad, who is anchored somewhere in the Mediterranean sea.

"You might be onto something." I drag my hand down my face. "This deal is sucking the life out of me. I'm trying to be on three continents at the same time, and it's never enough. There is always a fucker who delays shit, and things topple like a house of cards."

I play with my tumbler, the golden liquid swirling. It's so peaceful here, it makes me nervous. I don't understand how Conrad and Nora can live on their yacht longer than a week. Jesus.

On the horizon, the sun is setting, a large red ball tethered above the ocean. Even the view makes me edgy.

"You're too involved. Don't you have people to deal with some of that shit? Seriously, man, there is no point in making money if you have to work this hard for it. You're micromanaging."

Perhaps I am. I've always loved working. It's my go-to place where I thrive, but lately it's been pure stress.

I'm more involved than I've ever been, and things are going from bad to worse. This deal is taking up so much time and attention, that other things are getting caught in the landslide.

I'm working more because I'm avoiding my fiancée. I took the lead on two new acquisitions to keep my distance from Mila. And now I'm drowning in stupid details that are way below my pay grade.

We've been engaged for three months. I have successfully avoided her for most of it. Mostly to stifle the need to yell at her for ruining what we could have had.

Since my last and only serious relationship I haven't trusted women, and they continued to prove me right in my reluctance to let them in.

I always assumed I'd end up in a marriage of convenience, to secure myself an heir. Mila is the only one cashing in on the conveniences here. I've been dodging social invitations left and right, just to stay away from her.

"I can't have this fail. It's not even about money anymore. I'm not having fucking Corrado Napolis steal the deal out from under me. He's a mobster."

"I'm all for some good old competition, but a little perspective, man. This much work and hustle can't be good. When do you have time for your fiancée?" He snickers.

I grab my phone to check... I don't even know

what. Who cares? As long as I can avoid this line of conversation.

Making up business trips in the last three months has helped me stay away from her, but as much as I try, I can't get her out of my head. I'm irrationally mad at Mila for not being who I need her to be.

Every time I see her, I want to take her home and undress her slowly and make love to her. It irritates me. At least I found some restraint, and I haven't fucked her since the incident in the restaurant's closet. That encounter wasn't sweet or gentle, but still it was more intimate than I could stomach.

Conrad watches me patiently, knowing me too well. Knowing my silence speaks volumes.

"She's marrying me for money." I throw the phone on the table.

He chuckles. "Not this again."

"It's true. I went to grovel—your advice by the way —and she needed money and said yes before I even withdrew the proposal."

"Fuck me. I'm sorry, man. I thought she was differ-ent." He refills his glass. "Why did you go through with it?"

"I need a wife." I shrug.

I'll marry her, because in that moment when she kicked me in the solar plexus with her acceptance, I couldn't stand the idea of losing her.

Not that I benefited.

Not that she cares.

I want her to consider me the way she does her family. Everyone gets a piece of her except me.

I shouldn't have gone through with the engagement, but it's too late now. Everyone is excited. Lucky me.

I can't be with her, and I can't avoid her forever, so I'm locked in this weird situation where I have what I want, but I don't really have it.

"How is that working out for you?" Conrad's lips quirk up.

"Don't go there, fucker," I growl.

"Of course I'll go there. You've busting your ass working—more than your usual workaholic self. I know you better than anyone. The symptoms are too similar to post-fucking-Kimb—"

"Don't!" I clench my fist and down the scotch.

"Gio, talk to me. Or talk to her, but fucking talk."

"And what am I supposed to say?" I snap. "That it fucking hurts when someone rejects you? When you think they're different, but in the end they are not? I've lived for years, accepting my wealth and status always come at a price. Knowing I will have to marry an heiress or a socialite and lead a sterile life dictated by societal expectations—"

"That's where you're wrong, you idiot. You're not

old money. There are no societal expectations. Just because a woman fooled you years ago, it doesn't make you unworthy of love. It only makes you gullible. Besides, Kimberly fooled us all, so it's not even on you. We should learn from our mistakes, but you took that shit too far. Like the opposite side of the pendulum too far. Why are you really marrying Mila Ward?"

"Because… I fucking can't let her go." I grab the bottle and fill my glass to the rim. Classy.

He jerks it away from me. "Motivated by momentary obsession, or by love?"

I chuckle. "Don't be absurd. I'm attracted to her, but that's all. I thought she felt the same."

"Yet you're marrying her, and knowing you, it isn't because of your charitable heart. You're not marrying her to resolve her financial issues. You want her. Let's skip the motivation since you don't believe in love, but you want *her* to be your wife. And yet you run away, chasing deals that are not worth the effort. Working yourself into the ground."

"That's not true," I bark. "The deal is very important."

"Okay, then continue working yourself until you collapse. Look around, Gio. When Nora suggested this lifestyle, I had an allergic reaction, and then it took me months to detox the stress-related adrenaline. That shit kills you."

If I slow down, I have nothing left. I love my work. Though the pressure lately has been tainting that.

"Why don't you bring Mila and spend some time here with us?"

"And be reminded every day why she is with me?" Damn it.

"Fair enough." He pats my shoulder. "Stay longer then."

"I have to get back and deal with these projections, and my mother's monthly family summons. I missed the last two, and believe me the last thing I want is to get her on my case."

He laughs. "Understood. Bianca is lovely, but she scares the shit out of me."

I need to learn to live with Mila without this persistent feeling of betrayal. And without being horny and pissed all the time. She'll stick around for five years at least. I need to find a way to look at her without being disappointed.

Maybe I can try harder.

Chapter 27

Mila

"**A**ren't you going home yet?" Hilda pokes her head in my door.

It's seven o'clock, and I have to be at a theater opening night in an hour. I had a new dress delivered to my office, so there is no reason to commute to the house.

What's the point? It's not like anyone is waiting for me there.

Over the past three months, Gio has been traveling a lot. Mostly avoiding me. When in New York he stays at his club most of the time, and then comes home to tend to his bees, but that's it.

I accepted my fate and dove into the work. When I'm here, I forget about my loveless relationship. I've been spending a lot of time at Annie's.

Her new house is beautiful and full of life. Unlike

Gio's house. A place which is no longer his home because I'm intruding there.

"We're attending a premiere tonight. I'll be leaving shortly."

"The glamorous life of the young and wealthy." Hilda sighs dramatically.

Though she has contractual obligations to remain here, she's been nothing but amazing and we work well together. My initial assessment was right, and Hilda has become my business mentor.

"Frankly, along with the two events we're organizing this weekend, I could use a night off."

"Yeah, but it's nice you get to do something fun with your devilishly handsome fiancé." She purses her lips and looks at me suggestively while shimmying her hips.

Fun with Gio? What would I give for that? Or would have given, but with two hate fucks under my belt and an MIA fiancé, I kind of gave up on the idea of reconciliation and a happy marriage.

But as Hilda leaves, the suggestion persists. Gio hates socializing. After three months of almost radio-silence, we're going out tonight.

As much as I built walls around my heart, I allow hope to seep through. I can't imagine this particular theater premiere is that important—the first social obligation since we've gotten engaged.

Does he, in his twisted, prideful way, have an ulterior motive for this outing? Does he want to forge a better relationship?

We've been in this weirdly constructed partnership longer than we were ever in a normal one. I don't know anymore what's real and what's my imagination.

Perhaps I misconstrued how much he used to care about me. All the gestures and gifts and the weekend in St. Martin blinded me, and I might have fallen while he didn't.

"There is a delivery here for you," Hilda calls from the elevator bank. "Good night."

The door slides closed as I walk to the reception area, enjoying the silence of the office and the carpet under my bare feet.

A small package lays at the front desk. It has no card or return address. I open it gingerly. A jewelry box? I lift the velvet top and gasp.

A delicate chain with an intricate pendant. Tiny emeralds nest between the rose gold wires of a butterfly. There is no card attached, but there is no doubt who it's from. I didn't even know Gio noticed I admired the necklace at Saks on our first date.

The fluttering feelings in my stomach stem from both excitement and anxiety. Why did he send me this? What does it mean? Jesus. As soon as I think I'm getting immune to my reluctant future husband, he does this. Instead of words.

By the time I get changed and dolled up for the premiere, I'm so torn between fantasies and reality, I almost call Gio to tell him I can't attend. I have been reasonably good, avoiding this destructively hopeful spiral of thinking, but tonight I can't seem to collect myself.

Hope blooms, and as much as I try to protect myself and stomp all over it before he does, I'm a mess when I get into the car.

My driver texts Gio, so he's on the sidewalk to open my door when we arrive. My hand slips into his and he helps me out of the car.

Goosebumps.

Heat wave.

Heart palpitation.

"You're late," he growls instead of the greeting.

Cold shower.

The cameras blind me as we make our way inside. Gio puts a protective hand on the small of my back.

Whiplash.

We take our seats on the balcony. I wasn't paying enough attention before to realize this is a new production of *Anna Karenina*. Great. Now I have to suffer through a drama about love with a tragic end. All the while breathing through the accidental touches of Gio's arm.

"I promised Andrea we'd stop at his opening tonight. Are you tired?" Gio asks during the intermission.

"Whatever you want." Is this going to be my default answer from now on? Perpetually trapped between his mercy and my need to demonstrate I'm grateful for what he's done for my family.

"I was thinking we could skip the second half of the play and just zip by the gallery in SoHo. Do you want to watch the rest?" Gio adjusts his cuffs.

What is with him tonight? Is he uncomfortable? After the initial growl about my lateness, he seems... I don't know... less aloof, more protective, distant but still present?

Closer than in the last few months. I can't describe it, but suddenly I feel we're on the verge of a breakthrough. Or perhaps a breakdown.

"I know how it ends, and frankly the production is a bit underwhelming." I search his face for signs of... well, I don't know what.

He smirks. "You're right about that. Let's ditch it." He offers me his arm, and we leave as the happy couple that almost everyone believes we are.

The ride takes longer because of traffic, and the air fills with an awkward silence. I don't know how to break the ice, so I talk about my work. He's the primary investor, after all.

Flustered for no apparent reason—other than spending time with my fiancé after three long months of trying to reinforce my guard—I chatter on and on. He finally interrupts me, but it's not with a growl or dismissal.

"So you doubled the number of clients?" There is both praise and concern in his question.

I chance a look at him. He's not even holding his phone. Gio is looking right at me. I avert my gaze, because in the car's dimness I don't want to misinterpret the emotion behind his eyes.

I don't want to feed the hope, so I lean into the safety of our current topic. "Our projections are at twenty to thirty percent increase compared to last year. I had to hire more people, so the overhead is higher, but most of them work from home, which contributes to the bottom line."

"If you continue this way, next year we can consider an IPO. You should be careful about growing this fast, though. Smaller shops—"

"We have a committee looking into implementing necessary processes. It's important to Hilda, and me, that we stay small in terms of values and culture as we grow."

He continues asking me questions and offers

suggestions. By the time we arrive, my poor heart is galloping around, and my stomach is tied in a double knot.

I should be thrilled, but I can't risk it. I can't expose my heart. Allowing hope would be a suicide mission.

Perhaps his openness has nothing to do with me. He might have had a good day and I benefited. Still, as we walk to the gallery, I'm struggling to breathe. This can't be happening. I protected my heart. I can't have it shattered again.

The beautiful open space with floor-to-ceiling windows facing the street is packed with people. I can't imagine anyone can truly appreciate the art. It's more like a dance club, though the music is jazzier. Several well-dressed guests squeeze around us, leaving.

"Hey, guys. Good, you made it." Sydney pushes through the crowd to greet us. Her gorgeous boyfriend shakes hands with Gio.

"Quite a turnout." I try not to analyze Gio's arm around my waist.

"I'm not so sure that's good, and Andrea is high." Sydney pleads with Gio, and some undecipherable communication passes between the siblings.

"It doesn't seem like this is a crowd of art aficionados." Gio frowns. "Where is he?"

He's right. Most of the people here look like starving artists, hipsters, goths, bohemians. I'm not the one to judge by appearance, but this looks like a group of artists descended on the place. Not the typical crowd for a commercial gallery.

Sydney huffs with exasperation. "Somewhere here. I tried to talk to him, but it didn't go well."

A beautiful but somewhat frazzled blonde appears by our side. "Gio."

"Violet." He kisses her cheek. "This is my fiancée, Mila Ward. Mila, this is the gallery owner, Violet Mathison." We shake hands and Gio continues. "Why did you send so many invitations for the event?"

"I didn't," she pushes through her teeth. "The man of the hour did."

"Fuck me. Where is he?" Gio grabs my hand, and we follow Violet through the crowd, with Sydney and Hunter behind us.

There is some family crisis happening, that much is clear to me, but it's my hand in his that steals all my attention. Large, warm, protective. The most intimate touch we've shared in months.

The gallery consists of three interconnected rooms, and we finally find Andrea in the last one. In the corner, under a large colorful canvas, he talks to a small crowd of guests. His long fingers direct his monologue like a musical performance.

Around him, women are gasping at everything he says, and it's clear he relishes the attention, but behind the dilated pupils his inner torture is visible. When he flirted with me at Hunter's opening, his struggles were obvious. What drives him to drugs?

He lifts his gaze. The man is roguishly handsome. All the Cassinetti brothers are. Andrea has a lean body like Gio, but his form is not as filled out.

His jawline and cheeks could cut diamonds, all sharp lines of raw beauty. His cat-like, greenish brown eyes scare me, but I can see how they draw women into madness.

"My family," Andrea drawls and excuses himself. A collective sigh follows him as he joins us, his eyes narrowed and a cunning smile on his handsome face.

"What the fuck? You won't sell anything if you bring all the stray cats in off the street and nobody can actually see the art." Gio glares at his brother.

Andrea laughs and pats Gio's cheek. "Not everything is about closing deals and making money, bro."

Violet sighs and leaves to attend to a couple who seem mortified by the bursts of laughter and carefree behavior around them.

"Don't act like an asshole. Why would you jeopardize your own opening?" Gio insists.

"You haven't had a show in years and then you do this? Your friends could have come any other night." Sydney rubs her hand down Andrea's arm in a motherly gesture.

"I wanted to have my friends here. I don't give a shit about the so-called connoisseurs. Fuck them all."

His words carry to the couple, and they shake their heads and leave, despite Violet's obvious efforts to placate them.

Andrea sways a little and turns to kiss the cheek of a young woman who passes by.

Violet storms back to us. Poking her finger into Andrea's chest, she speaks quietly enough not to cause a scene, but with an authoritative tone that makes us all straighten up.

"You're a narcissistic egomaniac little boy hiding in a man's body. I gave you an amazing opportunity, and you fucked it up. All the possible buyers ran away because you filled the place with desperate people who want to be you, or who admire you because they clearly don't know you well enough. Next time you want a fan club, don't fuck with my gallery business."

She turns and leaves, her heels somehow echoing above the raucous crowd around us.

"I'm glad someone explained this to you." Gio shakes his head.

Andrea chuckles and cups my face. It's so unexpected, my arms flail up. Before I process what is happening or anybody can react, Andrea lowers his face to mine. "You chose the wrong brother, beautiful." He crashes his lips to mine.

His tongue slides in, but he's yanked off me imme-diately. Gio punches him in the face and Andrea stum-bles backward, loses his balance and collapses into a tall woman, taking her down with him.

A group gasp is followed by silence. Gio grabs my hand and drags me across the packed room until we get outside.

"Are you okay?" He scans me for injuries, as if Andrea's lips could have cut or hurt me. His concerned gaze fills me with a fleeting hope.

"Yes," I rasp. He stares at me, bewildered. Like the whole situation made little sense to him. "Are you?"

Instead of answering, he seizes my lips. I'm assaulted for the second time within minutes, but this time I welcome the invasion. Gio kisses me like a man possessed.

I don't know if he needs to erase Andrea's lips from mine. Or if he wants to re-brand me so I don't forget who I belong to.

Because he may keep pushing me away, but there is no doubt in my mind, I belong to him, whether he wants me or not.

Startled—that was the only emotion cruising through me during that millisecond of Andrea's kiss. His kiss had only one goal—to rile Gio. Well, mission accomplished. Had I known, I'd have kissed someone a long time ago.

I almost smile at the thought, but the cocktail of emotions coursing through my body right now is too powerful to let anything else seep through. I grab Gio's lapels and pull him closer, unwilling to break the connection.

He anchors me with his hands in my hair. Our tongues dance together. My heart dances too. And I hope it's pairs choreography because whatever happens after this kiss, I know I can't continue like we've been since the engagement.

"Let's go home." He steps away and turns, pulling out his phone. I watch his back, my hope disintegrating into a puddle at my feet.

Gio calls his driver. "He should be here in five." He doesn't look at me, but he weaves his fingers through mine.

I want to ask what's next, but our issues, the lack of trust and major miscommunication are too deep to just attack here on the street.

We get into the car.

Gio holds my hand the entire ride.

We're silent.

We don't look at each other.

The air between us crackles with energy that is sexual, but also full of anxiety.

The silence is weighted with unsaid words and unanswered questions.

When we enter the house, neither of us is talking. Gio walks to the bedroom and I follow, preparing my speech, but suddenly feeling completely unequipped to fight against his misconceptions.

I want to tell him I love him, but do I? After three months of adjusting to his demands and absence, I'm not sure anymore. Maybe I'm just jaded, rejected, and holding on to something that is only a part of my fantasy.

I stop in the doorway. Gio sheds his jacket, unbuttons his shirt, and my core tingles at the sight of his abs. God, I've missed that body, but I can't survive another hate fuck.

Not with this man. I might question my love for him because of the last few months, but I definitely don't hate him.

At that moment, I need him so much. And while unable to find the words, I decide I need to take back control.

I remove the distance between us and startle him when I yank the shirt off his shoulders. Gio observes me with raised eyebrows. While I fiddle with his belt, I nuzzle his neck and kiss him gently.

He lets out a sharp breath and leans down. Finding the hem of my dress, he steps back and pulls it over my head. His eyes roam my body as if he's seeing me for the first time. I finally figure out the belt buckle and yank down his pants.

We both stand in our underwear, staring at each other with anticipation and hesitation. His eyes drop to the butterfly pendant between my breasts.

I touch the fine jewel. "Thank you," I croak, the tiny stones burning under my fingertips. What a fitting symbol of our relationship. It grew from ugly to beautiful, and very tragically short-lived.

I pull him to me and brush my lips over his. A moan of frustration finds its way from his throat, and he deepens the kiss. The sensation that explodes in my body and heart has lethal properties. There is no way I can survive him.

I move toward the bed, and Gio follows without breaking the kiss. His hands are everywhere, a rough caress that bruises and vindicates. That makes me feel all the feels.

Tears prickle my eyes, and my heart hammers against my ribcage as I try to reconcile what this means. Can we forge a new connection?

Gio pushes me to the bed and lowers himself onto me. For a moment I relish in the solidity of his muscles above me, but then I take him by surprise and flip us. I straddle him, knowing this is the only way I can control the tempo and make love to him.

Gio rips off my underwear, and I lift to allow him

to enter me. He fills me to the hilt and I still, because...
Jesus.

"Fuck." The word is strangled on his lips, and it encourages me to rock my hips. Gio throws his head back. A beautiful man.

I move slowly, relishing the sensations attacking my body, looking down at him. At the man who has made me the happiest and hurt me the most. He squeezes my breasts, playing with them, drinking my body in, but never reaching my face.

Tears blur my vision as I ride him slowly, hoping to find the lost intimacy between us, but he doesn't meet my gaze.

I stop moving, forcing him to snap his eyes to me. We engage in a silent duel of pain, hurt, betrayal.

The L word is on my lips, but before I muster the courage to risk my poor heart, Gio's nostrils flare and he turns us over, and then rolls me on to my stomach and hoists my hips up.

He plunges into me and sets a punishing tempo. I can't see his eyes and tell him with mine what I want to say. He took control, and I lose mine completely as my orgasm builds up.

My limbs go liquid as I see stars, and Gio follows me shortly. He rides me through our orgasms, and then collapses on top of me.

Still in me, he kisses my shoulder and then lowers

his forehead there and exhales. His sigh is loaded with regret, and tears trail down my cheeks.

We stay like this for I don't know how long. I can barely breathe under his weight, but I don't dare complain because having him this close, this much mine, is the most intimate we've been since January. Even though he fought hard to avoid it.

Nothing has been resolved tonight. Nothing has changed, but so much has. When he finally pulls out of me, I mourn his loss immediately.

Gio stands up, leaving me exposed and conflicted.

I don't want him to see my tears. I have to be strong for this. I roughly wipe them away, and as I try to stand up, he appears and stops me, turning me on to my back. He hands me a washcloth. I stare at the warm fabric, my hands shaking.

Did we just take one step closer to possible reconciliation? I clean myself, strangely self-conscious as he watches me intently. He opens his mouth to say something, but then thinks better of it.

He takes the cloth from me and covers me with the duvet. "I'll sleep in one of the guest rooms."

Something dies inside me. Was this just a quick fuck for him again?

"Stay," I croak.

Our eyes meet. The dark brown abyss. Full of conflict.

Minutes tick by as we stare at each other. I squeeze the duvet and pull it closer to my neck, protecting myself. But no million-thread count fabric can save me from his words.

"I can't."

He walks away and I don't stop him. I finally made it to our master bedroom, and now I'm here alone. It doesn't feel like a win, but as the events of the night flicker through my mind, I realize it isn't a loss either.

In the morning, I find a note in the kitchen.

Unexpected business in LA. GC.

I tear the note apart, and for good measure throw a mug against the wall.

Chapter 28

Gio

The incident with my brother pushed me to her bed. She smelled so good, her body fitting against me. She took the initiative and... I felt used.

She spent our evening together blabbering about her work. Nothing else to say to me.

And then she seduced me. Why? To ensure I keep footing the bill? A part of me argues there was more behind her need. But that's wishful thinking. Mila doesn't want me for me. Nobody does.

I've been spinning in circles. Hating her and being pulled to her. She is like a fucking magnet.

I stayed true to my decision, to accept our co-existence without the resentment and unresolved disappointment. It would have worked.

But then she talked about her work, and I grew

impressed. In a few months, Mila turned the company into a cash cow.

While the opportunity was handed to her on no merit, other than snatching me in the process, she exceeded all expectations. As I listened to her, pride brewed inside me.

We were close in that car, discussing business. I felt even closer, holding her hand in the gallery. She was mine. She was mine after Andrea's stunt, but what happened later was too intimate.

Too real.

I can't afford to be vulnerable. So I ran. The hurt in her eyes when I refused to stay in bed with her has been haunting me for days now. But as alluring as she is, I can't trust her.

It's fucking exhausting. I buried myself in work again. My only salvation. Still, Mila is stealing most of my attention. I need to break this engagement. I can't trust women.

My life would be easier if she weren't so fucking sexy. I got engaged to the most beautiful, smart woman in the world, and now I have to avoid her because she is too tempting. Not just her body. Her mind. Her heart.

I don't even make sense to myself anymore. Fuck.

I get off the plane and two messages wait for me. One from my sister.

SYDNEY

Andrea is out of control. Go see him
when you get a chance.

The other one is from my mother.

MOM

You and Mila are expected today. No
excuses.

I love my family, but sometimes I wish I could love them from afar.

As the car pulls into traffic, my phone rings. Marnie?

"You don't trust Portia?"

What the hell? I groan. "Of course I trust Portia. What are you talking about?"

"She says you've taken on things I used to handle. She's considering leaving." Marnie's voice lacks manners. I might deserve that.

"I don't know what you're talking about." Okay, maybe I do know, and it has nothing to do with Portia or her performance.

"Where were you the last couple of days?" She really is pissed.

"California." I lean against the seat, closing my eyes. "Not that it's any of your business."

"And where was Portia?"

"How the fuck do I know?" I'm ready to hang up.

"She should have been in California. With you or alone, because she can handle the negotiations. Since when have you started micromanaging?"

Since I trapped myself with Mila. Everything has shifted on its axis since her smile, her scent, her voice, her body invaded my space. I can't find my equilibrium, and I hate that. Working, I can be myself. I can at least pretend things are as they are supposed to be.

"I got to go, Marnie." I hang up, because I won't explain my current funk to her. She has no right interfering.

I make several phone calls on the way to Andrea's house, fighting fatigue. This back and forth between several time zones is taking its toll.

When we finally arrive in Chelsea, I'm more ready to shower and sleep than tackle the issues with my brother, or any other normal functioning.

Of course, the fucker takes his time opening the door. When it finally flings open, I regret coming over immediately. He squints at me, blinded by the sun, and probably suffocating in the sudden intake of fresh air.

The odor coming from him and his place gags me. I push past him and get to the kitchen to start his espresso machine, while opening all the blinds and windows on my way. Like a vampire, he scurries around, shielding his face.

"What do you want?" He leans against the kitchen doorway.

I down a small espresso. "What the hell is wrong with you?"

"Many things, but I don't need you to come and remind me." He trudges into his sitting room and plops on the couch. "Go away."

I make myself another coffee and empty the tiny cup immediately. Fuck the jetlag. Andrea has struggled with substance abuse since we were teenagers. It got worse after his first exhibition, but after a not so voluntary stint in rehab, he'd been doing well. Clearly, that is no longer the case.

"Listen, dumbass, get your shit together. This struggling artist shit is getting old. Especially since you're rich and successful. Seriously, what's your problem?"

He snorts. "Fuck you. I didn't sell one piece that night."

"Yeah, idiot, because you're set on destroying your career. Why would you hijack your own opening? Violet Mathison is one of the best in town, and you scared away all the potential buyers. How bad is it?"

He turns to face the backrest of the sofa and rolls into the fetal position. *That bad.* I let out a long breath and drag my hand down my face.

"Andrea, if you don't deal with this shit, I'm

bringing Mother over." A low blow, but I don't have patience for his shit right now. He clearly needs help, though.

He growls. "Go away."

"Yeah, you said that already. Let's get you to the clinic, bro. I'll pick you up tomorrow morning, okay?"

"I can handle it." He tries to roll to face me but ends up on the floor, and starts chuckling like a lunatic.

"Are you drunk or high right now? Or both?" I stand above him with my hands on my hips, fighting the urge to kick him. Irresponsible asshole.

"You're just jealous because I kissed your lady." He pushes off the floor and sways, smirking at me.

"Shut up, you idiot. That's not why I'm here. But for the record, you pull something like that one more time and I'll fucking kill you." I'm not even kidding right now. Mila is mine, and I know he was just being an asshole, but I won't stand for him disrespecting her or me like that.

"Look at you, Mr. Nobody-wants-me-for-me, you're in love." He collapses back to the sofa, laughing. Bastard.

"I'm not." I walk away, looking for a box. I collect all the bottles I can find in the house.

Damn him. Of course I don't love her. She doesn't want me. She wants my money.

"I might be high and fucked in my head, but I can

see. You look at her in multi-color strokes." He flails his arm like he was holding a brush. "Also, you haven't punched me since we were in high school, which only proves you care."

"That's your proof? Multi-color strokes of my gaze?" I shake my head. "Be here tomorrow morning. I'll make an excuse with Mother today."

I go upstairs to make sure I got all the bottles. The state of his house is a concern by itself, but I don't have time to address that. At least I didn't find random women sleeping around, which in hindsight might be a bad sign.

As I walk around, opening more windows, I try to ignore the nagging feeling his words stirred in me. I can't love Mila. As I told Conrad, I'm attracted to her, but that's all.

Why does it hurt so much that she only wants my money?

Because I thought she was different. That's why. There is nothing else behind it. I need to keep my distance. That's all.

By the time I'm done, Andrea is asleep. I drop the box by the door and look for his keys. When I find them, I walk to his kitchen and check his fridge. It's fully stocked.

His housekeeper must have been here recently. Or

by the state of his house, he probably hasn't been eating.

Well, he can survive one more day. I reach the sofa and kick his shin. "Where are your spare keys?"

He shakes his head like a wet dog and then looks at me. Struggling to focus, he gives up and closes his eyes. "With my housekeeper. Why? Are you moving in with me?"

"I'd rather die, but I'm not letting you meet similar fate. I'm calling my security and leaving them strict instructions. You're under lockdown, bro. See you tomorrow morning."

"Don't you dare." His protest is weak. He doesn't even stand up.

I lock the back door, and then dial the clinic and make an appointment for the morning.

I get into the car and fall asleep on the way home. When my driver wakes me, I'm a bit disoriented. Jesus, I need some shuteye before getting to my mother's.

The house is silent. "Mila," I call, but there is no answer.

She's free to do whatever she wants. Perhaps she visited her sister, or is at work. Or anywhere really, but a part of me wishes she was here. I've no right to expect her to be waiting for me.

But I want to have the privilege. *What?*

I take a long shower, hoping to shake off the empty

feeling. Something has to change. Can I get past her motivations and pretend we're a normal couple? Does she even want that? She has no reason to spend time with me beyond the social obligations.

God, I wish I could plug this into a spreadsheet, asses the risk and opportunities. Without all of this unknown. Like a dance I haven't learned the steps to, this relationship forces me to trip over my own feet all the time.

We need to get out of this whirl of events, and all the pretense, or we need to call it quits. I can't afford this constant distraction.

I walk into my closet, glancing at the bed as I pass. Has she been sleeping here since I left? Has she returned to the guest bedroom? My fingers itch to grab the phone and call her. See where she is. Join her, even.

What is wrong with me? I get dressed and flop on my bed. I grab my phone. I have two reports to approve. I might as well read those before leaving.

An unopened message blinks on the screen. Mila. I let my finger hover for a moment before I open it. Since when am I worried about opening a message?

We've been lingering in this weird state of retreating and advancing for way too long. Everything has become awkward between us.

MILA

I'm sorry. I have a horrible headache.
Give my apologies and regards to
Bianca and the family.

What the hell? I sit up. Where is she with her headache? She hasn't had one since I've known her. Not that I know of. I call her, but there is no answer.

I stand up and pace around the room, my heart rate spiking. Where the hell is she?

I call my security company. Mila doesn't even know they're following her, but as soon as my engagement was announced, my security specialist insisted it's necessary.

"Where is my fiancée right now?"

Chapter 29

Mila

Aidan kicks the ball and runs, cheering. "He seems calmer and happier than ever."

Annie snakes her arm through mine and leans her head against me. "The new school is amazing. He's been thriving."

My heart swells. "I'm so glad."

"He... we have you to thank." The sadness in her voice chafes, but I gave up on making her feel better about my *sacrifice.* At the end of the day, I have a great job and my family is doing much better, so I have no regrets.

Well, I regret that things between me and Gio are still unresolved. My hope bloomed the night of Andrea's opening, but it was premature. Gio's hurt expression when he left the bedroom confused me.

Something else is going on with him. I don't know

what it is, but every time I look at the beehives in the garden or the pictures on his shelves I wonder where his distrust stems from.

Every time I replay the wonderful few weeks we spent together before our engagement, my mind and my body remember, and yearn for the man I still believe he is.

Yet every time I get a glimpse of that man, he retreats. What is he hiding from?

"How are you, Mils?" Annie interrupts my useless and by now way too familiar mental cycling. On a loop, I've been analyzing every conversation, every touch, every glare, every soft gaze, but I always end up more confused than before.

Annie's question is simple but loaded with layers of meaning. I've been keeping so much bottled up, I might burst.

She stops and studies me, and as much as I want to bravely withstand her scrutiny, tears prickle relentlessly behind my eyes.

"I'm as good as it gets. I love my job and bury myself in work most of the time. But I wish I could separate my life from Gio's. I could cope more easily."

"Feelings complicate everything." She sighs as she watches Ron chasing the ball with Aidan. She parks the stroller and sits on a bench. "Talk to me."

And I do. I settle next to her and tell her about my last encounter with Gio.

"So he punched his brother, fucked you, and then disappeared again?" Annie shakes her head and leans over to check on her sleeping daughter.

"He left, but he looked so beaten by it. And he said he can't stay. Not that he doesn't want to. Why can't he? I'm not even mad at him. I'm just miserable, sad, and so lonely, Annie." I wipe my tears.

"You need to confront him. His behavior makes no sense. He grouped you with the other gold diggers without really trying to understand your motivations. Or just assuming they are purely monetary. He treats you like a nuisance, then he takes you out. He gives you a necklace that commemorates your first date. It's like he wants to spend time with you, but avoids intimacy at all costs. And when he fails at that, he runs. It's exhausting to keep up with. You need to talk to him about it."

"I can't." I blow my nose.

"Why not?" She stands and picks up the ball that rolled to us. She pretend-throws it to Aidan and chuckles before she throws it for real. "You've never been timid." She joins me again.

"Annie, I'm scared he will reject me completely. I know he practically has, but I still harbor hope, and if I confront him, none of us will benefit."

"So, you are a gold digger?" she deadpans.

I gasp. "I guess I am."

"Mils, look, I'm benefiting from this the most, but don't you see that if you just silently accept his behavior, you're confirming to him the only reason you're in this relationship is the financial benefit?"

Have I been sending those signals to him? I have been so on edge, hoping for a change, for an opportunity, for some sort of new-found connection, and all that time I've been keeping things bottled up.

I might have lost Gio's respect after I said yes to him, but somewhere down the road I lost self-respect too.

"I just don't think I have the right to complain. I agreed to this arrangement." I shrug.

Voicing my belief out loud only confirms how irrational and twisted it is. I didn't lose my right to lead an emotionally satisfying life. I can't keep up with the constant whiplash his behavior gives me.

"Mila, for fuck's sake, you need to tell him how you feel. You're trying to protect yourself, but you've been silently suffering for months now, and nothing changes. Even if he rejects you, at least you'll have some resolution."

She might be right. Living by evasion is the worst possible way to function. But I'm not strong enough to accept that he doesn't feel anything for me. Though hoping we might reconcile didn't do me much good. It's been close to four months. I need to kill the hope.

Ron and Aidan join us, and we make our way toward the house. Like a nightmarish déjà vu, Gio's car is parked at the curb.

"Shit," I whisper.

Annie's eyes dart between the car and me. "What is he doing here?"

"I told him I had a headache and would stay home instead of going to his parents."

Gio gets out of the car and narrows his eyes when he sees us. Annie greets him and scurries away with the family. The traitor.

I fidget in front of him, wringing my hands as if he just caught me doing something wrong. My cowardice pisses me off. Just because our arrangement is... well, just that, an arrangement, I still have my freedom. My mind has it at least, because my poor heart doesn't belong to me anymore.

"I came to check on you. You said you have a headache. You never get headaches." His words suggest concern, but his eyes glare at me.

"I don't have a headache. I wanted to avoid you and your family." My voice wavers a bit, but speaking the truth liberates me.

I return his glare with confidence. He seems genuinely surprised by my rebelling.

He adjusts his cuffs. "You're obliged to attend as per our contract."

"Then fucking fine me." I spit out the words and fold my arms over my chest. I want to stomp my foot, but I'm aware my acting out is enough already.

He blinks a few times and fiddles with his cufflinks. "Is this about my brother's behavior the other night? He's not at my mother's today, and I can assure you he won't pull such a stunt again."

My nostrils flare as I try to compose myself. Is he for real? We haven't spoken openly in the longest time, so when we speak now this is the result. We jump to conclusions instead of listening.

"It's not about your brother. It's about you," I cry, and several pedestrians look our way.

Gio emits a deep sigh and opens the door. "Get in the car."

Not this again. The last time he issued that order, we ended up in this hateful vacuum, unable to move in any direction.

"No. I'm not going anywhere with you." I raise my chin, grasping at the remains of my dignity.

"What the fuck do you want from me, Mila?" He throws up his arms, exasperated.

We may as well get into it right now. I huff and get into the car. Gio follows, instructs the driver to take us to the Bronx, and raises the partition to give us privacy.

He turns to me, his jaw tight. "What do you want, Mila?"

My chest heaves. I can't tell him how I feel. I can't go back to hustling without the light at the end of the tunnel, struggling and seeing Annie and Aidan suffer. I can't risk their future. Or mine, for that matter.

"I want your respect," I whisper, and look down. My limbs are heavy with the spoken admission, even though it's just a small part of the truth. I'm not ready to bare my heart. He has too much power in this relationship already.

"Well, Princess, respect is earned."

With one sentence, he again throws me into a whirlwind of emotions. *Princess.* Oh, how my heart swells with that name. But then a slap, a vicious jab into my chest, reminding me I made a mistake. If he's not ready to forgive, I'm done.

I'd rather drop everything and lick my wounds until I forget him. But what about Annie? I let the tears roll down my cheek, staring out of the window, making sure he doesn't see my meltdown.

He doesn't because he's on his phone.

That's it. I'm breaking off this engagement, right after we leave the dreaded lunch with Bianca and his family.

* * *

"Where is Andrea?" Bianca spreads a linen napkin on her lap.

We're eating in the formal dining room. I thought these affairs were more casual, but clearly today Bianca decided to go all white china and shit.

I'm wearing my jeans and T-shirt from the park outing with Annie, and even without the conversation in the car and my decision to end things I'm utterly uncomfortable.

London mimics Bianca's fury and snaps the napkin open before placing it on her lap. Dominic, her boyfriend, taps her hand with his finger and she relaxes a bit.

I wonder if I'm the reason for Andrea's absence.

"Andrea is sick," Gio says.

"What's wrong with him?" Bianca frowns. "He could have at least called."

"Bianca, love." Micah smiles at her from across the table. "Maybe you can enjoy the children we have here with us today."

Her eyebrows jerk up. "You're right, darling." She returns his smile with such tenderness I wonder where the Bianca who just demanded answers went. The woman rules with an iron fist, and then melts at the sound of her husband.

Hot and cold. Just like her son. I decide to observe her a bit more during the lunch to draw the parallels.

To discover more about the man who has been closed off for months. Not sure why I bother, since I won't keep up this charade beyond this meal.

I play with my food while Massi updates everyone on Gina and their baby girl. I wish my friend was here, so I wouldn't feel this lonely. London and Paris dote on their father. I would enjoy the family dynamics if I wasn't so exhausted from pretending, and having my heart destroyed in the process.

"So, when is the wedding?" Bianca's question carries across the table, and I look up. Unfortunately, it's addressed to us. Gio tenses beside me. I return my stare to my plate, hoping the floor will swallow me.

The clang of the cutlery around us stills. I can't be sure, but I think all eyes are on us. Heat creeps up my neck.

Gio takes my hand and I almost gasp. He kisses my knuckles. He doesn't let go as he leans back. "In one month. We're getting married on July fifteenth at Lake Como."

Chapter 30

Mila

"We'll be leaving in the next few days. You're welcome to arrive as you please and use the house, but of course we expect you there for the fifteenth."

Gio's announcement causes a wave of excitement around the table. My heart thumps in my head, drowning all other sounds. I look at Gio who is talking, probably answering the questions coming from all directions. He keeps my hand in his.

To make sure I don't run? To give me support? To apologize for ambushing me with his announcement?

How am I going to break up with him now? Why did he just set the date? Without even consulting me?

I'm so conflicted about it all. As if the last few months didn't happen, hope blooms in my chest. The joy is tainted as I remind myself this is nothing. This is not real. He probably just caved in to please his mother and stop the questions.

The people-pleaser in me is defeated. Being engaged indefinitely was one thing. Getting married feels like a bigger commitment.

How do I get out of this?

Especially since a part of me doesn't want to.

"Mila, I can't believe you let him talk you into Como." London shakes her head. "He goes there every year and works. Calling it vacation." She deadpans. "Don't you want to go somewhere special?"

Yes, I do. I also want him to want to marry me. Not out of obligation, or because he needs a wife. But because he needs me. In that moment, for some outlandish reason, I decide to give this one last try. If not for myself, then for Annie.

"Actually, I'm thrilled about the location." I squeeze Gio's hand and smile. "He's told me so much about it, I feel like I love the place through his eyes already."

He never has, and maybe I'm so used to the charade I deliver the perfect line. Our eyes lock, and the soft gaze I haven't seen in so many months warms his face, a smile lingering.

We stare at each other, a silent communication, or in our case probably a lot of miscommunication, passing between us.

Maybe, just maybe, Como can be our new beginning. Our remake of St. Martin.

* * *

I didn't break off the engagement. I should have, but I didn't. Instead, I play the role of supportive fiancée, pining for my man who seems to give me some crumbs of attention to placate me.

After all this time, I'm at the same place I was with Brian. Blaming myself for everything in our relationship. Eager to please the man who only thinks of himself. It's even worse than that, because before I was oblivious to the pattern, but now I see it clearly.

And yet here I am, landing in Italy. A bride to be. I keep reminding myself it's for my family, but my heart isn't big enough to cope. And my self-esteem is too bruised to absorb the lies I've been feeding myself.

We rush from the plane to the waiting car. The gray sky mirrors the state of our relationship. Or at least my perception of it. The rain is pouring down in heavy curtains as Gio holds an umbrella above my head.

I wish he would let me get wet. The gentleman-like behavior is in some ways worse than a cold shoulder, or even outright aggression. The latter we seem to release with occasional fucking. Not that it helps our situation.

Something shifted at Bianca's house when Gio blindsided me with the wedding date. It's like he doesn't hate me as much, is making an effort to include me in his life, and not only through Lydia and the concierge.

We have a cordial relationship, much better than before, but nowhere close to where it should be. Where it could have been if... Argh, I'm tired of this constant analysis.

He might not hate me anymore, but he keeps his distance. Aloof and cold.

The car speeds along the highway, gray clouds stretching across the sky. Despite the dreary weather and my weary mood, I marvel at the majestic mountains in the distance. Their peaks are shrouded in fog and mist. The sight is breathtaking.

Maybe this beauty could do the trick. Could relax Gio from his work and rekindle what we lost.

But when I look at him, he's working. He's seen the scenery before, but for fuck's sake. This is not even about me anymore. How can he go through life missing out on all of this?

"Will you work the whole time?" I fail to hide my annoyance.

"This is not a vacation, Mila. More like workcation. I have a lot of work." He doesn't even look at me.

I'm about to snap when his phone rings, and of course he answers. With a sigh, I turn to the window.

Fucking rain. Fucking Gio. Fucking engagement.

Goddammit. I don't want to be this bitter person. I close my eyes and start counting my breaths. One, two, three...

I jerk awake at the sound of the gate. The car rolls slowly into a well-maintained yard. Somewhere on the road it stopped raining and the shy sun peeks now through the clouds.

Rows of cypress trees dot the well-manicured lawn. When Gio said his house was on Lake Como, I didn't expect it to be directly on the lake. We park at the side of the house, and the beauty around me caresses my soul.

I spy a pool and immediately think of St. Martin, and our first time making love. The lump lodged in my throat grows bigger.

It might be the breathtaking surroundings, but my soul sparks a little. What if I attack life with abandon? Stop hiding behind my mistake and my humiliation at needing his financial help. What if I show him normal again?

I won't let him hide either. I'll drag him out of his cave and force him to enjoy life. And if down the road he remembers he can trust me and enjoy my company, this journey might just be well worth it.

* * *

My plan has been derailed several times, but I'm persistent. Gio took me to town and had dinner with me. But that's the most attention I've coerced from him in the two weeks we've been here.

Gio has been buried in work and I have been buried in self-pity, planning our wedding and swimming.

I have calls with Hilda and my team daily, but the firm runs well while I supervise from afar, so I'm bored.

Too much time on my hands to contemplate how to plan a wedding I don't want with the man I want so much. Or a version of him that is probably by now a figment of my imagination.

In a week, the family arrives. I should just break off the engagement now. Before we embarrass ourselves. At least Massi and Gina are coming first.

I could talk to Gina about the situation. Tell her the truth and ask for her help. For the first time, I'll ask for the help she's been offering all along.

Every time we take a step forward, he pulls back, burying himself in work. I can't stand it anymore. He's stubborn and full of pride, so I guess it needs to be me that sets us both free. I wish I could keep the job, but this golden cage is not worth it.

My heart is breaking into a thousand pieces every day.

I start the music, sending my playlist to the speaker on the patio, and jump headfirst into the pool. I complete several laps before I sense a shadow at the edge. I reemerge and my eyes meet Gio's, scolding me.

I tilt my head, submerging my hair. I don't break the gaze. What is he pissed about? I push out of the pool and stand in front of him.

He's in a shirt, a vest and dress slacks. So handsome. I'm dripping water, my body tanned and barely covered with my skimpy white bikini.

Gio's eyes lick my body with a gaze that burns and leaves goosebumps at the same time. He licks his upper teeth.

"The water is wonderful. You should try it." I don't move to get a towel, ignoring my body's reaction to his presence.

Hard nipples. Check. Clenched core. Check. Elevated heart rate. Check.

"I had a conference call, and you're playing the music too loud." But his tone doesn't match the scolding in his expression. Probably because it's not just my body reacting. Tent in his pants. Check.

"Why don't you have fewer conference calls and more time by the pool? What happened on that call that couldn't have waited?" I put my hands on my hips, smiling. "It's fun here on the lake. You should give it a chance."

He glares at me, his eyes dropping to my chest more than he'd like based on the clenched jaw. He adjusts his cuffs and strolls away. Well, I can't call this a win, but it's a tie.

He retreats to the house, but before he disappears behind the glass wall of doors, I notice his fingers tapping on his thigh. The rhythm can't be mistaken for a nervous tick. It matches the music blaring from the speakers.

My smile grows bigger. Perhaps it's only patience I need to make this work.

That patience dies when Gio comes back out half an hour later and announces he has to leave for several days.

* * *

I spend the next few days trudging around the property and talking to Hilda about my potential future. I don't give her details of the state of my relationship and she doesn't pry, but she gives me some very good financial advice.

On the third day, I go to the town where I scheduled a tour with a local guide. I might as well tourist the shit out of it before I leave.

A young man—tanned, all muscles and delicious smiles—meets me in front of a cafe. He looks more like an underwear model than a tour guide, but God does it feel good to have a man smile at me genuinely. It's not the burning smile Gio is capable of, but this girl is starved for attention.

"I'm Ricardo." He kisses my hand. "Would you like to start with the funicular and see the lake from the mountain, or do you prefer a tour of the town, signorina?"

"Hi Ricardo. Call me Mila. I'd love to see the lake from up there." I shield my eyes with my hand.

"Let's go then." He puts his hand on the small of my back and I tense. But his intention is to steer me in the right direction, so I relax and let him guide me.

We spend several hours enjoying the sights and views, and when we finally return to the main square I'm famished, but also fully sated.

"Would you like to grab a meal, Ricardo?" I offer, because I don't want to eat alone again.

He takes my hand, winks at me and kisses my knuckles, bowing. "I'll be delighted to join you for a meal." I can't help but giggle at his over-the-top flirting. I'm not interested in him in the slightest, but it's fun, and over the course of the day with him I pushed my sadness to the side.

"Let go of her now."

We both startle and Ricardo drops my hand like it burns. My eyes meet Gio's. Dressed in his three-piece suit, his fists clenched at his sides. His nostrils flare, and his jaw might dislocate if he doesn't relax it soon.

I smile broadly, pretending to be unfazed by the encounter. Who does he think he is? After ignoring me for weeks, he pulls this caveman routine. "Gio, this is Ricardo—"

"I don't fucking care who he is," Gio spits, killing me with a look of hatred. "Leave. Now," he orders the guide.

Ricardo looks at me, wide-eyed, silently asking if it's okay to leave me with the lunatic in the suit. If I was smart enough to protect myself from Gio, I wouldn't be in Italy in the first place.

I curl my lips gently up and nod. Ricardo scurries away.

"What the fuck?" I snap.

"I leave and you immediately find yourself a boy toy?" He grabs my elbow and drags me across the square.

"Let go of me, you idiot. Maybe if you took an interest in me, I wouldn't need a boy toy." I don't know why I provoke him more, but Jesus, how dare he?

He halts, and while I have never been afraid of Gio Cassinetti, I think right now I should be. I'm not, but his look probably killed a few people around us like a drive-by shooting spree.

"I swear to God, Mila—" His nostrils inflate again. "Get in the car."

I jerk my arm away from him. "I have a car here."

He closes his eyes briefly, sucking in air. It does nothing for his composure. "I don't give a shit, Mila. We're having dinner with my friends. Get in the fucking car now."

I fold my arms over my chest. "Ask me nicely."

His chests heaves as he steps closer. Too close. The smoke and spice linger around me, wrapping me tightly in the essence of this man. I step back, but he snakes his arm around my waist and yanks me to him.

Crashing his lips on mine, he takes my breath away. And with my breath he steals so much more.

My resolve, inhibition, hatred.

This man has always taken what he wants, and I will always give willingly. That's how unequal this union has been.

I moan into the kiss as his tongue dives in, and my body tingles with recognition and need strong enough to knock me off my feet. But he's there to catch me. To support me. And for a moment, I let myself believe he will always be there to catch me.

"Get in the car, please." The word might be courteous by definition, but there is nothing polite in his tone.

Still, I slide into the backseat and close my eyes. There are so many reasons I should be pissed right now. And I'm upset. But the pathetic hopeful fool in me is also utterly pleased Gio acted the way he did.

Maybe it's a weird version of Stockholm syndrome. I've been trapped in this relationship for too long.

I don't condone the action, but the emotion behind it rings too close to jealousy. And while that's not a feeling I admire, my mind focuses on the motivation behind it. Does he care?

The car moves and Gio stares out of the window. He doesn't pull out his phone. It should please me, but it's almost scary. So unexpected I don't know what to think about it.

"How was your trip?" My words are light, floating through the car.

Gio whips his head round and studies me for a moment, like I'm a puzzle he can't solve and it pisses him off. "It was fine," he says through his teeth. "It was what awaited me here upon my return I don't care much about."

I roll my eyes. Seriously? Though he didn't really give me a chance to explain who Ricardo was. Let him stew. His mistake. "How did you even find me?"

He looks at me like I'm deranged. "GPS tracker."

Now, if he had slapped me, I wouldn't be more stunned. "You have a tracker on me?" I run my hands over my arms, because apparently I didn't know until a second ago and now I can detect it by patting myself.

Gio frowns, unimpressed. "On your phone. Of course, my security team has tabs on you. It's for your own safety. You're my fiancée."

Is he for real? "Am I? Am I really, Gio? Because it seems to me you're already married to your work. You told me respect needs to be earned, but you don't give me the time of day to even try."

He glares at me.

It's the look of a predator ready to pounce. Kill me. I'll take this brewing emotion over his indifferent behavior anytime. I raise my chin, taunting him.

The car comes to a full stop, and he breaks the gaze and opens the door. I scramble out behind him, gearing up for a fight, but I halt, my heart sinking into my stomach, when I see a helicopter waiting for us.

Chapter 31

Mila

Gio holds my hand as we take off. He's probably flown in a helicopter several times since our last and only ride together to Napa Valley. But for me, this is like reliving hell. At the same time, it stirs more than the fear of a crash.

It unravels all the memories after the accident, so many of them the best memories of my life. With this man who has pulled me closer, holding me in his arms. He probably thinks my tears are those of fear.

Our relationship practically started in a helicopter like this one. And as we descend to a helipad on a yacht somewhere in the Mediterranean sea, I'm pretty sure it might end with a helicopter ride.

I need to find the courage to leave. To figure out my life without him, because my life with him is nowhere close to what I deserve. I can't live in this state of conflict and confusion.

We land, and a stunning couple waits for us. I recognize them from the wedding photo in Gio's library.

"Mila, this is Nora Flemming, a smart woman who lost her wits at one point and married this fucker here." Gio punches his friend's arm.

He only raises his eyebrow and then smiles at me. "Conrad Hermann. It's a pleasure to finally meet you, Mila. Let me extend my condolences."

I blink, my hand unmoving in his.

"Well, you're marrying him." Conrad shrugs.

"Play nicely, boys." Nora chuckles and pulls me along with her. "Dinner is almost ready. Come help me finish the salad. I'll give you a tour later."

I have never been on a yacht, but I'm so riled up from the argument and the flight that I barely take in the luxurious surroundings.

The sea glimmers around us and the sun is rolling on the horizon, slowly setting into the water.

"Do you spend your vacation here?" I try to summon my brain and carry a conversation. Nora seems like a nice person, and I don't want to mope around her.

"You can say that. We've been living here for two

months now. Conrad is off-loading his business assets, and we're planning to live a less stressful life."

We enter a kitchen that could probably cater to a mid-sized restaurant, and Nora pushes a cutting board and a bowl of tomatoes to me. I get to work, appreciating that she doesn't have help and makes dinner herself.

"What do you mean?"

"He's been working too much, so I finally made him choose. Me or work?" She shrugs, her white teeth shining through her smile.

I'm irrationally jealous of her. Not for her looks or her riches, but because she got her man to see what matters more than constant work.

"That's not a concept Gio would ever contemplate." I shake my head and chop the tomatoes, sliding them from the board to a large bowl.

Nora pours olive oil and balsamic into a small dish and starts whisking it with several other ingredients, preparing the dressing.

"I wouldn't be so sure. It took me a while to get Conrad to take a week off, but slowly he started appreciating the benefits of a more relaxed lifestyle. The way Gio looks at you, my dear, I'm sure he can't concentrate when you're around." She winks.

"It's not like that between us."

"Nonsense. Gio Cassinetti is a proud man who sealed his heart after Kimberly, but you're the first woman who is thawing it slowly. That's Conrad's opinion. I only saw his lingering gaze on you when you arrived and the way he moved around you, and I agree."

I want to believe her so much. "Things are not always what they look like."

She chuckles. "That's Gio's motto after that wench took all his pride and faith in love away. I can't believe we never saw it coming. I introduced him to the conniving bitch."

"What happened?" I can't help asking. Whoever Kimberly was, is she the answer to Gio's locked heart?

Nora gasps. "You didn't know about her? Oh my God, it's not my story to tell."

"Too late for that," I deadpan.

Nora leans down and opens a cabinet. She takes out a bottle of wine and gets two glasses from another cabinet.

"Where is my hospitality?" She giggles and pours us both to the brim. "He should have told you, anyway."

She pushes one glass to me and takes a generous sip from hers. "Kimberly was Gio's fiancée several years ago. He worked a lot. In the meantime, Kimberly was screwing every male alive, including the pool boy.

She was such a cliche." With her finger, Nora draws circles around the edge of her glass.

"She wanted Gio for his money and influence. When he found out, he swore off women and started dating bimbos with as little personality as possible. At least with them, he was sure they were gold diggers from the start, and he could protect himself."

"Nora," Conrad's voice carries down from the deck. "Are we to starve here, woman?"

Nora rolls her eyes. "We're coming."

"I'm so glad you broke the unhealthy streak. It would be so much fun to attend events with you rather than those personality-less types."

I smile, agreeing with her while knowing we might not share time together ever again. We carry the food outside.

Shimmering sea and fairy lights accentuate the beauty of the night. The dinner is a lovely affair. We eat and laugh. The dynamics between Gio and Conrad are too much. With the help of wine, I relax enough to enjoy myself.

Gio is as relaxed as he was in St. Martin. It's bittersweet to watch. A part of me wishes Nora didn't tell me about Kimberly, but I'm grateful to know. To understand better.

Without realizing, I became another Kimberly when I took his money. No wonder he hates me. As we say our goodbyes and board the chopper, I squeeze Gio's hand.

He could give me so much more if he wanted to break the walls he maintains with such vigor. But he won't, and now I understand I can't have his respect or his trust. Let alone his love.

I deserve better.

Chapter 32

Gio

A tear rolls down Mila's cheek. I wipe it and pull her closer. I forgot she might still be traumatized by flying in a helicopter. Idiot.

Conrad and Nora adored her. Everyone adores her. My family, my friends, my employees, her employees. Even a fucking Italian asshole who is hoping to get into her pants. If he hasn't yet. Fuck.

When I found her giggling with him, I wanted to burn the fucking town down. She's mine.

Only she isn't. Clearly she doesn't even care to offer fidelity in return for my money. By the time we land, I'm sweating with frustration and anger.

I need to keep as far from her as possible. That's the only way this arrangement will work. I'll call Fatima to redraft the prenup to include fidelity, and then we'll conduct ourselves according to our deal. For social obligations only.

And let my cock fall off. Fuck. Meeting Mila Ward, getting close to her, was the worst thing I've ever done. I can't undo it now.

Conrad asked me tonight if I'm sure Mila needed me to sweeten the deal, because he feels she would have been with me regardless.

I almost punched him.

We arrive at the villa that used to be my safe haven. Now it's full of Mila. Her music, her swaying hips, her gorgeous, wet, half-naked body, those perceptive indigo eyes, her constant chatter and her giggles.

Every night I fist my cock and ask myself why the fuck do I still plan to go ahead with the wedding?

Every night I come imagining her. And I can't stand the idea of not knowing where she is. What she does. If she's doing okay. I've become a stalker. Fantastic.

I pour myself a glass of whiskey and almost drop it when I realize Mila is behind me. Deep in my thoughts, I assumed she had disappeared into her room.

"Can I have a glass of wine?" she asks, as if she wasn't drinking it freely before tonight. She doesn't need my permission.

"Chianti?" I offer, because she fell in love with the

local wine. I fucking notice everything about her. I wish I didn't.

She nods and saunters outside. My cock twitches. I've never been in an impossible situation. I can always find a solution to any problem.

Mila is a fucking unsolvable paradox. It's not even her fault. I'm frozen between rationally knowing we have to break up and being unable to quit her.

I join her on the terrace and put her wine in front of her. She has her feet on the chair in front of her, her skin glistening in the warm night.

"I love it here. It's so peaceful and beautiful." She raises the glass to her lips. Full, and so sweet. Mine, but not mine.

"Clearly you've been enjoying yourself," I quip.

She looks at me, her eyes tired and unimpressed. "Ricardo is a tour guide I hired to show me around. Today was the first time I actually spent a day *not* alone, and I will not let you ruin it for me."

I squeeze my glass. What the fuck do I really want? I don't even spend time with her, but I can't let her go. I'm torn, and I hate Mila for that too.

"You can stay here as long as you wish. I have to spend some time in California right after the wedding. We're selling the Wings, and then I fly to finalize the deal in Singapore."

All my hard work has paid off, and I got even better

deals than I hoped for. It took a lot of hours and sweat, but the win is so much sweeter. "You're welcome to return to New York or stay here for the summer."

She stares at me, her face passive, but something flickers in her eyes and then she stands up. "I better go to sleep. Gina and the family are arriving in the morning." She leaves her wine and returns to the house.

For the first time in years, I hate being here. I hate that the place is infused with the heaviness between us.

I hate that she can be so indifferent. I hate the silence that is more profound when she leaves.

I hate myself for the way I feel and don't want to.

What the fuck is that wailing?

A baby? I run my hand down my face, wondering why my back hurts. I must have passed out on the sofa, reading the projection for the Chicago condominium development.

Grunting, I push up to a sitting position. My mouth feels glued shut with rancid cotton balls. A half-empty bottle decorates the coffee table.

Oh, yeah, that would explain why I feel like a dumpster.

Walking out of my office, the sun blinds me. Massi

is bouncing his crying daughter around the terrace. I guess his wife and his grumpy teenage son are around as well. Having company is annoying at the best of times, but this morning... fuck me.

"Make it stop," I growl, leaning in the doorway.

My brother pins me with a look that I'm sure makes his famous consommé sour. "You look like shit. I thought I was in charge of your bachelor party."

If my niece doesn't stop right now, I might just drive them to a hotel. "I'm going to take a shower."

I make my way to the master bedroom. The guest bedroom door is closed. Is Mila sleeping? My hand hovers, but I decide to take care of my basic needs first. She doesn't need to see me like this, anyway.

I shower and get changed, feeling marginally more human. At least the baby seems to have gotten the message. When I return to the living room, I'm met by Gina's glare. I've never seen her appear this vicious.

She's feeding little Ali. Fuck. Now my house is a nursery.

"Your milk will go sour if you continue glaring," I quip, mostly because I'm an asshole. "Where is Mila?"

"Gone," she deadpans, looking at me like I've just drowned a litter of kittens.

"What do you mean gone?" I shake my head and go to make coffee.

I start the espresso machine and down the bitter shot.

Gina waltzes in, the baby now sleeping in her arms. "I mean she left you."

Everything goes still for a moment as I stop midway, placing my cup in the sink. Not sure why I think that turning in slow motion might make the words comprehensible, but I still take my time. In that slowed down moment, before I face Gina, scenarios run through my mind.

She can't be far.

She wouldn't have left without telling me.

She can't risk her family's lifestyle and health.

She did what's best for both of us.

No. No. No. She's mine.

When I meet Gina's glare, the truth sinks in. In my head I'm running for the car keys, getting behind the wheel and chasing after her. I just need to ask where she went.

In reality, I'm frozen. The only tangible certainty is the hollow, painful feeling in my chest. I'm having a heart attack.

Gina decides she can't stand the silence. "You ignored her, treated her like an acquisition you don't really want, and without respect."

"What do you know about it?" I snap. This can't be happening.

"Not enough for me to have realized sooner how you've been hurting her, you asshole. But enough to know she made the right decision. I wish we had spoken sooner than this morning. You're an arrogant egoist, Gio Cassinetti."

Massi walks in, his hair damp, freshly showered. He kisses Gina's crown and takes the sleeping baby from her. "What's going on?"

"The wedding is off." Gina folds her arms across her chest.

Massi raises his eyebrows and darts his eyes between the two of us.

"Yeah, Mila left," I growl. "Apparently all the money wasn't enough for her." Why does it hurt so much? I'm a sore loser, but I've lost before. I can cope.

"Is that what you think?" Gina grits through her teeth.

"She left, didn't she?" I shrug. "She signed the prenup and still left. Money wasn't enough for her. That's the fact."

"Are you for real? You're a fucking idiot. That's the fact." Gina looks at me like I'm garbage she hopes she doesn't have to get closer to.

Massi puts his hand on her shoulder and looks at me, unimpressed. I recall a similar situation when Gina was gone from his life and I sat across from him, not really understanding why he was so down.

Well, I don't think he even remotely hit the low I'm drowning in right now. "Where did she go? To her tour guide?"

"You have no right to judge her. It's not like *you* spend any time with her. She's done nothing wrong." Gina checks her watch. "By now she is over the Atlantic, I hope. I gave her our plane."

Massi's eyebrows almost reach his hairline, but he doesn't comment. I don't have time for this shit. I have a wedding to cancel and proposals to review and—

"Just get the fuck out of here," I spit in Gina's direction.

Massi raises his hand. "Hey, asshole, don't you dare talk to Blue like that." Him threatening me with a baby in his arms is pathetic. This whole situation is pathetic. I drop my head and shake it.

"Don't..." Massi warns, and I look up, startled to see Gina in front of me.

She jabs her finger into my chest. "You want facts? In December, she got you off the screen because suddenly there was something else to care about. Fact. For the first time in your workaholic life, you took time off and enjoyed life. Fact. She was the first woman who cared about you for you. Fact."

"The evidence suggests—"

"She left you this." She pulls an envelope from her back pocket and plasters it against my chest. She takes the baby from Massi. "I'm going to have a nap with her. Don't let us sleep too long, love, so we adjust to the local time."

They kiss. "I'll join you shortly. Sebastien was sleeping when I got out of the shower."

The cook/housekeeper arrives and stops in the doorway, unsure if she can enter. Massi tells her something in Italian and she laughs and gets busy. What's so fucking funny?

My brother pulls me outside and pushes me into the chair. "Read what she has to say, and then we can talk about how you're going to salvage the situation."

I meet his eyes. He doesn't even consider the option of me just letting her go. Everyone is on team Mila. Well, I can't blame them. I'm there with them.

Massi leaves, and I stare at the lake, hoping to draw solace and strength from the view I've admired and enjoyed so many times before. It looks blank right now. The sun is warming up the tiles, but the only burning thing is the paper in my hand.

I tear the envelope open, but I don't start reading. Reading her words has the air of finality. She took matters into her own hands, and I don't like relinquishing control.

Ironically, I admire her for that. I don't want her gone, but fuck, I admire the shit out of her for standing up to me.

I admire her for more than that. For the loyalty to her family. For her business acumen, and her ability to attract clients and work with people. For her easygoing ability to put everyone at ease. For being the only sliver of normal I've had since I remember.

My dear Gio,

I didn't accept your first proposal in January because I wanted it to be real. Not a business, not a convenience. Just us.

The second time, I accepted out of desperation. But I can't go through with it, Gio. You have been generous, and I could easily get used to such a lifestyle. I could accept it and learn to be content.

But you will always think less of me, you will always negotiate, because after all, we have a deal.

You once told me that when things don't go as expected with an acquisition, you cut your losses and move to the next venture.

I'm cutting my losses now. Not moving to the next venture, because I expect it to take a while to recover, but I can't stay and hope.

Last night after you suggested I stay here was the last straw, confirming how you feel about our arrangement.

There was nothing wrong with what you were saying—I signed the deal after all—but there is so much wrong with what you haven't been saying. The words I long to hear so much.

You've done nothing wrong. I have myself to blame for not speaking my truth sooner. I put my family and my financial needs first, and you couldn't forgive that.

Please, I don't blame you for what happened between us. You were always honest about your expectations. Your conditions. It's me who breached our contract, so to speak.

Falling in love was never in the terms. I'm sorry about the mess with your family regarding the canceled wedding. I hope you can forgive me in time.

I love you, my beautiful Gio,

Mila

A glutton for punishment, I read the letter three more times. Each word slices through my chest with the precision of a surgeon. Give it to Mila not to be mad, or blame me for the way I ignored her.

When I finish reading for the fourth time, the gravity of my loss finally sinks in, carving a hole in my chest.

Massi comes back and leans against a pillar shading the terrace. "Do you want a drink?"

I shake my head. No amount of alcohol can numb or solve this.

"Thank God. I'm so jet-lagged I'd drop after one sip." He sinks into a lounge bed and sighs. The bastard is enjoying his vacation. "So, I reckon the wedding is off. I hate tuxedos anyway."

"Fuck you." I lean forward, resting my elbows on my knees. I drop my head into my hands. My stupid brother chuckles.

"She really wanted to get as far as possible if she took my plane, but her family lives in your house and she manages your company, so I'm sure you can talk to her again."

Is he taunting me right now? Because I would punch him in a heartbeat.

I stand up and punch the pillar instead. Wrong fucking move. The pain sears through my fingers up to my shoulder. Massi raises his eyebrow.

"Gio, you clearly care about her, so why are you acting like she is the nemesis in your story? Go, find her. Tell her you care. Or even better show her, because if you try to express it in words, you'll fuck up again." He chuckles.

"I hate you." I hold my hand close to my chest.

"Feel free to aim your stupidity at me. It won't make you feel better. There is only one person who can make the hurt go away—and I'm not talking about your hand." He taps at his chest. "I suggest you pull your head out of your ass and admit you care."

I do care. I do fucking care so much. Shit.

"And while you're pondering your future, I'd get that hand iced." He closes his eyes and turns his face to the sun.

Happy fucker with his beautiful family. Jesus, I can't watch him. But he's right, I need to ice my hand. Not the only thing he's right about.

In the kitchen, I shove my hand into the freezer. Fuck, it hurts.

Fishing my phone out of my pocket with the other hand, I dial my concierge. "Get my plane ready. I'm flying to New York."

"Of course, Mr. Cassinetti, when would you like to leave?" The overly sweet voice grates on my nerves.

"Right fucking now!" I hang up.

"I wouldn't do that." Gina appears from out of nowhere, and I jump. Jesus, as if my heart needed more rebooting. "Give her space."

"I don't have time for that. I need to be in California in a week and then in Singapore." The words, my plans, sound foreign.

Gina looks at me like I'm an idiot. I probably am. Definitely. "If that's your plan, don't even bother. Your flight to New York will only add to carbon pollution. Nothing else."

I pull my half-frozen hand from the freezer and bang the drawer closed with unnecessary force. The housekeeper eyes me warily and mutters something under her breath. Gina continues to glare.

"What?" I snap.

"Is Mila really just a pit stop between two business trips?" She pushes around me and leaves to join her husband.

I trudge around the house mindlessly, unable to gather my thoughts. Everywhere I look Mila's presence is too evident, laughing in my face.

Her hair elastic in a bowl on the counter. Her towel draped over the chair. Her lavender scent filling the air.

I look at the happy couple outside, whispering and touching under the sun, and I call the concierge to cancel the flight.

Chapter 33

Mila

"But you wanted to retire, Hilda. I can't accept your generosity." I sip from my extra-large triple vanilla syrup iced coffee. No amount of sugar can sweeten my life since I left Italy a week ago.

Gio hasn't bothered to contact me. Nor has Lydia or any of his staff. I'm left alone, which is even worse.

He hasn't fired me either, which is great, but I feel like I'm working on borrowed time. As much as I don't want the reminders of Gio in my life, I love the firm too much.

"I'm not offering my time anymore, just money. With my financial contribution and guarantee, the bank is going to look at your loan application with more receptive eyes." Hilda smiles and squeezes my hand.

"Thank you." I try to curl my lips up, but it's more

of a tremble. I've been blinking away tears a lot. It's kind of ridiculous, but I can't stop the waterworks.

I was devastated after Brian, but now I know what I felt for him didn't even resemble love. My heart is cracked. Irreparable. I hope one day I can breathe again, but with the constant pain numbing me, I doubt that will ever happen.

Every day, I put on a smile and go to work because I feel safe and needed there. I enjoy working, and it helps me survive each day. In a stupid twist of irony, I can now better understand Gio. Working helps to dull the pain, or at least ignore it for parts of the day.

The breakup was necessary, but the gaping wound it left constantly reminds me of the emptiness my life has been since I returned from Italy. That's another irony right there, because for the past few months my life has been quite empty, waiting for Gio to come around.

Hilda heads home after our meeting, and I walk to my office. It rained last night and the air is pleasant, cleared of the smog and humanity, a nice break for the concrete jungle.

I've grown to like this city, but I wish I could still listen to the splashing water of Lake Como. *Stop it, Mila.*

When I get off the elevator on my floor, an uncomfortable prickle smarts my nape. My receptionist sits straight like she is expecting to be scolded. Breathless, she slides her eyes toward my office down the hallway.

Since I always keep my shutters open, the glass wall immediately reveals the reason behind the heavy atmosphere. The investor is in the building.

My eyes land on Gio. My heart stops for a moment before it starts beating faster than ever. The sweet latte rolls in my stomach.

He's sitting at the long conference desk in my office, working on his phone. Of course.

His jacket hangs on the chair behind him, and he's only in his white shirt and a navy blue vest. A vest. Just my luck. As if my defenses needed another hit.

His hair is rakishly mussed, and his beard has grown in, but it doesn't hide the sharp lines of his face. I miss him so much.

The light from the screen glows against his face. His hand is bandaged in a sling.

What is he doing here? He must have come to fire me. I thought he had business in California and Asia. I thought I had more time.

Panic coils up my spine, but I can't just leave. Can I? I need to be brave, face him, and hopefully get him to give me more time. I take a deep breath and walk toward what I hope is still my office.

My heart races with every step. As I get closer, he looks up. His eyes fix on me, and my chest clenches.

Those deep brown eyes. Here to swallow me.

My office has never felt so far from the elevators. It takes an indecent amount of time to finally reach the door. I enter, close it behind me, and remain standing there.

"Mila." He sighs. Like he's waited his whole life to see me again.

"What happened to your hand?" Why I focus on that, I'll never know.

"I punched a wall." His eyes burn my skin. "After you left."

Jesus.

I swallow hard, trying to hold back my tears. "I know I have no right to demand anything, but would you consider keeping me here as the CEO? I have the track record to prove it's not a burden on your bottom line—"

"Shut up," he growls, and I gasp. "Please." He adds, his voice hoarse. "I'm not here to fire you."

"Oh." I don't think my heart rate is at a healthy level anymore. "Why are you here?" I deliver every word with care like they could detonate between us, though I'm not sure I want to hear the answer.

"You were wrong." He stands up and starts pacing. He adjusts his cuffs and runs his hand through his hair, leaving it disheveled. Unlike him.

"About?" The air is filled with an anticipation heavy enough to suffocate us both. Why is this so hard?

"In your letter you said I've done nothing wrong. Fuck. I've done everything wrong. I made assumptions about your motivations. I held your desperate situation against you. Against us. I don't know how to deal in the absence of hard data, so I assumed. I didn't offer what you deserved. Not even what I really wanted to give you. I offered what I thought you wanted. I was wrong."

He stops and drops his head, inhaling sharply, and then meets my eyes.

The lump in my throat grows bigger, the tears running down. "What do I deserve?"

"Everything. You deserve everything, Mila." He doesn't hesitate for a moment. "Definitely not the asshole I've been. But I want to give you all you deserve for the rest of my life. Princess, I'm a selfish asshole, and I can't let you go. I can't."

My poor broken heart. "Why?" I whisper.

He comes closer. "I can't because it's not the rest of my life, it's just the beginning of ours."

I swallow a sob. "What are you saying?"

He looks at me with the softest gaze I've ever seen on him, his features dark with pain, but his eyes shining with adoration. "I want to cut my losses and focus on a new venture. I want to forget the arrangement and dive into the unknown with you, not because it's convenient for me and my social status, but because I love you, Mila."

Now I don't swallow the sob anymore. It tears through me with all the pent-up emotions of the past six months. "You do?"

He steps close and cups my face. "Don't leave me, Princess. We don't have to go through with the wedding if you don't want to, but please take a chance on me. Take a chance on me, even though you know I'll fuck up again. I'll get side-tracked again. I'll say or do the wrong things, but rest assured, Princess, I'll always do them with the best intention, because you matter to me. More than anything in this world."

I heave with sobs as we stand there, my tear-stricken face in his hands. I want to kiss him, but I have to protect myself. He hurt me, and just because he regrets it, I don't know if I can trust that he won't continue in his ways. Shying away from my affection and hiding at work.

I step back, and the broken look on his face almost shatters my resolve. "Nora told me about Kimberly."

"Fuck her. Kimberly is inconsequential." He reaches for me, but then thinks better of it and drops his hand.

"And yet you compared me to her." I don't know if

there is a chance for a real reconciliation, but if there ever might be, we need to address this topic.

He opens his mouth, all his features ready to argue, but his vehemence dies as soon as he realizes I'm right. He hangs his head, defeated. Broken. I never imagined I'd see a day when Gio Cassinetti would bow down.

"You were wrong. Kimberly wanted things from you because of her greed. For me, it was a question of survival." I sigh. "It never was the reason I wanted to be with you."

He says nothing, just accepts the truth, pleading with his eyes. Dark brown abyss. So desperate, it breaks my already fractured heart.

"I love you, Gio. I love you so much it hurts. But you hurt me, neglected me, made assumptions about me, and yes, I never tried to explain my feelings, but that didn't give you the right to behave the way you did."

"Tell me what to do. Do you want me to beg?"

"Stop it. Don't be ridiculous. When you told me you're allergic to a beesting and you fight that by getting close to them, I admired you. When it came to me, you didn't want to get close. I don't know if I can trust that you would let yourself feel. That you wouldn't hide behind work."

He looks at me, and it's not the thirty-four-year-old man, it's a boy, lost and scared, who pleads with me.

"I can't promise you anything, Gio. Not right now."

* * *

The next day, I return from an afternoon client meeting to find Gio waiting for me. Not in my office. In the seating area at reception.

The receptionist nearly needs resuscitation, pleading wide-eyed that I remove him from her vicinity.

I stifle a smile at her freak-out and walk over to him. He stands up and, damn it, the dimples. He is shaved and dressed casually in khakis and a polo shirt. God, he's gorgeous.

"What are you doing here?" I fold my arms across my chest, mostly because I want my hands to stop shaking.

"Hey, Princess, I'd like to walk you home." He wiggles his eyebrows. Gio actually wiggles his eyebrows. *The self-assured bastard.* My mind says, *Oh my God, oh my God.* My heart flutters. Stupid heart.

I bite my lip. "You should have called. I have work to do."

He shrugs. "That's okay. I'll wait."

I narrow my eyes, studying him. What's going on here? "Don't you have a deal in California or Singapore to chase?"

"Not important." He shrugs again. "I'll be here whenever you're ready." He sits down, smiling. The king in his court.

I sigh and go to my office, honey-dipped wings fluttering in my stomach. It's another four hours before I'm ready to leave, and he still waits there patiently.

We walk for several blocks and talk about my day. I live with Annie now on the other side of Manhattan, so we finally take a cab. Gio walks me to the door, asks about my sister, and then kisses my hand.

"See you tomorrow, Princess."

We continue the same routine for almost a month. A few times we stop and eat from a vendor in the park, or a hole in the wall restaurant. Twice I accompany him to a charity event. Most evenings we just hang out.

Normal.

Gio Cassinetti is doing normal. My defenses are nonexistent by now, and I'm keeping my distance more, because a part of me worries things will return to his usual way of life as soon as I cave.

Though I can't help but enjoy his attention. No longer is he taking me to shop for things I don't want. He listens, and then surprises me with little things. Tickets for a Pink concert because I was humming her song. Flowers from a corner mom-and-pop shop I frequent to help the elderly couple. Many, small, thoughtful gestures.

My heart is ready to give in. My body craves his touch. My mind still needs to address one last thing.

Two of my team members are with me on the call, but my focus is stolen by the handsome man at reception. At one point during this courtship, he rearranged the seating out there, so he could watch me.

It's wonderful to see him off the screen, but it's wonderfully nerve-wracking having him stare at me with attention and reverence. Needless to say, I have to get the most important stuff done in the mornings before he comes. I'm useless once he enters the premises.

We get off the phone and debrief quickly. As soon as I'm alone, I take out a yellow folder. When I asked my assistant to print the document, she brought it back in the yellow folder and I laughed at the irony.

I hit my intercom.

"Yes, Mila, what can I do for you?" she chirps.

"Please ask Mr. Cassinetti to come to my office."

I see her stand up and glance my way in surprise before she gets him. Gio enters, a dark grin on his face. I want to kiss that mouth so badly.

"Please sit down." I gesture to the opposite side of the table from where I stand.

His eyes tighten around the edges, and he studies me for a moment. I bite my lip. Jesus. I'm no match for him in the boardroom. He opens his suit jacket and sits down.

Heart hammering, I push the folder across the table.

He stares at it, the typical, indifferent expression of professionalism I haven't seen in a month settling on his features. I sink into the chair, keeping my hands under the table.

He opens the folder and reviews its contents. "You want to buy this firm from me?"

I swallow hard. "With our previous agreement, the firm is yours. So, yes, I want to buy it. With Hilda as a minority partner."

"Why?" His gaze stirs hesitation inside me.

"I love the company. And I need to be financially independent." From you. I don't say that, because under his scrutiny I'm not sure I can pull it off. But I raise my chin and meet his challenge.

He frowns. "This is not financial independence. This is you getting deep into debt with a bank." Of course, he assumes I'm taking out a loan. He's not wrong.

I look out through the glass wall at the firm that Hilda built, and I feel a sense of ownership and pride. I took her baby and made it better, stronger, more profitable. I'm not a failure.

I look back at the handsome man in front of me.

Tilting my head, I lick my lips and enjoy its effects on him. His eyes darken and he runs his tongue over his upper teeth.

"Perhaps," I breathe. "But I'm not in love with the bank. I don't want to fuck the bank. I don't want the bank to do things to me—"

"Give me the pen," he growls, and signs the deal.

Epilogue

Gio

"Are there any problems, Portia?" I tap on my glass desk, ready to log off the call. It's Saturday, for fuck's sake.

Portia blinks a few times and clears her throat. "No, no problems. I-I thought I'd walk you through the negotiation strategy—"

"I completely trust you, Portia. When is your meeting?"

"On Monday morning." She fidgets, clearly unsure what to make out of this situation. We just started this meeting, after all.

"Good, then enjoy Singapore and we'll talk after your meeting. I got to go."

It turns out trusting people pays off. It gives me more time for other things. Especially today.

I have been dating my former fiancée for three months now. Best fucking months of my life. We're taking things slowly, but my patience is running out. I want her here with me. I need her here with me. I want the world to know she's mine.

I grab the basket and my carry-on and throw everything into my Lambo. A sense of déjà vu overwhelms me, but I mentally flip it off. Because this time around, I won't fuck it up.

I tap the steering wheel to the music blaring through the speakers. I'm ridiculously happy. What a novel emotion.

It evaporates when I arrive at Mila's, or rather her sister's place. They're still living in my house, but they're moving out soon. Ron got a new job somewhere rural, and the family is moving with him. Annie is planning to homeschool the kids while she finishes her degree online.

Mila is equally happy and sad about it. After she bought the company from me, she's been really busy, but she still finds time for her family. And for me, thank God.

She's been apartment hunting for a month now, and while I've been supportive of her almost one hundred percent, I've been faking my support in this matter. If things go as planned this weekend, she won't need an apartment.

When she comes down, I'm hit with the most beautiful sight, and a wave of ownership, pride and adoration. Every time I see her, it's a mixture of familiar and completely new, undiscovered.

Perhaps life has always been like this, if I'd bothered to look up.

"Hey, handsome." Beaming, she bounces to me and wraps her arms around my neck. I always thought I'd get sick of the lavender. I was wrong. I was wrong about so many things when it comes to this woman, I can't believe she gave me another chance.

I bury my nose in the crook of her neck and bite her gently, squeezing her ass. "Hey, Princess."

"So, what's the secret plan?" She wiggles her shoulders in excitement.

"We're having a picnic." I kiss her.

"A picnic? Like you're going to sit on the grass?" She chuckles and I yank her closer, nibbling on her jaw.

"Of course not," I growl half-heartedly. "Sophisticated people have a picnic blanket."

She throws her head back and laughs. "Isn't it cold for a picnic?"

"Not where we're going." I open the door for her. She raises her eyebrows, but doesn't push.

* * *

"What the hell, Gio? Where are we going?" Mila half-bounces with excitement, but chews on her lip at the same time.

"To have a picnic." I shrug and get out of the car. She doesn't wait for me to open the door and rushes out.

"Where is the picnic?" The wind flaps her hair around.

"It's a surprise." I get the basket from the boot and push it into her hands.

The valet comes to get my car and my luggage. Mila's luggage—she won't like that I bought her a new wardrobe—is already onboard.

I take the basket and her hand and drag her across the tarmac.

"Gio, I don't like surprises."

"Since when?" I stop and peck her before beckoning her toward the stairs.

"Since right now."

I laugh. "Okay, then we're flying to St. Martin."

She turns around and almost knocks me down the step. "Gio!"

"Yes, Princess?" I nudge her to move. We won't fucking ever take off at this speed.

She climbs the stairs, smiles at the flight attendant. "I'm not packed, and I have meetings on Monday. How long are we going for? One night? That makes no sense. It's too far for a round-trip like that. And I—"

I seize her lips. I don't mind her babbling as much as I used to, but shutting her up with my mouth is satisfying. She tenses, flailing her arms, but then melts into me. Heaven.

"We're going for a week." I eat her protest with my lips again. God, she's delicious.

"You don't have any meetings. I made arrangements with your assistant," I continue, stopping her words with my tongue. "You're packed, Princess." I nibble on her neck, fist her hair.

She moans. "I am?"

"Yes, Princess, I took care of everything for this picnic, and if you stop protesting, I might even fucking sit on the grass later."

She giggles and takes my cheeks into her hands. "Thank you."

"Good. Now buckle up so we can finally take off, and then I can take you to the bedroom, because my cock remembers the last time you slept there alone and demands retribution."

* * *

We're swaying, completely out of rhythm while the music echoes around a small patio. Mila talked me into visiting the town again, and I can't say it's all that bad. Just like the first time here with her, it doesn't matter what we do. As long as we're doing it together.

"I don't want to go home tomorrow," Mila murmurs into my ear.

"We can stay longer." I yank her closer.

She chuckles. "Who are you, and what have you done with Gio? We can't stay longer. We both have work."

"I'm rich enough." I shrug, and she laughs again. I'm only half joking. It's not realistic to stay in our little bubble here, but we could stay longer.

"I have London's gala and seven other events this fall." She cups my cheek. "Besides, I'd like this place to be special, and if we stayed here it would become common."

I kiss her senseless, because I love her and because she is perfect. My cock strains against the zipper of my slacks. "Okay, woman, let's go."

"One more dance." She raises her hands above her head, shimmying. It doesn't improve the situation in my pants.

"No, we're leaving," I growl.

"Jesus, you know how to kill the mood." She rolls her eyes but follows me.

I'm like a horny teenager, suddenly unable to wait a minute longer, so I drag her up the street to the villa.

"Slow down, my feet hurt," Mila whines.

I scoop her up and, ignoring her squeals, throw her over my shoulder. She complains half-heartedly, but I don't stop until we get to the house. I march through the living room and drop her in the pool.

Spluttering, she laughs and protests. I shed my T-shirt and shorts and join her, sending ripples of water over the edges.

I pull her to me, and Mila wraps her legs around my hips, kissing me. "Something feels very familiar about this situation."

"Hm." I rip off the front of her dress and sink my teeth into the lace of her bra, tasting the salty water and her nipple.

Mila moans and grinds her hips against me. I walk backward to the edge of the pool, find purchase with my back, destroy her panties and finally fill her. We both moan, pleasure and need mixing.

Our eyes meet and we still for a few beats, just soaking each other in. Mila rocks her hips, and we make love in the pool where our story kind of started.

Two or three orgasms later, she is cuddled in my arms on the lounge bed. "Do you want something to drink?"

She sighs. "Yes, but I don't want us to move."

I kiss her temple. "Don't move. I'll be right back."

We've shared many special moments here, but none of them have seemed perfect enough. And since we're leaving tomorrow, I can't wait anymore.

I get a bottle of champagne and the velvet box then rejoin Mila.

"I'm cold when you're not here," she murmurs.

I prepare two glasses, sit behind her and lean back, wrapping her in my arms. She puts her glass to her mouth and then stiffens. Is that good tension or bad? Why am I nervous?

Well, asshole, you've never closed a bigger deal than this one.

She turns, her indigo eyes darting between the glass and me. She gulps down the champagne and carefully removes the ring from the flute.

Fuck. My heart hammers against my chest, looking for an escape. Time stretches painfully, and Mila's face is too serious.

"Many times since California, I thought you were pushing me for your own good. All the while, you were trying to help me grow into a better version of myself. I know that now, Princess. I have nothing to offer, but I swear I'll try to push you to grow into a better version of yourself, support you, love you, listen to you, catch you when you fall. I'll stand by you when you make mistakes and, fuck, I'll sit on the grass for the rest of my days if that makes you happy. Because you, Mila Ward, are a fucking queen."

She sobs and blinks away tears. "We're naked."

What? "I was hoping you'd go for a one-word answer. In fact, yes would improve my current heart failure situation."

She sniffles through giggles. "When I say yes, this will be our engagement story. We're naked."

"Fuck that." Jesus. Several minutes in and I still don't know where this is going. "Can we get to the actual answer?"

"It's not like you asked me the actual question, you idiot." She laughs through the tears.

I roll my eyes. "Mila Ward, my naked queen, will you marry me?"

She throws herself at me then. "Yes."

"Finally." I seize her lips, and then put the ring on her finger.

"It's beautiful. It looks like those cufflinks you always wear." She admires her finger.

"They belonged to my grandfather, and this ring was my Nonna's."

Mila starts crying, hugging me with way more

strength than someone of her stature should have.

"I love you, Gio."

"I love you too, Princess."

"I love the ring, but what about the other one?"

"Pawn that shit. I don't want a reminder of how poorly I treated you. It will never happen again."

* * *

Andrea

A few months earlier

Strong arms yank me away, and I register Gio's face before pain blossoms in my jaw.

He punched me. He fucking punched me at my own exhibition opening.

Not that I can blame him. I'm not sure why I kissed his fiancée in front of everyone.

The poor woman must be gagging now. I can't deal with all the attention, and then I do this shit.

Shit that helps me numb the fear. Trouble that makes me feel alive, real, fearless.

Amidst gasps, I lose my footing and tumble to the floor. A delicate groan reverberates through my mind.

While my brain swims with alcohol and who knows what other substances by now, it still registers a blur of yellow, and the silky skin belonging to that fragile sound.

I brace for impact, but I land on a soft... body. Shit. I took someone down with me. Now the gallery owner won't be happy about that. Not that she's been happy about tonight to begin with.

After agonizing over my first exhibition in years, I've ensured it won't be a success. If I fuck it up on purpose, I can't be blindsided by the critics and other schmucks who call themselves art connoisseurs.

I push up onto my elbows, and meet huge eyes.

The darkest of brown with sparkles of gold in them. They shine with mystery and... pain. Damn it. I probably hurt her.

Still, I can't move, mesmerized by the beauty underneath me. Her rich, tawny skin tone glows with natural radiance. She's not wearing makeup. How refreshing.

Bold and defined, her high cheekbones beg to be caressed, accentuating the alluring air around her.

Her curly hair is tamed into a bright yellow scarf matching her top. My eyes drop to the bee-stung lips and, Jesus... She's a vision.

Her lean, long legs are tangled with mine. Shit, I'm pressing my thigh into her center. I should move, but I can't let go. Not yet.

My hand itches to draw her. To paint her. To

sculpt her. To depict the feeling she is spreading through my veins.

"You're hurting me," she croaks.

I shake my head, but it doesn't bounce me back to reality. "You're beautiful."

Her eyes widen, and I realize the rhythm tapping against my chest is her heartbeat.

Some idiot grabs me again as several people try to help us up.

I don't fucking need their help. I shake off the hold that belongs to my sister's boyfriend.

I don't want to lose the connection. This powerful moment. I want to remain frozen in time with the beautiful gazelle. I need to capture her essence.

She groans as she straightens up.

"Are you hurt?" Sydney disturbs the magnetic moment with her concern.

I should be concerned as well, but I'm too awestruck—and high—to act like a gentleman. Or kindly. Or like a human.

"I'm okay." She keeps staring at me with those shining eyes, and only now do I notice the innocence in them.

"I'm sorry." I finally find the appropriate words.

She smiles, and it hits me straight in my chest. She must be a dream.

"I must go." She turns, moving with grace and

fluidity, commanding the attention of the room without even knowing it.

Without trying. Long and slender, her body disappears into the next room.

I'm rooted to the floor.

"You're such an idiot, Andrea. What were you thinking?" Sydney's voice drags me from my stupor.

"Who was she?" I rasp.

"Who? The girl?" Sydney looks toward the arch that separates the rooms.

"Who was she?" I demand again.

"I don't know. You invited all these people." Sydney sighs.

"I have to go." I push around my sister and pursue the illusion. The living work of art. Completely captivated, I roam the rooms, looking for her, but she's gone.

My muse.

Mine.

Well, well, well, has Andrea Cassinetti just met a woman who will heal him?
*While you're waiting for their story, **Reckless Hunger**, read how Violet Mathison, the gallery owner, found her happily ever after in **Chosen by the Billionaire**.*
In this enemies to lovers romance, the socially awkward hacker brings trouble to Vi's steps, but their love story is

"*an excellent read from beginning to the end*", *according to a reader's review.*

Mila and Gio start their **honeymoon,** but their plans get derailed. Read all about it in this bonus scene here: www.maxinehenri.com/deal or scan:

Also by Maxine Henri

Untamed Billionaires Series

Tempted by the Billionaire (A Fake Relationship Romance)

Chosen by The Billionaire (An Enemies to Lovers Romance)

Chased by the Billionaire (An Age gap/Innocent Heroine Romance)

Stolen by the Billionaire (A Forbidden Love Romance)

Reckless Billionaires Series

Reckless Fate (A Second Chance Romance)

Reckless Desire (A Single Dad Romance)

Reckless Dare (A Fake Relationship Romance)

Reckless Deal (A Grumpy/Sunshine Bosshole Romance)

Reckless Hunger (An Age Gap Romance)

If you loved this book, please spread the word and leave a review. One sentence is enough to help other readers and make me very happy.

Author's Note

This book was released only four weeks after Reckless Dare (London & Dominic) and you may be wondering if I'm some magical speed-writer. I wish.

It came out so fast because I faced my fears of being seen.

It is one thing to write—and I love it—but it's a different beast to let people read my words.

I usually take my time and sit on a final version of the book. And while there might be some solace in aging the story like a delicious wine, I had to accept that's not why I'm writing.

I write stories to entertain, to provide escape and hopefully inspire if stars align. Not to hide them in my drawer.

So I released Gio and Mila into the wild and I

hope they will make you cry and smile and swoon in a similar way I experienced while writing their story.

Dear reader, I appreciate you and value every single one of you. I truly do.

Love,

Maxine

About the Author

Maxine Henri is a contemporary romance author who infuses her stories with steamy passion and complex characters. When she's not crafting stories that will have you swooning, she can usually be found sipping on a cup of black tea while reading a good book. Or traveling to new destinations.

Maxine believes that stories matter. They facilitate emotional journeys, inspire and entertain. And when it comes to books and fiction, stories are a great escape and probably the most beneficial addiction on this planet.

Her billionaire romances are the perfect escape, offering a taste of luxury and adventure. Maxine introduces heroes who may have a dark past, but are always balanced by a lighter side. And her leading ladies? They're strong, independent women who may be a little broken, but always find their way in life.

You can connect with her on any of these platforms: